HARKFAST

The making of the king

Robbed of pride and spiritual direction after Rome's departure, Britain's scattered tribes are prey to savage marauders. Only one Druid remains alive—Harkfast, a wonder worker of limitless vision. He seeks to unite the fractious clans by breeding a new line of kings. To inherit the mantle of glory, he selects and trains an orphan Pictish boy, Ruan.

Accompanied by a tormented prophet, a renegade centurion and a grizzled Pictish dog-master, the Druid and his protege go in search of the talismans of Celtic legend, by whose magical influence Harkfast hopes to raise and control the heroes who lie in the halls of the dead.

Battle, ritual magic and haunting beauty mark this richly imaginative novel which traces the Druid's quest through the territory of the barbaric Smerteans to the brooding Isle of Sketis. There, in the ruins of the ancient warrior school under the command of the majestic Mother Hag, a final great battle is contrived to restore a flickering splendour before the mists of the Dark Ages obliterate all trace of the mystical Celtic realms.

Also by Hugh C. Rae

The Rookery (1974)

HARKFAST

The making of the king

Hugh C. Rae

ST. MARTIN'S PRESS
NEW YORK

To
Rosemary Sutcliff

Contents

Part 1

The valley

1

The Bull of Seven Battles

The war boats grounded on a brown sand spit near the head of the narrow loch. Mata was first ashore. He swarmed over the blunt prow, sword unsheathed, ox-hide targe strapped to his arm, an iron spike clenched in his teeth. Tiny pig-eyes glinting, he grunted in his throat like a boar in rut. After a long, dreary winter entombed in a crannog on the Bog of Tara, shunned by King Niall, who had grown jealous of his mercenary's fame, a rough sea crossing had set the seal on his temper.

Twice now they had struck on the coast of Erragail, his lust for conquest honed by the burning of a steading, a mass hanging and the writhings of the Pictish virgin he had raped on the night before last when the spring moon was hard and frost still held. Thaw had set in since, though, and the moon guttered in mist and greasy cloud. Because he could see in the dark like an owl, Mata stormed the beach alone. Besides, was he not Mata, the Monster of the Boyne, the Bull of Seven Battles who loved killing even more than rutting? Behind him the crews dragged the curraghs on to dry sand. The light, shallow-draught boats slid easily up the slope above the neap-tide line, out of reach of any sudden squall which might claw them from a mooring and strand the plunderers on this foreign shore. The boats secure, the men grouped in pairs, spread out to make awkward targets for arrow showers or volleys of spears. They would await Mata's command, however, before they attacked. It was an honoured tradition that the Bull slew the first of the enemy whatever the weight of odds.

Crouched by the rocks at the edge of the herd-track from the beach, Mata calculated the worth of the flock which drifted uncertainly along the pasture in the direction of the weems. It was early in the year for so many horns to be openly cropping,

11

and with the lambing ewes still confined to the underground shelters the haul was promising indeed.

As yet there was no sign of defence, no watch or guard. On the strength of information extracted from a Connemara horse-trader, Mata had singled out this loch for attention. Allegedly its shores were peppered with mixed-blood cantons, sleek and secure in the comparative peace that had descended on this province since the last uprisings had been quelled and the Romans had brayed south, abandoning the walls. Small thriving settlements, under minor chieftains, always gave good sport. If it happened that the horse-trader had lied, he would run the man to earth somehow and geld him like one of his own miserable nags.

A sound caught Mata's attention. Instinctively he tilted back his helmet to protect the nape of his neck. He remembered now how the Caledones fought when they had advantage of numbers. They went in like a mongrel pack, gouging and slashing with their shears, making a particular target of the spinal cords that bound the skull to the body. A groove on Mata's right shoulder was proof, one of many scars collected in battles and murderous combats as far afield as Gaul. His squat body was a calendar of wounds. Naked, he displayed them proudly, flaunting them to excite women with evidence of his stamina and courage.

There would surely be women today, young girls and plump wives. The living was fat on this coast, even at the rump of the season. Most cantons were well enough organized now to endure a winter in comfort. Better for the natives, though, when communes were small and scattered; then folk had sense to scuttle into hiding when the war boats came, allowing their cattle to be stolen and their steadings fired but at least escaping with their lives. To stand up to Mata, or any wild rover from Erin, was to invite death. The possessive pride that settlers had developed of late would serve them ill in the end.

Lowering his shield to cover his groin, Mata slunk through the withered weeds that fringed the cropping. Half-caste tribes were small of stature, like swarthy dwarves, and could lie low in cover that a normal man would find scant. Sword poised, Mata lurched on to the pasture.

12

Sheep trotted nervously ahead of him, stringing out along the base of a low cliff. If he played the stalk with caution the mutton would eventually lead him right to the gates of the weems. The raiding crews would have moved silently across the beach, as eager as their leader to come to grips with prey, insatiable in their appetite for booty, for gold and silver ornaments, for meat and drink, for captives to sell as slaves on the Leinster block, and for women, always, eternally, for women.

Mata was forty steps on to the level sward when the herders struck. They rose like wraiths from the grass, from under the bellies of the sheep, their sudden rush bursting the flock in panic. Mata was buffeted by a dozen frenzied rams before the enemy reached him. He had sense enough not to use his sword on the muttons. Thick fleeces might ensnare the blade and leave him helplessly disarmed. As it was he had hardly regained balance before the dwarf horde swarmed upon him.

Scything his sword, Mata dropped instantly to one knee. Hoisting the targe to bear the brunt of the spear thrusts, he swept the blade close to the ground, and felt it bite. A body slumped over him. Shears lacerated the crown of his left shoulder, an area so often torn that the flesh was crimped and almost bloodless. Even so, the wound ignited slumbering madness in the mercenary's brain. Charging from under the spears, deflecting them with sword and shield, rebuffing dirks with his studded armour, he retreated to the head of the track, leaving three Picts dead or wounded behind him.

Pulling the spike from his mouth he bellowed the command which brought the bullies scrambling from the rocks and, being Mata, swung round and charged again into the thick of the shaken herders. With the short chopping action that was the mark of his personal style, he butchered two more dwarves before his cohorts, Dagg and Fiach, carried the rank abreast of him and ran on in a line like a trolling net along the pasture to claim the weems and breach such paltry hedges as the canton lords had thought fit to erect.

Picts popped up on knolls at the funnel of the sward. In spite of the darkness Mata detected the flight of short arrows, weaved

13

away from them or glanced them off with his targe. One stripling raider, on his first voyage, screamed, skidded to his knees and fell headlong behind the loping warriors. Without turning, Mata knew that the Picts would converge like flies to hack him to pieces, imagining that one death was an omen of final victory.

Remnants of the sheep flock streamed into a shallow depression which led past an alder brake on to the plain where the steading stood. The weems lay between the brake and the hedge, turfed hummocks with poles already dropped and a brazier lighted: only one, though, and with hardly a flame to feed the swinging pots which, if properly prepared, could drench a man with scalding fat at a distance of thirty paces. As expected, the outlying guards had buckled, running like hares to warn the chieftain. The weems' wardens too had already deserted their posts to seek shelter within the scraggy ring of thorn.

Mata hooted as he ran, leaping pitfalls and discarding missiles almost casually. Laughter and hooting was taken up by all the bold running bucks until the dawn was full of noise. Their mocking clamour drowned the urgent cries of the herders' leaders and the screeching of women torn from blissful sleep to face the prospect of a torturous death or the alternative of life-long slavery. Better dead, my beauties, thought Mata, transforming thought into word and bawling out, in the ugly Latin tongue, 'Death'.

In his own dialect, he shouted the word again. The rallying cry was instantly adopted by his men who, as they dispersed to the calculated chores involved in breaking a siege as swiftly as a stag breaks a sapling, communicated with each other by chanting, DEATH, DEATH, DEATH, DEATH, until the growl of the first of the fires in the thorn swallowed up their voices and smoke carried the invocation skywards like a druid's prayer.

Mata steered himself away from the main party. Dawn tinted the pallid mists which skirted the chattering river and lifted on the inshore breeze to expose the terrain as far as the roots of the mountains which towered above the valley. The altar stone was not difficult to find. It stood on a tongue of grass above the riverbank. As he had hoped, four armed guards had gathered there to make heroic gestures to their piddling gods who, they prayed,

14

might yet blink their eyelids and swat away the nasty lads who had come to destroy the canton and cram the otherworld with a fresh supply of disillusioned acolytes.

Slowing to a walk, Mata swaggered away from the industry that went on within and around the thorn hedge, from the mopping up of dreamy shepherds trapped in the weems. He had no interest in the perfunctory despatch of enfeebled fools. He would amuse himself with something that almost resembled a soldiers' band, seek diversion in combat with a quartet that, to judge by their grim visages, were prepared to die upright and armed. He slotted the iron spike into his mouth again. The flat of a blade rattled on the helmet could crunch a man's teeth to powder or cause him to bite his tongue in half; the iron prevented that, and gave an extra weapon to hand if the need arose.

Ruefully Mata approached the paltry garrison. The rock was a huge grey boulder dislodged from the ice that would fill the corrie in a hard winter, to roll and rumble down to this flat spot. It was smooth and inviolate except on the short flank where a series of niches had been painstakingly chipped into a ladder of steps worn shiny by years of use. The exact function of the stone did not concern Mata. It might be a council rock or a watchtower for all he knew or cared.

The guards were crowded on top. They did not know what to make of his casual approach. There was no meeting of minds, or of wills. They fought only to defend their possessions, and could not understand that battle and slaughter were ends in themselves.

After a whispered conversation, one guard leaned on his spear and, in the Scotian dialect, enquired, 'What is it you want of us?'

Mata removed the spike, said, 'To slay you, of course,' and put the spike firmly back between his teeth.

The four conferred again.

Losing patience Mata deliberately lumbered to the base of the rock and set foot on the ladder of niches. He peered up from under the snout of his helmet, scowling as the guards jabbed ineffectually with their spears. Solemnly he groped for the holds and ascended four more steps, parrying the uncertain blows lightly

15

on his shield. He was astonished by their lack of sagacity in allowing him to mount to the summit of the boulder before massing an attack. By that time, he had positional advantage, and they were cramped in a corner of the stone.

Mata laughed, shook his head and wagged his sword to watch them jump.

It was, in the end, a grand fight, rapid and bloody and unexpectedly dangerous. In spite of strong weapons and armour, the guards were without skill in arms. Mata hacked them up piecemeal, countering their assaults as solidly as if he was rock himself. When two were downed, and dead, the remaining pair lost faith and poked and swung with a feverish despair which made Mata snigger louder until, at length, out of pity he dropped his sword, discarded it and lured them on that way.

Spitting the spike into his right hand, the mercenary trapped the long-shafted spear between his chest and the targe, locking it there by pressure. Hauling the spearman to him he spiked him in the eye and throat, two swift punching motions. The young man gurgled and fell back. Before the corpse could separate itself from the shaft, however, Mata swung it like a sack on a pole, smothered the swordsman's desperate charge and gained the space required to execute the steps of his next sally. Spike against sword, Mata deftly punctured the Pict's arm in three places. With a last forceful thrust he shattered the shoulder bones completely.

But the dwarf was full of burning fear, the mad courage that accompanies desperation. It never occured to him that he might escape death by leaping to the ground. Mata grinned, snorted through his broad nostrils, and moved in for a killing sequence. The Pict's speed deceived him. Quick as a lizard the man ducked in under the targe, grabbed the waist of Mata's breastplate and, aided by slippery puddles of blood on the rock, flung the raider on to his back. Grappling with his broken arm to stave off the plunge of the spike, the Pict buried his right hand in the flesh of Mata's throat. The thumb, like a rivet, bored into the raider's windpipe and blocked his supply of air.

Clouds rolled briefly over Mata's brain. His pig-eyes, red as rust, lost vision. He struggled to dislodge the hand that starved him of breath. It was outrageous for Mata, the Bull of Seven Battles, to be snuffed out by a nameless black leech.

Sweating with effort, Mata hugged the guard close. Though he could not break the stranglehold, he shifted position just enough to dip his head and rub his cheek against his assailant's neck. Prizing open his jaws Mata fixed his teeth into Pictish flesh, biting the vein until blood spurted and flooded his mouth, biting until the tendons were gnawed through and, as fingers quivered and slackened from their lethal grip, wrenching his head backwards to rip out the side of the throat. Contemptuously he tossed the leaking corpse aside as if it had been nothing all along but an effigy of tarred straw.

Mata jerked his head and spat, spewing out gouts of bloody flesh and drawing in racking sobs of air. He spat again and filled his lungs, struggled to his knees and groped for his sword. A wave of exultation engulfed him, a sensation of appalling strength as if he had sucked his victim's life force through that gaping hole in the neck. Now he had truly learned how to kill. He had banished the last rags of honour, and would be the mightier for it.

Rising, Mata flung out his arms and bellowed loudly to the gods to mark his feat, to reel and tremble in their meek and cloudy halls in case the Bull of the Boyne chose to raid them too one day.

Blood smeared his lips and stubble beard, painted the tired emblem on his leathers a fresh and vivid colour.

Now he was Mata the invincible. Nothing could harm him: nothing, no man or woman, god or goddess, prince, king or mumbling priest.

Still roaring his triumph, Mata glanced down and saw the boy sprawled at the base of the rock. Even as he looked, the brown and innocent eyes turned upon him and the Bull of Seven Battles felt unaccountable fear enter his heart.

2

The morning of the deer

In half light Ruan wakened. It was not yet dawn. Mist shrouded the mouth of the river valley between the high and snowy shoulders of the hills. Strange sounds spooned the boy from sleep. He lay motionless under the bed fleece, listening intently. His mother snored peacefully behind the wicker screen and from beyond the steading wall came the rattle of the river which ice had held dumb until the waning of the moon. Now a torrent jingled the remaining icicles and soon, with the coming of the sun, a thunderous cascade would leap past the settlement, flaring and wild like the manes of a massive stallion herd driving relentlessly towards the sea. It was not snoring, nor the river that had wakened him.

The sound was slighter, more subtle, like the music of the Silver Branch which his father had put into many tales when they talked man to boy in the brush tent on the ridge in the season of the high grazing. Awe caused Ruan to curl his long legs into his belly and clasp them tightly in the shape of a babe in the womb or a bondslave roped for burial. The music sweetened, bringing more pleasure than alarm. Throwing back the bed fleece, Ruan pulled on his breeks and sark, stepped over the mongrel which guarded the door, and left the roundhouse, already as helpless as a slave shackled to a filigree chain.

The music drew him to the gap in the thorn hedge, a hole which the children had made to avoid the cuffs of the irascible gateman whose lodge overlooked the main portalis. Ruan was no longer a child. Recently he had filled out and promised to be tall, unlike his father or many of the Poltalloch Picts. His mother claimed Hibernian ancestry. Ruan had no reason to doubt her. Over the years the main branch of the Poltalloch had drifted back over the mountains or into the deep forest, driven away by an influx of Scotians. Ruan was too young to understand the intricacies of breeding but sometimes when the rain stank in the fleeces or the ewes were particularly surly, he sensed that his heart was not in Culln's hold but off where battles raged and hot blood nobly spilled, wherever that might be. In colouring, he was a fine mixture of Hibernian and Caledone. His skin was fair and took the sun redly like a rowan berry, but he was barely a handsbreadth shorter than his father and walked straight as a spear among the shepherds.

Dropping on all fours, Ruan wriggled through the spiked hedge and made his escape undetected. The music continued to lure him, steering him away from the weems' guard into the mist. Mist brushed his chest and wetted his hair. He thought of it as the breath of the river which snaked out of the mountains to an unseen mating with the sea. In the invisible mountains, wrapped in kilts of sleet, the winds called *lisssssssten* as if they had commanded the haunting strain to allay the tedium of their winter courts.

The music had taken full possession of him now. He trailed it unquestioningly, forsaking fires and cooking pots, the father and mother who had fed and clothed him and guided him towards acceptance of his humble rank in this brief blink of life between lives. The cold did not affect him, nor sharp flints and slivers on the ground prick his feet. He was oblivious to the world his body occupied as he wandered closer to the base of the mountains where no man ever went because the peaks were rumoured to fuse with the sky.

As Ruan reached the river bend, however, the music faded and died away, leaving him with an ache of longing for its return.

The period of emptiness was brutally filled by the screams of the outlying guards and the thunder of many feet upon the pasture below the weems, the hoarse shouting of unfamiliar tongues and the pathetic bleating of frightened sheep. Once, when little more than an infant, Ruan had been whisked off to hide in the hills. Since then the encampment had been lulled by a long peace. Even so, Ruan understood at once what was happening.

19

Flanking the hedge, he headed back for the vantage point where guards kept watch over the river ford and the funnel from the sea loch. From this quarter, so his father had told him, the plunderers had come in the days before the hedge was grown. Hedges would not stave off raiders ravenous for meat and women and loot. They loped out of the mist like wolves, running in a line, and split around the hedge within which, in a matter of minutes, all the living members of the canton's nine families had gathered to defend the round-houses and long huts, even though the weems had already fallen and the flock dispersed.

Frantically, Ruan ran to throw his lambsweight of courage into the defence of his home-place. No defence was possible, of course. The attack had been too sudden. Members of the clan who had squared up to the raiders had been hewn down. It made no matter that they were kith of the plunderers, Scotians from the same racial stock. In the end all would be slain, herders and warriors, elders and infants, women and striplings.

Ruan saw little of the actual slaughter. He was drawn to the ringing scrape of hand-to-hand combat, a sound which stirred him in regions of his soul that no music could ever reach. Shouting incoherent challenges he sprinted towards the fighting, possessed of a rich, intoxicating hatred that dwindled only when he reached the rock.

The beast was more terrifying than anything the boy had ever imagined. It shrank him instantly to lad's size, snuffing out his manly courage as sand smothers a burning twig. The beast rose from the guardstone, all patched and crusted, hoary as the rock itself. Four corpses, the remains of the watch, draped the stone platform. Blood dribbled down the flanks and slavered the creature's jaws. Ruan's senses refused to accept natural explanations as the beast propped itself up on its sword and disgorged blood from its mouth. Ruan slithered and fell, sprawling beneath the base of the rock, staring up in horror at the entity which howled victoriously at the sky.

Its snout was tusked, its eyes fiery, and matted locks ruffed the leather helmet. Broad as it was tall, its torso was encased in a carapace of leather, shiny brown and hard as crabshell, shoulders bulging under iron link-mail. By comparison its shanks were bowed and stunted. A short sword stood out stiff in its fist, the blade steaming. Horrified, Ruan lay where he had fallen until the brute caught sight of him, started and, with a gobbling sound, leapt bodily from the rock and shambled towards him. Its sword flickered in the air, sighing as if the thirsty soul of the weapon and the raider's passion were united. Ruan had no will, no volition. The beast reared and struck. Only then, did Ruan fling himself away. The blade's edge trimmed a neat whittle of skin from his heel, awakening him finally from his trance.

Ruan ran blindly round the guardstone, the beast lumbering behind him, and, robbed of alternatives, struck out along the riverbank. Glancing back, he saw the brute on his trail, hunched, horny and hideously ugly. Ruan ran harder. Soon his speed outstripped pursuit.

Mist blotted out the canton from his sight and he was safe, safe, at least, from the sword, if not from the madness that had briefly infected him in that red hour of dawn.

At no time, after he made the river crossing, did it occur to Ruan that he could return to the security of Culln's hold. He had learned enough in his eleven years to realise that the plunderers would leave nothing but charred ruins and mangled corpses behind them when they moved on. He did not weep for his parents and friends. He was wary of self-pity in any guise.

If the day had been fair he might have chosen to head for the forest, to make contact with his father's tribe. But in a half day's march to the east the great green sea of trees barely came within sight. He knew he might starve before he found friends, if he survived the many dangers that lurked within the forest. The trees sheltered bands of the dark ones who paid homage to no king or chieftain, still tattooed their skins and preyed on travellers as their grandsires had once preyed on the hosts of Severus and Antonine. In addition the forest was full of fierce beasts, bears, wolves, boars and the striped cats that everyone feared.

Discouraged by all that he had heard of the forest, Ruan headed into the foothills above the river, up the staircase of scree which spilled down from the bowl of the mountains. He ran without rhythm and staggered to a halt when the faint trail petered out among giant boulders.

From the glen floor came piping shrieks that signified that the hedge had been razed and the steading breached, thin forlorn cries like those of curlews on the wind. Ruan heard no more from Culln's hold. By rights he should have died with the rest, ended his life in manly defence of the home place. It was the music that had cheated him, spirited him from the swords to wander and die of cold in the high barren hills. If that was how it was to be, he would at least follow his fate with courage.

Pushing on upwards, he discovered that the cloud eaves were not so dark and impenetrable as they seemed from below. But the cold and steepness soon sapped his strength and, weakened by despair, he stumbled and lay on all fours on the scree. Being young, he could conceive of no life more sweet than he had known in Culln's hold and, rolling on to his back, covered his eyes with his wrist and wept in sorrow for all that had been taken from him. He cried until no more tears came, then wiped his nose on his fingers and propped himself on his elbows.

The deer stood close, ears pricked; a young animal, obviously female, soft, timid and dainty and with a remarkable pure white coat. Skittishly, as if the boy's attention embarrassed her, she moved off a little way and stopped again. Snow flakes melted invisibly into her pelt. It seemed that the doe was waiting for him. Cautiously Ruan got to his feet. The deer moved again, and waited. She *was* guiding him: he realized it as if she had spoken to him. Obediently, the boy followed her.

The trail was difficult, around craggy overhangs and angled snowfields where the sleet blasted hard against him. Without the deer to guide him he would undoubtedly have slipped and plunged to his death. Sometimes he lost sight of the little animal, would be left to track her cloven spoor, then would come upon her again, watchful and waiting, her slender neck bent across her shoulder and her black liquid eyes quizzical.

Noon came and went. Still the doe did not rest. She seemed weightless, tireless. Indeed there were moments when Ruan fancied that the rock had run out entirely and that the doe ascended steps dabbed out of the sky, clambering up and up to seek a blessing of the sun, the favour of warmth to tint her white coat and make her one with the rest of her kind. Finally his guide stood upright on the saddle of the pass, pale against the vast blanket of cloud. Ruan hauled himself exhaustedly to the summit. The mountain was less hostile than he had imagined. Perhaps the gods had chosen to grant two small insignificant animals safe passage over the sky bow and would steer them down to places where men dwelt on the far side of the range.

Below the saddle the gradient eased. The doe trotted ahead of Ruan as if the scent of pine cones tickled her nostrils. Charged by her alertness, Ruan struggled to quicken his pace, but he was too weary and his legs bent like kail stalks and he slithered and fell and rushed down on his back and shoulders. Eventually, the ordeal ended. The deer picked up her hoofs and broke into a trot, racing fast over ground that was as flat now and green as summer pasture and the mists parted before her and in the far distance Ruan saw bright yellow flame. Strength sprang into his legs. He ran too, ran with the doe, his hand stretched out to span her neck and touch the sleekness of her rippling snow-white pelt, drawing more energy still from that wonderful contact. Deer and boy ran together out of the mists on to springy grass, past trees and budding shrubs towards the blossoming fire.

Gathered round the blaze were the men who had summoned him. Ruan supposed them to be his ancestors come to welcome him to the third portion of his life. But, as he came closer and the deer veered away and ran off into the mists again, Ruan saw that he was mistaken. There was nothing fine and handsome and noble about the men. They were aged, ragged, gaunt and suspicious, scowling at him with eyes like holes burned in goatshide, baffled too by the forces which had brought him to this place.

Behind the elders, layers of rock were fretted with blackened caves. Beyond the rocks, another range of mountains jutted implacably into the sky. Ruan's tongue stuck to the roof of his mouth and his legs turned to jelly beneath him. Reeling, he tottered forward and sank to the grass, whimpering in fear.

One tall elder hurried forward and stooped to aid him. Ruan clung to the stranger's cloak which was warm and musky and, like the man's arms, full of a strange healing strength. In an instant Ruan realized that he *was* wanted and would not after all be driven off to die in the mournful mountains.

Free of anxiety, he relinquished himself to darkness and the security of the stranger's arms.

3

The elder caste

A seamed, bearded countenance masked the light of the oil lamp and a gentle hand coaxed Ruan's shoulders from the pillow. The bed covering was a decayed deer hide. A second hide screened the mouth of the alcove in which he lay. A mutter of voices floated from behind the drape, dry, dull, petulant voices.

A dish touched his lips. He drank thin soup, squinting at the person who held the cup. The man's beard was long, but neither beard nor hair were rinsed with lime or hogs fat to give the bulk appropriate to high rank. The nether lip was like a little roll of soft red leather and the nose large and hooked. The eyes were unique, sharp as winter stars, with a remote, glittering grain in the centre of each pupil. It was impossible to guess at the man's age, older than Ruan's father, not so old as Culln's venerable sage. A forefinger touched a spot behind Ruan's ear and for an alarming moment Ruan's blood seemed to pulse in rhythm with the stranger's.

'Drink it all.'

Obediently Ruan emptied the spouted vessel which the man then placed on the shelf by the lamp. His features relaxed and became almost jovial.

'Are you afraid?'

'No, sir. Who are you?'

'I am Harkfast.'

Ruan could not formulate a question which would be free of unseemly curiosity. 'I am Ruan,' he murmured, lamely.

'From the settlement of Culln.'

'Ay.'

'Culln's hold is destroyed now.'

'I saw it, sir. I was there.'

'Did you encounter the raiders?'

'Only one of them, sir.'

'You were afraid of him?'

Ruan was tempted not to confess to his cowardice, but he suspected that the stranger already knew of it. 'Yes, sir.'

'That's as it should be, Ruan. You need have no fear now. You have found me, and will remain under my protection. Even if my companions snarl and insult you, you have no cause for alarm.'

'Are they displeased with me?'

'Ach, they are old men, and old men are given to vanity, believing that they have witnessed all earth's wonders,' Harkfast said. 'I see you are bristling with questions. That's all to the good. Your mind has recovered from shock and fatigue and soon you will be fit enough to chase answers for yourself.'

'Answers?'

'Where you are, who you are, and why you have been brought here,' said Harkfast. 'But now it is night and you must sleep again. Tomorrow I will show you that which must be shown and accordingly let you be seen.'

'By whom, sir?'

'Sleep, I tell you.'

Ruan laid his head on the pillow and allowed the stranger's fingers to lull the restlessness from his brain. As he stroked the boy's brow, Harkfast chuckled and murmured to himself.

'When I told them to build a fire, they accused me of squandering kindling. When I set watch upon the mountain, they complained that their eyes were tired. When my little navigator brought you safe into the valley, they were angry that I had proved them faithless. Alas, they have all forgotten what faith is and how to trust in forces which lie outwith their poor, depleted means.' The voice was gentle, soothing. 'We will teach them to trust Harkfast once more, will we not, fosterling?'

Sleep itched in the corners of Ruan's eyes. He struggled to stay awake. The tall man bowed gravely over him and made a swift perfunctory tracing of the thumbs. Peace and warmth filled the whole alcove and Ruan snuggled down deep under the hide.

'Tomorrow,' said Harkfast, to the sleeping boy, 'I will show you to the King.'

Harkfast helped him dress, replacing his torn clothes with a
tunic of saffron wool tasseled with weasels' tails, a flowing cloak
fastened at the throat with a foreign brooch, and sandals. His
tangled hair was curried with a bone comb until it capped his
head like a helmet. Ruan was astounded at the richness of the
vestments but said nothing during the robing. It would not do to
appear vain. When the robing was complete Harkfast steered
him into the outer cave which was dappled with morning sunlight. Hand on his shoulder, the old man conducted him out into
the crisp light of the day.

Ruan walked tall, as if he had no fear.

The sky was as clear as water, an iridescent surface which
rippled above them as if they were salmon in the current of a
stream. The sun and his daughter the moon stood together.
Ruan made the sign which his mother had taught him, crossing
his hands over his mouth, though somehow the gesture was less
casual and humble today. Harkfast was gratified by this reverence in his fosterling.

The valley was beautiful and apparently fecund. From the fragrant spring air Ruan inhaled a royalty of spirit that lifted his
poise and made him fit the robes that Harkfast had fastened on
him. Harkfast's fingers tightened. Bracing himself, Ruan
dragged his gaze from the mountain peaks and looked directly
into fourteen pairs of eyes which gaped at him as if he had tumbled new-born from the belly of the lady moon.

'I have brought you the boy,' said Harkfast.

The fourteen men appeared older than Harkfast. Clad in
soiled cloaks, all had raised their hoods as if afraid that the sun-
shine would addle their brains like a clutch of goose eggs. They
were priests of some order, Ruan thought. In Culln's settlement
there had been no priests. Culln's sage had assumed the labours
of instruction and minor ritual.

'Here is the boy I promised,' Harkfast went on. 'Delivered on
the appointed day. Here is the youth into whom the essence of

the King will pass in favour of the infant who lies silent.'

Harkfast raised his arms. Sunlight infiltrated his hair and beard transmuting the strands to fine gold. 'This youth is Ruan of the canton of Culln of the tribe of Poltalloch of the Pictish race. On his mother's line he is of the warriors of the Red Branch of Conor MacNessa of Emain Macha. The descent through the paternal clan reaches back to one of our own, the Druid Pirilla of King Rimmen of the Decantae, into the loins of the aristocratic warriors who subdued all in years which lie on the edge of memory.'

'How did you make this divination, Harkfast?' growled one surly elder.

'I have pored over the life of the boy in dreams, and heard the Tongue speak of him when Mungan was with us in the broch by the Sea of Herons before we were guided to his valley. I have fulfilled a long-standing prophecy with all the forces at my command and in obedience to the greater forces which command us all.'

The elders grumbled and tucked their heads deeper into their hoods. Ruan was amazed at the references to his ancestry which was a great deal less humble than his parents supposed. Ruan had never heard of Pirilla or Rimmen, but every boy in Drumalban could reel off the histories of MacNessa's Red Branch. He could not, however, be sure if the man spoke the truth or merely wished to impress the elder caste.

'Now I must give the boy to the King,' said Harkfast. 'Our King will understand that it is time to die and be father in the otherworld to the sons who preceded him, husband and lord to the fallen warriors of Gairesa who await the hour when he will fulfil his portion here with us.'

Again the elders mumbled, neither confirming nor denying outright their belief in Harkfast's claim.

Harkfast scowled and shouted. 'Do you doubt me?'

Ruan was prepared for a lengthy debate between the caste members and was surprised to be nudged in the small of the back and guided across the sward to the wide mouth of a cavern which lowered under the rock ledges. The cave narrowed quickly, and darkened. As Harkfast pushed him out of the sun fear returned. He could not retreat. The tall priest and the elders shuffled after him, crowding the cave mouth.

Resolutely Ruan faced the inner recesses of the cave, heart thudding, mouth parched, nostrils shrinking from the odour which he recognized as the stink of death. He rounded a gable of living rock, and halted in his tracks.

Taper-lit, framed in a canopy of skins, were two adult corpses and the wrinkled body of a tiny babe. The woman lay on her side on a litter of oak branches draped with scaly furs. On the ground around her all her treasures were spread out, a gilded torque, a mirror plate, five combs of painted bone, four rings of precious metal, ruby stones and hair beads, bowls too and similar vessels, a large cup carved from stuff like moonlight crusted over with blue pearls. Her body was wrapped in a scarlet robe. Garlands of water flags and meadowsweets graced her limbs. A wreath of oak and ivy leaves entwined with sprigs of mistletoe dangled on a straw from her neck-torque. In the centre of such munificence, her face was as plain as a withered leaf. Though carefully and elaborately painted, death had robbed the pigments of true tone, and only the eyelashes remained black and bright, like spikes of blackthorn. The babe had no furnishings of its own. Tiny and ill-formed, compressed by tight swaddling ribbands, it sat upright in the crook of the woman's knees.

The third corpse, propped in a chair of birch-rods and webbing, was draped in a purple cloak bordered with badgers' paws, the hood like a huge pocket shaped to contain the head. Clasped round the wattled throat were seven smooth rings of gold. On the left hand were seven matching finger ornaments. Feet and ankles were shod in untanned hide. Once the head had been noble, now it was mottled and degenerate, skin pasted to the bones like sack-cloth on a withy frame. The nostrils were pimpled and unclean. Warts protruded through the stubble beard like lambs' dung on frosty grass. The eyes were packed in swollen pouches and the hairbraids were little more than wisps of limewash teased out to cover the ears.

The King's rude stone dais centred on the cavern floor, all

29

three cadavers confined within a narrow space. Man, woman and child could have been roped by a goat's halter and noosed into a bundle like kindling.

Prodded by Harkfast, Ruan inched towards the trinity.

Studying the King, Ruan felt that this wallet of flesh should have been decently interred. Burial was the right of every man, whether of high birth or low. He had heard of clans who treasured the severed heads of heroes and bartered and fought for such talismans. In the world beyond he would no doubt stride lithe and tall, even more noble than he had been in the prime of his days on earth. Pity calmed Ruan's loathing and much of his fright.

Feebly, the corpse's fingers trembled, crooked and beckoned.

Ruan jumped back.

The King's eyes, yellow as knuckle-bones, stared straight at the boy. Awe and hatred and other qualities which Ruan could not fathom glinted in the pupils.

Ruan would have ducked and scurried from the cave, fleeing from the old King as he had fled from the beast of the rock if Harkfast, hard behind him, had not barred his escape.

'King Pasard,' Harkfast began. 'Ruler of a people who are mighty even in death. Lord and overlord, sleeper in purple shadows, I have procured the boy. I bring him for your approbation. The year quickens and our time together is short.'

Though Harkfast's tone was respectful, the cavern arches seemed to drain it of sincerity, so that the flattery was slight and the statements definitive.

King Pasard uttered no word.

The forefinger twitched again.

Harkfast edged Ruan closer to the throne.

Now Ruan could smell the death-scent, quite different from that which oozed from the Queen and the babe. Repelled and fascinated, he watched the kingly buttocks labour to find purchase on the webbing of the throne, saw the trunk crane, the hand rise slow as a lobster-claw from a boiling pot, float through space and alight on his shoulder, as if there was no arm within the sleeve to support it. Pasard's grip was not welcoming. Holding him firmly, the King gave him a thorough inspection, making the assessment without a grain of wasted effort.

Ruan steeled himself as the fingers crawled over him, measuring the strength of his arms and chest and the depth of his ribcage. It was not the touch which really judged him, though, but those all-seeing pus-coloured eyes. Though only a stripling, while undergoing the judgement of the King, Ruan judged the merits of the King in turn. Pasard's forefinger pressed the cleft which had lately begun to shape the boy's chin, and suddenly Ruan identified the quality in Pasard's eyes which had so far eluded him—humour. He, Ruan, was a wry, dry joke which Pasard and Harkfast had fashioned between them. Ignoring the assembled elders, the King spoke directly to Ruan, murmuring secrets which leapt light-footed across the generations. The hostility was gone. Ruan felt himself closer to this ruler than he had ever been to any living thing. The affinity was too fragile to endure. Even so it touched Ruan deeply, meant more to him than the accumulated wisdom of Harkfast ever came to do. It was as if the King had already donned the mantle of destiny.

'Boy,' Pasard said, 'you have been chosen out of stark necessity. The Druid may tell you that *he* chose you, but that is only a part of the truth. Harkfast is merely the instrument of a greater process of selection, the master of intelligences determined to lead you to me on this day. Nine days have I waited since my true son, the final fruit of my loins, tugged his mother back into the place too beautiful to leave. You, Ruan, have been brought out of mists and mountain snows to fulfil *his* future. Ay, I see you, child. I feel a hot male heart beneath your boyish skin. I say to all that you are indeed my choice, fit to contain the essences which time, grief and hardship have not wrung out. Soon Harkfast will call you his own. For a period, it will seem that you do belong to him. But listen! Listen and remember forever that which I tell you now, that which no Druid will ever confess—not even honest, wily Harkfast. Listen, Ruan! When you are made the vessel of all that is in me, then even priests and Druids will be your vassals. The power which flows from my bones into your bones will be *our* power. It will endure until the hour arrives

31

when you and I meet once more to talk of what has been accomplished, how well deeds mated with intentions and where all faults and fealties lay. Come that hour, it will be sunset for you too, and the essence will again be passed on. I pray that the day is far distant, that your life may be long in the sun, and glorious, that the deeds of it will be spoken of forever.'

Air seethed into Pasard's rotting lungs. He slumped back into the recesses of the chair, lids wearily closed.

'Mighty Pasard?' asked Harkfast cautiously.

'Ay, Harkfast, my Druid, you have done well; better than well. Is the snow gone?'

'Gone from the floor of the valley,' Harkfast said.

'Let the boy answer.'

'It lingers on the hills, my King,' said Ruan.

'And the sun smiles?'

'On all the grass and trees.'

'And the moon?'

'The moon rests, sire, for it is morning.'

Pasard smiled wistfully, as if the imagining of sun and moon in unity had soothed his troubled mind.

'Harkfast.' The voice was urgent. 'Give me the babe.'

The Druid plucked the bundle from the lair and placed it tenderly in the hollow of the King's cloak. Pasard's features softly receded into the hood until nothing was visible of his flesh save the gnarled left hand which cradled the little bat-like body to his breast. Sighing in satisfaction, his head fell slack.

Ruan did not need the elders' lamentations to tell him that Pasard was dead. The very instant of the King's passing was recorded deep in the honeycombs of Ruan's being, not in sorrow but with gladness beyond measure, as if some part of him too had won through to the sanctuary across the waters in the land beyond time

4

The weathers of the mind

In Culln's hold Ruan had witnessed death in many forms. Each of the victims had been mourned according to his station with a calm and stoical dignity. He was not prepared for the extravagant mourning of the elder caste, however. The old men scattered from the cavern clucking and squawking like hens. They threw themselves to the ground and writhed and contorted their limbs as if sorrow was a contest of eccentricity.

Ignoring the elders' antics, Harkfast took Ruan's hand and led him back to the cave where he had been robed early that morning.

'Sit.'

Ruan seated himself on the ground.

Rummaging under skins, Harkfast produced a clay jar, the broken seal plugged with beeswax.

The Druid picked it out with an antler awl.

It was hot in the cave mouth. Ruan sweated under his woollen robe. Harkfast poured a small quantity of wine from the jar into a clay dish. Ruan was beset by hunger and thirst. Catching the boy's eye, Harkfast handed him the dish and let him drink first. Ruan had never lipped wine before, only water, and a beaker of ale which one of the herders had left on the grass last Beltane. The wine was not bitter, not sweet, not sharp, not dull: it hardly served to slake his thirst, but, oddly, immediately satisfied his hunger. Harkfast decanted a dish for himself, drank it in one swallow, replugged the jar, hid it away again, and lowered himself to the ground too, legs outstretched, shoulders against the wall. Outside, the elders pranced and scampered, their wails diminishing as fatigue overcame them.

'You may take off the cloak,' said Harkfast.

Thankfully Ruan slipped the pin-clasp and dropped the garment, folded it neatly and laid it by his side. The robe probably cost more than Culln's eldest son had owned.

'I would offer you meat,' said Harkfast, 'but we have little of it here. Tonight there will be broth and jelly, though that will not fill your belly or give strength to growing muscles.'

'I am not hungry, sir.'

'You must call me Druid, or Harkfast, but not "sir".' Harkfast raised one eyebrow. The effect was intentionally comic. 'As the wise King told you, I must always be the vassal—though we will not delve into the intricacies of that matter just yet.'

'What did the King mean?'

'By what?'

'By telling how he had . . . had waited?'

'For a lad who should be dead,' said Harkfast, licking the wine dish with a long pink tongue, 'you have an uncommonly lively mind.'

'The King could not have known of me. Until yesterday—or was it the day before?—I had never been far from my father's . . .'

Ruan hesitated. Already he had almost forgotten his parents.

Harkfast pushed away the dish.

'Ruan,' he said quietly. 'They are all dead, your kinsfolk.'

'The plunderers?'

'The plunderers will have sailed off by now, leaving nothing alive. You have my oath on that, Ruan. By the *Glainnader*, the magic egg I owned once and lost in a flood, I swear that you did not desert the canton.'

'There was a beast—'

'Ach, they are all beasts,' said Harkfast. 'The Scotians—dwell-at-homes, sea-skimmers, wives, concubines or warriors—they are all beasts of one order or another, mostly shrews and weasels, with an occasional bull flung in.'

'Did *you* make them attack?'

Harkfast was obviously startled by this question.

'If you, Druid,' Ruan persisted, 'brought the music to my ears and sent the roebuck to find me, then you . . .'

'Did *I* do those things?' asked Harkfast, innocently.

'Ay, I feel that you did.'

'You learn more quickly than I have wit to teach,' said Harkfast. 'It is true that I exercised certain disciplines to locate you, but the power which utilizes music and deer is beneficent and could not be yoked to murder and rapine. Nay, Ruan, though it is a sign of perception that you ask such a question, I tell you truly that I helped you escape from certain death only because it was told to me, to the very dawn of the very day.'

'Told?'

'Enough! Enough!' said Harkfast. 'You push forward too rapidly. You have much of the owl in you, to mingle with the hare that knows when to run and, if the Tongue speaks clearly, with the boar that never shirks a battle.'

'The history of my ancestors,' Ruan persisted, 'is that true or false?'

Slowly Harkfast hoisted himself to his feet.

'True in substance,' he said. 'One day you may hear the whole song sung, young Ruan. But not now. I have many duties to perform. Those twigs of priests outside will be of no help and perhaps much hindrance in the progress of it.'

'Am I to stay with you?'

'Do you wish to stay with me?'

'If all my people are dead.'

'They are.'

'Then I wish to stay with you.'

'It is fortunate that you do,' said Harkfast. 'I fear there is no help for it now.'

'It cannot be changed?'

'Fosterling, I am a man who loves to talk. Indeed, I almost failed in the lengthy disciplines of silence when I was an acolyte and striver. But you, it would appear, might drain me dry of words. Ruan, do not pose another question until I give you leave. Already I am beginning to hear the King's voice in yours, and the plague of all *his* inquisitions warming up again.'

'*Can* it be changed, Druid?'

'Hoh! So you *must* have your answers as you require them,'

35

said Harkfast. 'Ay, it *can* be changed. Patterns are set in the position of stars and the circulation of gods through the firmament and across the earth. But patterns are never immutable. Time and again, Ruan, they *must* be changed, or all that is good here will wither and perish like roots starved of rain. Now that is all; do you mark me? Come, I have work for you, fit work for a lad, dull enough to tire you and distract your mind from matters of too much weight for one so recently fledged.'

'Druid, why do the old men thrash and wail so loudly?'

'To express that which they cannot deeply feel,' said Harkfast curtly.

He dug Ruan with his elbow, pushing him back from the cave mouth.

'Now go inside,' he ordered. 'I will show you what I require you to do.'

'But—'

'*Ach!*'

With difficulty Ruan held his tongue throughout the rest of the morning and, when evening came, found it more prudent to listen than to make himself heard.

The task which occupied Ruan's fingers if not his busy mind throughout the course of the day was intimately associated with Druid ritual. Harkfast did not tell him so, of course, but Ruan understood it. Milky and supple as wool, the bulls-hide cloak was too beautiful and ancient to be a secular object.

The Druid installed him in the alcove, provided him with four whippy willow-wands, a glove of bark-like material, a vial of scented oil and a buffing cloth cut from red deerskin. Ruan had watched Culln's tanner at work often enough to know how to use the tools. He beat the cloak carefully with the wands, rubbed the lining with oil, stroked the hair-side with the glove and circulated the cloth over the whole skin until the cloak gleamed and shimmered like new.

While he laboured he listened, and brooded on all that had happened to him. The din of the elders faded. For a while there was nothing to hear but the chipping of a rock-pippet and that sound of wind in empty spaces which emulates rushing water. The sun's shaft inched from the cave mouth and shadows carpeted the sward. Ruan did not venture from the cave. Though the Druid had not prohibited it, the boy sensed that he was being kept out of harm's way.

The sun was low before Harkfast returned. He praised the boy's work, took the cloak over his arm and vanished again, leaving Ruan alone, and idle.

When the wind dropped it was utterly still in the valley. Voices carried clearly, bringing words in languages which Ruan did not understand, others in intelligible accents. They were frequently angry words, shrill and hysterical; it seemed that the argument he had expected that morning had finally broken out. Surprisingly he heard nothing from Harkfast. Curiosity pricked him. Shedding his sandals he stole to the cave mouth, now black with dusk, and crouched down close to the opening. A communal fire flickered on the tarry stain of last night's blaze. Cloaked against the chill, haggard by their exertions, the elders gathered round it. A few were standing, others lay full-length, chins cupped on palms. There was no meat or drink to be seen and no instruments. Only the petulant whining of voices, singly and in unison, gave point to the convention. Far back, out of range of the firelight, Harkfast sat upon the ground, resting his spine against a smooth grey boulder, saying nothing. It was a strange encampment, without women, dogs, goats, swine or cattle, with no visible tools of hunting, herding or fishing. Did these ancients live on water and grass, or were they, for all their girning, so divine that they could exist without substance at all?

Ruan quickly picked up the gist of the argument. As he suspected, *he* was the source of the quarrel. To a man the elders were opposed to Harkfast and whatever the Druid had proposed.

The voices quaked with emotion, craked like crow-calls, twittered and broke and mixed together.

'Pasard is dead, a sign that we must leave this valley.'

'Starved long enough.'

'Came to sanctify the birth-ritual, watch a prince born, not to

37

'be blighted.'

'Evil influences.'

'Meat!'

'Drink!'

'Cold!'

'A boy of unknown origin.'

'Cannot accept him.'

'Blame Harkfast.'

'Harkfast did this to us.'

On and on the complaints continued, rising in pitch, until Ruan could hardly contain himself and wanted to leap to his feet and command the Druid to answer the charges against him. It was not that Ruan feared for his life—the elders would not have the strength to catch him, let alone kill him—he feared that Harkfast might be swayed by their collective will and, for the sake of peace, do as they wished and cast him again.

'Bury the King.'

'All honour and rites befitting.'

'Oak and ivy, where can we find them here?'

'Has anyone an ivy wand?'

'Who will trench the barrow? I cannot; my back aches so sorely.'

'My hands will not bend to hold a stone.'

'Harkfast must build the barrow.'

'Harkfast.'

'Ay, Harkfast.'

'My belly hurts.'

'I die with hunger.'

'Harkfast, we will stay no longer.'

'Take us from this barren place. Let us disperse, disguise ourselves, do what we can to find a place in the world again, eat food, drink mead, and laugh.'

'You promised us more than this.'

'You have failed us, Druid.'

Harkfast leapt to his feet, the action so sudden that Ruan scuttled back into the cave's recesses. The priests too were startled, shrinking away from their leader as he bounded into the

38

firelight, arms raised.

'You *cannot* go back to the company of men,' Harkfast bellowed. 'You are priests. You are Druids of the Elder Caste. Would you relinquish your vows, all that you have learned, pretend to be but poor seniors, begging hoof-gristle and fish-heads in a community of strangers, slaves to causes in which you will be allowed to take no active part?'

'Harkfast, we are starving.'

'We do not wish to die like the others.'

'Harkfast, there is no reason now.'

'The reason is in that cave,' said Harkfast.

'He is but a shepherd's boy.'

'He is the elected one,' Harkfast told them. 'He is chosen not by me but by the King. Have you grown so frail that you cannot remember how it was when our power brought down the Eagles of Rome?'

'We were young then.'

'What is age but a withering of the body!' Harkfast retorted. 'Druidical spirit is what makes you strong. Your limbs may drop off, eyes turn to glass, ears block with wax, bellies shrivel like toadstools, *but you will still be Druids*. Not only now, but tomorrow, and the year after tomorrow and the years after that, down and down into the wellsprings of the future—there you will have your reward.'

'We will not live so long.'

'You will live *always*,' said Harkfast. 'The heritage of the generations who follow in your wake and the unchanged holiness of the great vocation will be your organs of life. Pasard is *not* dead. Pasard has gone to the land beyond the waters, and has left behind him everything that you once pledged yourselves to protect.'

'The infant prince did not wish to live.'

'The infant, flesh of Pasard's flesh, was born too late to live,' said Harkfast. 'The Queen had no will to bear and suckle after her many tribulations. Besides, it was told that Pasard would sire no more sons.'

'It is not relevant, Harkfast. We must do as we must.'

'Druids built the universe,' said Harkfast. 'They were the masons of the gods. The canons of a twenty-year novitiate must have taught you that. I think you learned it only with your heads, not your hearts. Have you too been corrupted by Roman lies?'

'No, no. But we deserve a little peace.'

'You will have peace, all of you, very soon,' said Harkfast. 'All I ask is that you remain here in secrecy until the boy becomes a man. It is not long, an eighth part of a lifetime, seven summers in all. Protect him with your skills and sciences, teach, train and mould him so that he will lead us again and give us back the full rights of the Druidship. Without him we are lost.'

'Most of us will die long before he reaches manhood.'

'That is true,' Harkfast admitted. 'But at least you will have died as warriors of the oak, in battle against the powers of darkness and confusion.'

'Battle?'

'Not with swords, not even with satires and incantations, but with the full purpose of your being aimed at the survival of the order,' Harkfast cried. 'Druids, priests of Pasard, what else is left to us but to engage in this last magnificent battle?'

'I have a wife and children among the Maeatae. I have not seen them for twenty years.'

'*Now* you remember them,' said Harkfast. 'You did not care to recall them when all was well with us and we worked great magic. They will have forgotten you. They will not appreciate your resurrection. Ach, I am sick of you all. It is because of your weakness that the order has slumped into this parlous state.'

'It is because of the Romans and the women of the Picts, and the changing times.'

'The sword changes times, and Druids are the counterweights of warriors,' said Harkfast. 'Why is it that we were given the care of the lineage of the kings of the world? Why is it we have been granted the gifts of the ogham and the dream, shape-shifting, incantation, and the ability to make nature our weapon?'

'We have no implements left to exercise the rites.'

'Hah! Do you pine for the nudity of the virgins, then?' asked

Harkfast sweetly. 'Implements are but twigs of power. The true source of all might is locked in the mind.'

'We no longer believe you.'

'I am the Arch-Druid. I am Harkfast, the elected Chief.'

'We . . . we have talked together of that, too.'

'What is this you say?' Harkfast demanded.

'We have . . . have toppled you, Harkfast, by legal vote.'

'And which of you will take my place?' asked Harkfast.

'None would dare.'

'Yet you would depose me?'

'Ay.'

'Is this the will of the majority?'

'Ay, unanimously.'

'But you cannot leave a void in the command,' said Harkfast.

'It is . . . inevitable.'

'For an idle moment of earthly peace,' Harkfast said, 'you would destroy the last vestiges of the priesthood, leave it to be debased by wailing bards and taken over by jugglers.' He covered his face with his long fingers. A shudder shook him as a breeze stirs the leaves of an oak. 'You would hide your amulets and wands, deny your gods and the grace of the gods, all for a full belly and a dry bed.'

'We cannot hunt and game is not plentiful.'

'Yet there is enough,' muttered Harkfast, through his fingers. 'Enough to retain the spirit in your body for ever.'

'After Pasard's burial rites we will make our way from this valley.'

Harkfast lowered his arms slowly. He tilted back his head, beard jutting ferociously before him. 'If you attempt to leave, you may find peace sooner than you realize, under the snow's white shroud.'

'It is summer, Harkfast.'

'It is not summer, brethren,' said Harkfast. 'Outside our lovely valley it is still winter.'

'Do you threaten us?'

'How can I threaten you? We are equals, bonded in antique faith,' said Harkfast. 'It is my duty to warn you, that is all.'

41

'Tell us the particulars of your warning, then?'

'I tell you only that there are many more ways to sanctuary than through the barrows and the oak groves and the sacred tunnels of the tumulus,' said Harkfast.

'The boy—'

'The boy discovered steps over the mountain—but he approached from a different direction,' said Harkfast.

'Our way lies downward.'

'Ay,' said Harkfast. 'It does indeed.'

'And the feet travel faster on that incline.'

'Alas, that is all too true.' Harkfast shook his head. 'Can I say nothing to dissuade you from this course?'

'Nay, nothing. We are of one mind in the matter.'

Harkfast's hands shifted from his face into the position of the clenched fists, a gesture symbolic of his right to be the prime voice among them. His face was terrible, not in its rage, but in its sorrow, deep and guarded but utterly sincere. Ruan was to remember that sorrow, how the cold grains in the Druid's eyes melted at that moment.

There was no hint of submission in his attitude. Ruan wondered, perhaps, if this parting too had been told in advance by the mysterious Tongue.

'You will assist me in the final rites to our King?' asked Harkfast.

The old men mumbled. Ruan would not have accepted it as any sort of an answer. Harkfast, however, appeared to be satisfied. His fists dropped slowly, ponderously, to his sides. With the lowering of the hands the elders' respect was replaced by furtiveness.

'So it must be,' said Harkfast.

The fire had burned low during the long harangue, but no one, not even the fire-keeper, saw fit to load it with kindling. A stray gust of wind from the ice field almost snuffed it out.

'We are . . . we are sorry, Harkfast.'

'You must not condemn us.'

'I have no need to condemn you.' Harkfast bowed his head and turned, the robe sweeping out behind him as if it had grown longer. Shoulders hunched, he skirted the circle and strode silently towards the cave.

Hastily Ruan scrambled back and seated himself innocently on the bed. It was almost totally dark within the cave now. Perhaps Harkfast had forgotten him.

As the Druid entered the cave mouth, Ruan heard him murmur to himself, 'I fear, my brothers, that you are condemned.'

Ruan scraped his heels in the dust to make the priest aware of him.

'Ruan?'

'Ay.'

'Have you been listening?'

'I heard . . . some words.'

'Do not lie to me, fosterling.'

'I heard much, and understood little,' said Ruan. 'That is the truth.'

In the silence, Ruan felt the Druid's hand upon his hair. His face was drawn down into the musty cloak.

'There is no soup,' said Harkfast. 'They will go hungry tonight under the moon, saving what little they have for the journey.'

'Are we leaving soon?' asked Ruan.

'Ay, soon enough,' said Harkfast. 'Here, boy, curl into my cloak. You will sleep then, in spite of your empty belly. If you waken to strange sounds, do not pursue them into the darkness. It will be a form of darkness which swallows all things without discrimination, a great white darkness over which I have no power.'

'I do not understand.'

'Hush!'

Ruan closed his mouth: suddenly he discovered that he did not want to understand. Touching the Druid's cloak brought a drowsiness against which there could be no insurrection of the will. Clinging to the folds, he succumbed to it, slipping down into sleep.

Harkfast lifted him, laid him on the ledge and covered him

43

with the musty cloak, and Ruan slept like one dead until the coming of the moon began another day.

Ruan realized that he was no longer the simple shepherd lad he had been three days before. King and Druid had released dormant strains in him which, if his life had run to common course, might never have been freed at all. Boldness, intelligence and courage were faculties which could rust like unanointed dirks in iron scabbards. Though he did not know how this magic had been accomplished, belief in its veracity was strong. Wakened in the night by strange sounds, Ruan was no longer afraid of enchantment. Indeed, he had become a shade arrogant in being allowed to share the secrets of such powerful men.

What he saw that night taught him a valuable lesson. He learned that Harkfast held in the tip of one finger more knowledge of the workings of limitless forces than any upstart princeling could ever hope to acquire. Also he gained a new respect for the Druid and from that night on could never be sure that Harkfast was merely a bystander in the arena of the inevitable.

When the noises disturbed him, Ruan struggled out of bed and crept to the cave mouth. Harkfast was nowhere to be seen. One glance, however, was sufficient to tell Ruan that the elder caste were abandoning the camp. Obviously they did not trust Harkfast whose capitulation roused their suspicions that he plotted some dire ritual to cheat them of freedom. Though they had legally deposed him as their Chief, none had the temerity to call himself Harkfast's peer. Though Harkfast had been insulted, it was clear that he had not been defeated.

The last resort of the elders was stealth.

Lugging pitiful bundles of ritual accoutrement, they stole from their holes singly and in pairs, crept round the ledges and pointed their noses to the rising sun. Their promises to Harkfast and King Pasard were abandoned. They would not allow Harkfast another day in which to wreak his will on their fuddled brains. They had existed without the luxury of authority for so long that all recollection of the intensity of their vows and the

44

laws they had sworn to obey were forgotten. In fact, few could even sustain the simplest of chants or swing the bull-roar accurately. Now they would crawl down from the icy sanctuary, seek food, shelter and cheer, a welcome in the coastal settlements where former pupils might remember them, and the bards, if any bards remained in the troubled land, would plead for charity and wheedle a lowly stool for them among the bondsmen. Charity was better than frost and rowan-jelly. If they were fortunate, they would live out the brunt of their lives in impotent peace.

Shades against the rock, the elders slunk away across the valley floor, not in the direction from which Ruan had come, but up towards the smooth, harmless snow-fleeces which draped the hanging crags and, higher still, the thighs of the mountain range. Charted with stars, the sky was liquid clear. Far round behind Ruan's right shoulder, the moon silvered the snows. The straggling file of priests showed plainly—nine, ten, fourteen figures, tiny as shrews upon the bland landscape, limping awkwardly with age and baggage.

Wandering from the shelter of the ledges, Ruan counted up on his fingers: all the elders had left.

He walked a little distance after them.

The wind was faint but cold, crinkling his cheeks and making his breath raw in his chest. He hardly felt the cold though, aware that he would never see such a sight again. He was not mature enough to recognize in the flight of the elders the loss of his own kingdom. After all, they were old, old men, worn out and useless, not fit subjects for a young king. He supposed that they would reach the pastures below, separate, return to homes that no longer existed, to wives that were dead, to chieftains long since deposed, to sons who would spurn them, and daughters who would pretend that their fathers were warriors and had died long ago. Punishment enough for their disloyalty, Ruan thought, and hoped that they had left some food behind.

By now the first of the train had reached the summit of the pass. Light touched the snow around the leader faintly blue, like sea-fire. The priest seemed no larger than a mote of dust floating in the cold, wintry air. Below him, the rest of the band toiled

45

laboriously upward in sprawling files.

For an instant, as the wind dropped, the silence was intense, then cracked as ice cracks, sharp and sudden. The little men-things scurried hither and thither, darting round and round in frenzied circles, bundles dropping behind them like the dung of crazed cattle.

At first Ruan could see no cause for panic, other than the taut sound, which, like the snapping of a bowstring, was audible only for a moment; then he heard a second, louder crack, not like a string, but like an oak riven by lightning, and the thunderous quake of its fall. The thunder gathered, accumulated echoes and choked on itself. A line of spray, like a sea-wave, ribboned the mountain face close to the high crest. It shifted sluggishly and at first seemed as weightless as froth. But when the deluge struck the rocks' upper strata, it swept all before it and rushed on down into the pass. Minute balls of snow scampered before the wall of debris. Spits of icy dust enlarged until they sank exhausted to be devoured by the long irregular comb of the wave-wall itself. Soon the hissing mass, gathering momentum with every yard of descent, was laden with uprooted boulders and ice-blocks. Behind it the slopes were torn and naked. Scree-skirts and fine particles like a sleet-storm dragged in a veil from its head. More jagged cracks sounded above the rumble of the tide, webs of sound laced across sound, as the tide swamped the pass and roared over the frenzied figures, flattening them like weed-stalks, plucking them up and absorbing them into its core. Before the torrent piled deep against the far shore of the pass, it had consumed them all.

Only when the avalanche drove in upon itself did Ruan become aware of its volume. More savage than any sea he had ever gawked at from the headland of the kyle, it smashed and fell back, and smashed again as the moving mass of ice heaved and dislodged from unperturbed levels more great scores and claw-ings of snow. Then it was over, nothing visible in the base of the pass but a sifting dust which fogged the skyline and transformed the first rays of sunlight into a crescent of vague colours. It had lasted only as long as it takes to draw ten breaths. But in that space it had captured and drowned all the elders in its roaring peace. Already dissolving, the rainbow aura was a mingling of fourteen pale souls unhoused from their ancient, uncomfortable retreats. Rather than release them, the gods of the valley had swallowed the elders whole.

Ruan gave a wild shout, turned and ran down the trail to the caves in search of Harkfast. He was afraid to look at the ledges, afraid that the snow-tide would swerve down the floor of the pass and engulf him too. Only Harkfast could protect him. More than anything he wanted to bury his nose in Harkfast's cloak and steal sleep from its folds, sleep and waken and pretend that he had not seen the unveiled wrath of the mountain gods.

The lamp-wick clung to the lip of the bowl. The oil was impure and the flame spluttered and held shadows, filling the entrance of the cavern with a stink of burning. The one lamp on the floor gave barely enough light to show Ruan the Druid's brown-skinned heels, naked under the bulls-hide hem. King Pasard, his Queen and infant son were quite invisible in the darkness beyond the puddle of yellow light. Harkfast was on his knees, bent, beard brushing the ground, arms stretched out behind him, fists clenched. Sleek with grooming, the cloak covered the whole of his body, pinched round the neck with a torque of gold, forming a flare of hide to cover his head. The wand, of bright and slender stuff, was buried upright in the earth, an arm's length visible, capped at the tip by a hard round stone the colour of blood. Four bowls stood round it, each containing oak-fruit, leaves and bark. A fifth bowl, smaller than the others, held fourteen shrivelled berries of the mistletoe.

Not knowing if the rite was open to him, Ruan crouched down too, and bowed his head. The rhymes droned in the air, bee-dull, lazy, unimpassioned, unceasing. Though raging with impatience to inform Harkfast of the elders' deaths, he did not dare interrupt the ceremony. The Druid continued to intone, lips hardly moving. The ribband of words, unlike a bardic song such as Culln's sage might make to cheer the flight of the departed, had no particular inflection. The language was strange, formed at the back of the throat. Instead of being soothed by it, Ruan was greatly agitated. Harkfast's voice sawed at his nerves. Wriggling closer to the Druid's heels, he peered up at the hood of the cloak, willing Harkfast to give him attention. Though Harkfast's eyes were wide open, they did not remark the boy. The elongated ears with drooping lobes were deaf to everything except the messages which rang in his brain, which he was enjoined by his profession to formulate and make audibly manifest. The words hummed faster and faster, then, abruptly, ceased.

If Ruan had still been watching the Druid's features he would have seen a natural light return to his eyes. But the boy was crouched very low indeed, afraid that he had disturbed the ritual and would be punished for impiety. Though the chant was concluded, Harkfast did not rise. Listening, Ruan heard the supple creakings of the Druid's cloak. He would have preferred to sidle away out of the cave at that point. But Harkfast was no longer blind and deaf. Ruan curled himself into a knot on the ground to show how contrite he was, and almost forgot his news of the wonder of the tumbling mountainside. Brow tucked to knees, Ruan tilted his eyes. The Druid's fists were close to him now, the left shut up as tightly as the shell of a clam. But the right had slackened a little. The grey fat between the knuckles had changed. It was not fat at all. A drop of liquid dribbled into the hairs of Harkfast's wrist.

Ruan gasped.

The hands opened. In the hollow of each palm was a rib of snow, melting and moist.

'*Ruan!*' Harkfast's voice boomed in the silence.

Ruan jumped, tripped and sat on the ground.

'Ruan, return to the sleeping cave.'

'But . . . but the old men.'

'God in the Sky!' said Harkfast. 'Will you go, boy, or must I *kill* you to preserve the mysteries.'

Ruan rose, turned and fled. He hid under the brown blanket at the back of the sleeping cave, thumb in his mouth, fear in his belly, his mind boiling with the wonder of all the things he had seen.

*   *   *

When the Druid returned to the sleeping place at noon, Ruan wakened from fitful dreams. Harkfast had exchanged his ritual robes for working garments. His manner was brisk, not hostile. Even so, Ruan was still afraid, too afraid to ask questions. Throughout the course of the day and the rites and labours of the day following he did exactly what he was told to do, and kept his mouth shut.

The weather had changed. There was no warmth in the atmosphere. Above the ledges, the aftermath of the shifting mountain filled the valley all the way to the saddle of the pass. The mass was still now, glazed and glittering in the glassy blue light of day.

The effects of his last two days in the valley were beyond the horizons of Ruan's intellect. Most of what he was ordered to do was labourers' work, the remainder enigmatic. Carefully he followed Harkfast's directions in every particular, though the Druid gave him no explanations and, in all that time, hardly uttered twenty words to him. The work of the first afternoon was to gather kindling, drag twigs and deadfall branches back to the mouth of the cavern. There the Druid examined the fuel to determine its suitable properties. At dusk, Harkfast allowed Ruan to rest, and fed him braised hare which did not taste fresh. Too hungry to be fastidious, Ruan ate it all, sucking the bones, washing down the meal with a mouthful of scented wine from the jug. He was not permitted to sleep, though. By the light of four lamps he carried the chosen wood into the depths of the cavern and piled it round the king's throne When that was done to Harkfast's satisfaction, the Druid spread the bulls-hide cloak between the bowls of oak-mast. The shrivelled berries and the wand had been taken away. Shuddering with cold and fatigue, Ruan stripped naked. Harkfast wrapped him tightly in the cloak and extinguished the lights.

Ruan slept deep, deep down in darkness, and wakened warm at first light.

On the second day he toted stones to the cavern mouth. At noon the Druid lit a small fire and steamed a tasty soup out of stringy hare meat seasoned with roots and herbs. Ruan ate greedily, then returned to his labour. All afternoon until dusk he lugged stones to the cavern. While he worked he had strength in plenty and only when he was given leave to rest did he find himself weak with exhaustion, dimmer than the dimmest little star in the silken sky.

That night Ruan stripped and once more wrapped himself in the Druid's ritual cloak under the king's throne. Once more he slept. Dreams troubled him, however, fantasies of power unlimited, words issuing from the wrinkled lips of Pasard, the cadaver, which stood watch over him, preserved against decay by the cold air.

Come morning Ruan felt surprisingly strong and calm, larger than he had done yesterday. He determined that he would stay awake that night to listen to Pasard's verities, to be filled at last with funds of knowledge suited to a king.

But there were no more nights in the valley.

That midday, after a helping of reheated broth, Harkfast donned his ceremonial vestments, brought out the wand, a sickle of gilded wood and a curved knife with a bronze blade. He entered the cavern alone.

Ruan was ordered to build a wall, the pattern of it scratched out for him in the dirt. In his newfound maturity he was able to work without supervision, piling the stones high against an osier framework. His task was near completion, hours after the Druid had entered the cave, when Harkfast's sobbing rose from within. The sound caught Ruan completely off-guard. He paused, a heavy speckled stone in each hand, to listen. He felt his heart cramp with sorrow for the Druid, whose loving had reached beyond duty, who had lost not only a king but a companion. After a time, Ruan went on with lifting and laying, balancing the boulders with extreme care now that the wall was high and half the height of the cavern mouth closed off.

A first wisp of smoke slithered along the roof out into the air. It curled and coiled like a tuber root into the sky, blue-grey against the pure blue infinity. It was quickly followed by a puff of thick grey-brown smoke which alarmed Ruan and made him step back from the wall. Another billow followed the first, denser, alive with the crackle of burning twigs and the sappy hissing of branches.

Climbing over the dike, Harkfast duly emerged from the smoke, his white cape smeared with ash. He was chased by a blast of heat and tongues of scarlet flame which licked the cavern ceiling. In a bulge of his cape, the Druid had accumulated his personal artifacts, but oak-bowls, votive offerings and all the rich things of the King and Queen were left to the fire.

Eyes streaming, the Druid wept. Ruan drew in a mouthful of the scent of the incineration, found it fresh not acrid. It expanded within his chest and made his head light. Arms by his sides, chest naked, Ruan inhaled the final invigorating essences of the King, absorbed them into the fibres of his body and brain. When the rock turned white and the cave roof split like a dragon's beak and let the earth vomit out, he did not step back. The dike had been cleverly constructed to contain the slumps and voidings and close off the cavern completely.

For a moment longer Ruan heard the fire gorging, until, replete at last, it sighed and died too. A few straggling feathers of smoke, black as raven's down, whisked upward on the breeze.

Man and boy left the valley two hours before dusk. They carried little except the Druid's tools, a pot, and a heavy object tied in a leather sack, which Harkfast would not allow him to touch.

They did not converse.

They did not glance back.

They walked across the flanks of the slope towards the pass, snow firm underfoot. They stabbed at the surface with their toes, bypassing the great jumbled hummocks under which the elders slept, digging into the hard fluted snow climbing higher and higher into the rising wind.

When it was night they were far past the saddle on the downward track. Here were trees in leaf and a chattering stream and shelter in the brush.

But no moon.

Never again, Ruan thought, would there be such a sun and moon as stood over the hidden valley in the four long days it had taken him to be born a king.

Part 2

The forest

1

The shield of time

A night and day of fast foot travel carried Ruan through the depths of the forest to the cattle-herders' lonely settlement on the borders of the province of Cairncha. There he spent a night, and a day and a night, in the plump, brown arms of Rea, and spurred her four times. For some mysterious reason the return trip took twice as long, and almost a week passed before he again came to the edge of the clearing of Domgall.

In spite of his size, Ruan approached so quietly that not even the dogs caught wind of him. He was downwind, of course. He had learned never to arrive at an inhabited plot, even the home-place, in any other manner. Still within the shelter of the tree-ring he paused and studied the scene. Quiet enough, almost too quiet. The three stone-and-wattle dwellings seemed deserted. A spiral of smoke purled lethargically from the thatch-hole in Harkfast's retreat. By its slight shifts and the imperceptible floating of insects over the dung clouts in the bush, Ruan judged the drift of the evening air. In spite of the peacefulness, he was not entirely at ease, and did not for the moment move openly into the clearing.

Seven summers had come and gone since first he clapped eyes on the place. He was then so hungry and sore that he could hardly drag himself across the earth towards the appetizing aroma of cooking meat. Not much about the place had changed in the intervening seasons; the camp had grown one more shelter, and he had swelled and sprouted like a healthy thistle to become strong in body, intellect and in spirit. Though Ruan was blissfully unaware of it, he had also grown in arrogance. Even Domgall, his wizened little instructor, occasionally found Ruan's pride insufferable and wished that he was still small enough to cuff across the rump with a dog-leash. To remonstrate now with the tall young man was hopeless; Ruan merely laughed at chastisement.

At first he had been afraid of Domgall. The Pict was small and swarthy, scarred and gnarled. The scrawls of the warrior still burrowed under his flesh like coloured worms, a sign of age and ferocity. Even the greatest of the warrior Picts, who inhabited strongholds on the coasts and the lush grazing lands beyond the forest, no longer prodded clay into their flesh, though they still painted their bodies for feats of combat, clashes of arms, and festivals.

The wheel-shaped houses were in good repair now, turf and thatch well-knit. The long rectangular weems, which had been there for such a multitude of years that Domgall had no notion as to who had done the digging, had been extended and raised two tiers above the ground. The dogs occupied the upper floor. The lower was used for storage and to stable Domgall's four shaggy horses during the wettest quarter of the year. Dogs were the coins of Domgall's trade, defenders of the encampment, and its overlords. The Pict bred, reared and trained them, then traded them off at markets or in private barter for mead, wine, ale, cornflour, salt and other luxuries which the forest did not provide. In one of the round-houses Ruan lived with Domgall. The second, smaller habitation belonged to Harkfast. Sparsely furnished, it sheltered not only the Druid but his garments and tools and the puzzling wedge-shaped satchel he had brought from the valley, and which had hung unopened on a peg on the rooftree since the hour of arrival.

The trek from the mountain to the forest clearing had taken five days. It had happened so long ago that Ruan could not even remember in which direction the mountain range lay, though the events of his stay in the valley were packed in his memory. Occasionally, when he had pilfered an extra quart of mead from Domgall's hoard, he would find the recollections very sharp indeed, would steal off to a private place in the forest, kneel, and call out to Pasard to inform the king that all was well with him.

For Ruan, all *was* well.

The young man did not dwell on the past, or seriously contemplate the future much beyond his next trip with Domgall to deal off a brace of hounds, or a quick foray to spur Rea or one of his other women. He was a king in early exile, and found the state extremely comfortable.

The seven years, however, had not been squandered.

Domgall had trained Ruan in the crafts of hunting and war, had taught him to use stealth and observation, to hurl a bone-tipped throw-spear, to fire an arrow from the handsbreadth bow, how to angle a dirk for a quick killing, how to maim a man with bare hands; all the sundry skills that went with such an education. At first Ruan had been trained with the dogs, like a dog, in fact; beaten when disobedient, rewarded when he did well. Ruan knew most of what there was to know about the husbandry of hounds. Horses too were no strangers. But such subjects were secondary to acquiring the high arts of a warrior.

Domgall's maternal grandsire had been a kern, a mercenary, for the Eagles and had guarded the wall of stone and fought in the Orcades, Thule and Hibernia, until seasickness and love caused him to desert. Domgall's father, and Domgall too, later changed sides, fought with the Atacotti, which was no tribe at all but the best of the paid men of all clans and races. Such experiences Domgall distilled and poured out to Ruan—thrust and parry of the man-spear, the distance javelin, the short sword, and the long sword; the defences of the spiked shield and the round leather targe; footwork and the use of guile. All these lessons Ruan loved. In spite of his insolence and mischievousness, he did nothing to make the Pict ashamed of him, and administered many stinging whacks to his tutor's shaven crown with the flat practice sword as signs of affection and respect.

To Harkfast, of course, fell the principal burden of instruction; not only in religion but in history and ritual, oratory and invective and the use of language in many tongues. The Druid hardly ever left the clearing, except to visit the oak-groves beyond the horse pasture to make prayers in the shadows of the boughs. He spent most of each day indoors, though he was not morose or withdrawn. Sometimes he would venture out to watch drills and mock combats between Ruan and the Pict and laughingly egg on Domgall to brain the young man if he could.

Four years ago, at Harkfast's instigation, Ruan had chosen Cailleach as his personal goddess. Though an ugly deity of winter and a female to boot, she was also the mother of all forest creatures, as loving and as fierce as any animal mother. Her worship and lore had roots in time so ancient that even Harkfast did not know much of it.

Ruan always found it difficult to concentrate on the Druid's words while the dogs barked interestingly and the insects sang and the confidences of the wind told him that salmon would be slapping over the river rocks and stags browsing on the tender shoots along the open trails.

As he grew older and left the camp more often as Domgall's companion, however, Ruan found that learning was not an end in itself but had many useful applications. On visiting the thriving communities of the coastal region he discovered that he could understand the voices of the motley men who gathered to trade their wares. He might have haggled with brewers and weavers and sellers of salt, chatted with potters and wheelwrights and the workers of black and red iron, with Saxons from the long ships and the Picts from the Long Island, all with equal facility. But Harkfast had forbidden him to use more than two dialects, one Scotian and one Caledonian. Even so, this combination allowed him fair licence to charm merchants' daughters and free women whose function in the pleasure bed he had learned early. Domgall did not inhibit his amorous adventures. The Pict believed that exercises of the flesh had many manifestations, all of them vital to health and amusing into the bargain. Between trading excursions, Ruan lived alone with his Druid and his instructor, ate meat in plenty, drank mead and barley ale, dressed in warm furs, and dreamed less of glory than of the big stags of the plains country and the soft, warm, willing girls of the lonely settlements. Few strangers ever strayed into Domgall's clearing. Harkfast had strewn the periphery with powdered seeds and breathed instructions to the friendly trees, appointing them guardians over the secret place. The spell had so far been highly potent; Ruan could not remember when the last unknown visitor had happened upon them.

That evening, though, all was *not* as it should have been. Standing by a lithe birch in thinning underbrush, only fifty yards from the weems, Ruan intuitively sensed that the peacefulness veiled danger. He was not afraid or seriously alarmed, though the bands of muscle over his torso tensed a little.

Reaching behind him he crushed the leather satchel and cramped bow, spear and four arrows together to deaden all sound. The rush of the evening breeze passed along the pine-tops and stimulated the finger of smoke above Harkfast's house. In the pasture the small, shaggy horses contentedly cropped the summer turf. The dogs in the long-house were dumb.

That was it! The dogs were completely silent.

Ruan faded back into the trees.

Stooping, he unlooped the satchel from his shoulders and tugged out the thong. He must choose between the bow and his hunting javelin. The javelin was narrow and flexible but not particularly strong, quite unsuited to hand-to-hand combat. On the whole it would be better to vote for the bow. He dallied, undecided, then obeyed whim not logic and took up the spear. An iron dirk was strapped to his back, the sheathed point tucked into the waist of his breech-clout.

It would be dark in an hour. The sun had already faded from the clearing. Pigeons cooed and whirred in the forest branches and across the glade a thrush spun a complicated saga to the evening moths. Ruan shifted through the underbrush. He would not wait for dusk; many things could see better in the dark than man. As his angle on the clearing altered, he detected other signs that something was amiss in the home-place. The flavour of roasting pork was sweet in the atmosphere. Domgall, like many of the clansmen of the north, was prohibited by taboo from the eating of pig-meat, and Harkfast would not kill and cook a swine for himself. There was another scent too, reminiscent of clover honey, but not so sharp. Moving cautiously round the clearing, Ruan soon found more evidence of disturbance. Close by Harkfast's door, six large gouts of earth had been howked out of the grass. The hide drape was dropped across the door opening; also strange, for the evening was warm. Perhaps the Druid was about the preparation of some magic. Ruan soon quelled that notion by observing that the curtain was lowered over his own sleeping-hut too and that the grids of the weems were fastened.

The dogs were audible, moving but not mouthing. The pups whined and whimpered a little, and pliant tails swished against the wicker walls of the whelping stalls. He went on again, not pausing until he reached the path by the stream. Here, squatting, he studied the moist earth and tall grasses and squinted through the leaf-tunnel to the fish-scale of the water. There was no rank wolf smell and, though he did not have any first-hand experience, he doubted if a bear would be so stealthy a marauder. Domgall's teachings came clearly to mind. This had the appearance of a trap. He would treat it as such, cunningly not boldly. He came to the bank of the shallow water so quietly that nervous minnows did not even dart away but stayed flickeringly still browsing on cress and drowned flies like tiny tags of leather stuck to the stones. He crossed the stream at the mossy ford, circled away from the path through the trees over spongy pine-mat, and emerged in the birch-brake where hewing and chopping was done in fine weather. There he found what he sought, an extension of the six gouts of earth leading back from Harkfast's place, through the sparse brake and back over the stream.

It was a large horse, certainly not one of Domgall's. It had carried the weight of a man. The depth of the tracks indicated that it had been burdened by pack-panniers so heavy that, even in the dry, the horse had driven down hard with its haunches to struggle up the slope. Droppings, containing seeds and stems, were firm and well-shaped, not like the slop of grass-fed ponies or the palfrey of a common trader. If the rider had alighted this side of the clearing, he must be as weightless as a froth-bubble. So, a laden horse had been ridden up to Harkfast's door. But what then? Where had horse and rider gone? Why were the drapes lowered and the dogs muffled?

Widening his arc, Ruan recrossed the stream, steering well clear of the home-place, until he reached that zone where the night-wind wavered and changed from right to left. Giving the weems his scent for a few moments he was rewarded by a chorus of barking from within—then silence—a growling outbreak— silence again.

Only Domgall had that kind of mastery over the dogs. Domgall must be in the weems, holding the whip and showing the animals his fist. Why was Domgall hidden in the weems? Was the proud little Pict a prisoner? If the captor had sense enough to muffle the animals, he would surely interpret the bout of barking as a sign that someone had broached the clearing. And where was Harkfast? Had he been taken too?

The natural avenue into the camp lay between the round-house and the weems gable. A breathing slot in the gable might enable him to peer inside. But was just as likely to land him with an arrow in the eye. Crawling like a newt, he came out of the brush on his belly, and stopped before the grass cover ran out.

Somebody had broomed out the round-house. Domgall performed the chore twice a month or so, but swept straight into the main compound, not round corners. Ruan scowled. The trap was a true trap, a hunter's trap, almost undetectable. Ruan doubted if he would have noticed it at all but for the hint of the sweepings and a keen instinct in such matters. A man's length by a man's height square, the coating of the pit was neither unduly damp nor dry. The sweeper had cleverly disguised the matting at the hems. Below the lid would be spears or staves to disembowel the unwary.

Hah! It would take more than a pitfall to bring Ruan down. Pride and guile blended in him. He was relieved at the banality of the adversary's strategy.

Creeping backwards, Ruan again hid himself among the pines, back against the trunk of a favourite tree, a spot to which he adjourned when he wanted to dream undisturbed of woman-flesh. Moths were becoming increasingly luminous; a half hour of light remained of the day. Possibly he might outwait the ambusher. But the men of the tribes had a surfeit of patience in their livers, legacy of years of rain, bitter winters and thievery. Some could outlast a hedgehog in a seasonal sleep if they put their minds to it. Nay, he could not afford to wait. Besides, it was not in his nature to be passive.

Glancing up at the twined branches, he caught sight of the whisking red tail of a squirrel as it darted out of range. Ruan grinned suddenly, hoisted himself to his feet, and returned to the last rank of pines before the clearing. He scaled the tall tree with ease, making less noise about it than the squirrel. He crept along the branch until the bushy tip bent and dipped, four or five feet short of the roof ridge of the weems. It would do. He propped his spear in a fork, and lowered himself to the ground. Back in the forest, he found a large stone, dug it from the sponge, tucked it under his arm and carried it back to the pine tree. It was very difficult to prevent the branch shaking as he manhandled the boulder into the lower branches. He had learned a similar method of boar-baiting, however, and applied the grip of one sole against the other heel to keep balance. As he could not attain the end of the branch with the boulder in his arms, he braced himself firmly against the trunk and lowered the stone into his hands like a soup dish.

Below him the dogs were whimpering again; the whelps could not keep quiet for long.

Ruan lifted the boulder, bent his spine, and hurled the missile accurately over the gable end of the weems on to the lid of the pit-fall. It crashed through the covering in a cloud of dust and a din of noise, increased by Ruan's simulated screams of pain.

Released from Domgall's command the dogs broke into a furore of barking. Ruan did not hesitate. He danced along the sappy bough, snatched up the javelin, leapt, and landed on the roof of the weems. His heels cracked the thatch but the ladder of poles supported him and he ran quickly up the rafters to the ridge. Knee and foot upon it, spear poised, he watched Domgall race from the doorway below and swing towards the crumpled pit. Domgall was followed by a tall, well-muscled man. His hair, cut short like cloth of gold, his bronze colouring and the crested bridge of his nose indicated that he was a Roman. Ruan could easily have shot the javelin through him at that range. But the stranger was unarmed, and Ruan would not make a thrust

62

through the back. Shouting, he caused the stranger to whirl, saw green-gold eyes, like the lights of a wild cat, split by narrow black irises, wide with astonishment.

Ruan uttered a venomous cry, and projected the hunting spear with all his might. Domgall yelled at him, but Ruan was deaf to everything save the whistle of the rotating javelin.

The barb struck the stranger in the centre of the chest, ripping the toga-like garment. The man grunted, flopped backwards and sat down upon the ground. His thighs were full, bunched with muscles, his feet shod in blond leather sandals clasped with silver medallions. The medals would look well, thought Ruan, draped on the house wall.

The stranger, however, was far from dead yet.

The barbs had failed to penetrate. The blunted javelin had bounced to the grass. Under the toga was a bronze breast-plate. Ruan cursed the impulse which had directed his aim at the heart and not the gullet or eyeball. With a hoarse shout, he dived from the roof-ridge. He did not hurl himself directly at the Roman who, while apparently stunned, might still have enough wit to tug out a knife. Clasping the dirk in his fist, Ruan landed in a crouched position, whirled and lunged.

The whip stung his wrist, wrapping fire up his forearm. In spite of the searing pain he did not release his dirk, drove on relentlessly at the Roman. It was not until Domgall reined him down, tossing his weight back into the whip-stock, that Ruan swerved from his course. Even then, with Domgall dragging him, and his dirk-hand useless, Ruan managed to reach out, grab the stranger's patrician beak, yank him forward and stamp down a heel on the nape of the golden neck. The blow, however, was not forceful, Ruan was badly off-balance—which may have been as well, for the heel-jab, if properly delivered, would kill a man as effectively as a dirk.

Bawling, Domgall reeled him in on the whip like a ferocious pike from a bog lochan. Obviously Domgall was party to the trap, anxious that Ruan do no more harm to the stranger. The whip-coil scorched his flesh. Angered by the pain, Ruan could not bring himself to leave the matter as it stood. Cocking his

wrist, shortening the Pict's hold on the lash, he canted his elbow
and shook the leather stump from Domgall's fingers. Swinging
the whip, butt-foremost, he clipped his instructor across the
shins with it. Domgall scuttled back, limping, tripped and
padded off on all fours like a cowardly hound. Though the spleen
was out of Ruan, he did not end the game yet. Pivoting, he whis-
tled the lash over the Roman's head, forcing the stranger to drop
dizzily to the ground, one arm folded over his head and the other
wagging in a desperate signal of submission.

Ruan unwound the whip from his arm, switched and cracked
it, stingingly but with no great weight, across the stranger's
upraised buttocks. Laughing now, Ruan dropped the lash and
kicked it away. There was more laughter behind him. Helpless
with mirth, Harkfast leaned against the flanks of a large corn-
coloured mare which, to judge by the state of the lintel thatch,
the Druid had just led from hiding in his own cramped house.
Ruan laughed louder, slapping his hip. And Harkfast laughed so
much that he slithered to the earth and kicked his shanks in the
air like a spring foal. Eventually the Druid and his fosterling
wound down, gulping, gasping and sobbing, then, worn out,
ceased their laughing fit.

Showing a tight, unconvincing grin, Domgall limped over to
his pupil. 'Ay, Ruan,' he said thinly, 'indeed you did well.'

'Who is the Roman?'

'Come, meet him,' said Domgall.

The handsome man had hauled himself to his feet by now,
though he still held his hand up in a *pax* sign. Ruan judged him
to be in the prime of life, forty summers or a little older. There
was no bitterness in his smile, though wariness loitered in the
gold-green pupils. The irises were narrow. The white teeth
striped with gold in two places. On his fingers were golden rings.
If he had ridden unescorted through the forest laden like a treas-
ure-boat, then he must be a brave—or foolish—man, indeed.
Brigands would kill without compunction for a hundredth part
of the hoard he wore on his person.

'By Nemon, Juno and Old Black Annis, you *are* an ingenious
young man.' The Roman spoke in the language of the Britons,

though he used Latinate nominal forms for the gods. His lazy, drawling tone mixed all the words together, like corn flowing from cupped hands.

'Are you a "guest" in the place of my friend Domgall?' asked Ruan, in Latin.

'After a fashion.'

'Then I am sorry if I did you hurt.'

'No, Ruan,' murmured Domgall, 'Gadarn has come far to reach this place and the trick was his idea.'

'I deserved what I received,' said Gadarn. 'However, that was only a sport, a jest. Tomorrow we will try a little harder.'

'I do not understand,' said Ruan. 'You are a games-master?'

'Not quite!' said Gadarn.

'Tomorrow,' said Domgall, simply, 'Gadarn will kill you. That is the nature of his brief.'

Ruan stared incredulously from Domgall to the stranger, then glanced round to seek Harkfast. But the Druid had gone. The huge, golden-maned mare stood alone peacefully cropping a handful of windfalls.

When he looked back at the Roman, Ruan knew that Domgall had spoken the truth.

The white spiced pork was succulent. Ruan could well believe Gadarn's tale that the meat-gift came from a piglet suckled on mead and fed on ripe chestnuts. The Roman also produced a tall amphora of wine pressed from grapes grown on the Isle of Oranges which was set in a warm blue sea near the land of the sand-oceans. Though the wine was sweet and heavy as honey, Ruan rationed himself to a single beakerful, mindful of tomorrow and the demands that would be made on him.

Gadarn was the son of a pure-bred Roman centurion who, stationed at Eburacum, had married a minor princess of the Brigantes. Her father, Gadarn boasted, had been the most famous swordsman in the legendary regiment of the Votadini. When hardly more than an infant, Gadarn's Britonic mother had died. His father remarried and left, with his new wife, for a tour of

65

duty in Hispania, virtually abandoning his first-born son to the care of a bondsman. Perhaps an unsettled childhood had something to do with Gadarn's subsequent behaviour. Though he had fought well and commanded intelligently, he never truly regarded himself as a citizen of the Empire. He cultivated an interest in food and wine and women to a degree which, for a military man, brought him into disfavour. When the garrison of Eburacum, under control of the loutish Emperor Constantine, was marshalled to quell the uprisings of the barbarians in Hispania and Gaul, Gadarn left the service. Whether he was given leave to retire, or whether he simply deserted, Ruan never discovered; nor did he unravel the link between the Roman and Harkfast which had brought the man from his wine-trading in the region of the Dumnonii and the short sea crossings.

Harkfast did not share the supper. He remained shut away in his own house. Ruan was under no illusions; this was a device of the Druid, an initiation test. All three men had conspired to put him through a preliminary challenge merely to see if he was prepared. 'The jest' had almost cost Gadarn his life, though Ruan had been in no serious danger himself; the pit was shallow and filled not with staves but with dung from the weems.

When prudent, Ruan excused himself from the table, and went across the compound to Harkfast's place. The curtain was still drawn. Ruan stamped his foot on the worn step before entering. The Druid was seated on the ground, back against the roof-pole. An oil lamp burned wanly on a hook. In the lap of his robe was a leaf full of hazel nuts, the last of the winter store. He ate them one at a time, nibbling with his front teeth. He did not seem surprised to see Ruan.

'Is it true, Harkfast?'

'It is.'

'Tomorrow that man will try to kill me?'

'It will be a fair contest, bound by strict rules.'

'Did you summon him here for that express purpose?'

'Fosterling, you cannot be protected by the shield of time all your life long.'

'I see,' said Ruan. 'It is a test?'

'In nineteen days the eve of midsummer equinox will be upon us. The stars and portents declare this period as the most advantageous for you to receive your rites of initiation, to become a man.'

'Not Beltane?'

'You are no common herder now, Ruan,' the Druid told him. 'Beltane is not the best festival for you. Midsummer will be the day of your acceptance.'

'If I survive, that is?'

Harkfast nodded solemnly.

'Will Gadarn really kill me?' Ruan asked.

'If you give him an opportunity.'

'Single combat?'

'That would not prove enough.'

'If it comes to it, Druid, may I kill him?'

'If it is necessary to defend your own life.'

'Why is Gadarn doing this?'

'I need the services of a stranger. Domgall will help him, but one cannot depend on your instructor's ruthlessness. Gadarn will have no mercy.'

'What is his reason, Harkfast? Are you paying him?'

'No. I will tell you soon,' said Harkfast. 'For seven years I have held my peace; another moon is not too long to wait for answers.'

'What is the form of the contest?'

'You will be instructed tomorrow.'

'Harkfast, what will you do if I am killed?'

'Mourn you,' said the Druid. 'And find another fosterling.'

'I thought as much,' said Ruan. 'Why don't you prevent it?'

'Do you ask out of fear?'

'I have no fear,' said Ruan.

'Then that will be one of your lessons. Fear is a quality you must re-learn.'

'Gadarn will teach me?'

'He has much experience.' Harkfast nibbled another nut, found it sour and spat the mush on to the floor. 'It is imperative that I put your learning to the test, Ruan. It is not enough to forge a sword; it must also be tempered in blood.'

Ruan held up his hand. 'Never fear, Father. I will temper hard and straight and as flexible as a withy wand.'

'I believe you will, fosterling.'

Harkfast, hazels in each palm, fashioned the sign of the thumbs over the young man. Ruan bowed, then lifted a blanket from Harkfast's cot and went out into the forest by the edge of the pasture. He slept there, under the infinite sky, slept deeply without dreaming until Domgall wakened him in the hazy light of dawn.

2

The black dogs of Domgall

A faint mist lay over the underbrush. From it the pines soared upwards towards the innocent sky. Bracken, gorse and woodbine cocked tendrils from the haze, each spur and frond glistening in horizontal strands of sunlight.

Ruan blinked and sat up. Domgall stood grimly above him, the Pict's body dyed carmine, the coloured worms which nested in his skin revivified by clay and berry-juice. In one hand he held a coiled dog-whip, in the other his bow. A kirtle of otter fur hung from his waist to his scrawny thighs; otherwise he was naked. Wordlessly he signalled. Ruan rose and followed him into the weems.

There Ruan stripped and laved his body in purified water from an oak-root tub, shaking himself dry. The dogs yelped and called on the level above his head, full of a new day's energies. Domgall gave Ruan a fresh breech-clout, a narrow leather belt and a sharp dirk. That was the extent of his arming. He was led outside again into the sun.

Harkfast and Gadarn waited on the training sward. The Druid was clothed in a crimson robe and wore a chaplet of oak and yew leaves around his brow. He carried the wand in his right hand. Gadarn wore breeks like a Caledonian warrior, and lamb-skin boots. But his plump-muscled chest was smooth and bare, crossed only by a leather band to support the sword-sheath snug behind his left shoulder. He carried no shield, helm or armour. Casually he bowed to Ruan who touched his brow with his thumb in polite reply. The four men kneeled. The Druid intoned a short prayer to Lugh, and another to Ceridwen, to whose worship Gadarn subscribed. A final prayer was offered to Cailleach. Though careful not to beg for intercession on the young man's behalf, Harkfast did not neglect to commend his foster child to the goddess as a devout follower. There was no sacrifice. Harkfast did not favour the practice, save on occasions when ritual left him no choice.

After the ceremony, Ruan stood again, and studied the ring of trees. The haze was no more than a feather over the stream bed, and dew had dried from the leaves. What little wind there was blew from the west.

Gadarn and Domgall retired to the weems, and Harkfast addressed himself to Ruan.

'I have made a magic,' the Druid said, 'which informs me that a white roe has been caught and killed by hunters who are not of our faith. The deer has left behind her an unweaned fawn. The fawn is too young to stray and lies now in the ligging where its mother placed it, afraid, abandoned and in danger of starving. You, Ruan, will find that fawn, bring it here and place it at the base of my wand.'

The Druid pressed his weight into the metal rod and sank six inches of it into the earth.

'In a day, a night and a day, the fawn will die of hunger. Before that, if Cailleach wills it, the little creature may be found by a wolf or other wild beast and gobbled up. The sooner you discover it, the more chance the fawn will have of living.'

'I will find it.'

'That is the basis of your initiation,' said Harkfast. 'However, it must be more than a mere test of your hunting skills. Even as you seek the fawn, Gadarn will seek you.'

'Does Gadarn know where the fawn lies?'

'No, nor does Domgall,' said Harkfast. 'Gadarn and Domgall will hunt you and if you are careless they will kill you. The Roman is an excellent warrior, though his forest lore is not the equal of your own.'

Ruan searched the Druid's face, but found no consolation there.

'Will Gadarn be horsed?' the young man asked.

'He will be on foot.'

The horseman's muscles were strong but not fleet; it would be easy to outdistance him.

The baying was dark, deep and anxious.

Ruan turned as Domgall came past him.

'Domgall will be Gadarn's packmaster; the black dogs his cohorts,' Harkfast said.

The Pict strained against a leash which forked out to the choke-collars of four black hounds, the pride of all the pack. Though mongrel in origin, they were the crop of ten years' careful breeding, their ancestry studded with pups dead and deformed: six of them, five dogs and one elderly bitch. The four on the leash were the fittest, black-muzzled, glossy-haired, snouts pouched and puckered, devoid of the grizzled hair which fringed their spinal ridges, ribs and deeply arched bellies. Their large, flat paws were usually fringed with hair too, but Domgall had neatly shaved it off. The hounds' jowls drooped and slavered, slitted nostrils as wet and black as cave-snails. Only Domgall could control them. Even Ruan was not their friend. On the few occasions when he had fed them they had seemed more interested in gnawing off his arm than in the chunks of venison and hare which flopped from the basket on to the straw of their den. Domgall had not yet sold a black dog. Perhaps he never would, though they would fetch much in barter because of their strength, stamina and handsomeness. The real worth was in their noses. They were endowed with the ability to track down game in any weather and over any sort of terrain. Trained but untamed, they would rip and tear at any creature which came within range of their jaws. In one bloody festival two had broken loose and almost pulled down a pony before Domgall had whipped them into obedience again. Ruan had not counted on the use of the dogs. He felt a prickle of apprehension at the very sight of them. Perhaps the lesson of fear *would* be well learned before nightfall.

The Druid came forward and opened his palm. A polished pebble fell from it and, casting his glance at the sky, Harkfast shifted it on the ground with his foot until it stood in position not far from the base of the wand. With the shadow measure set for a fifth part of the morning every moment was precious.

71

Briskly, Ruan put his arm round the Druid's neck. The beard brushed his shaven cheek. Harkfast's nose pressed against his naked shoulder. The crimson robe smelled sharply of yarrow.

Ruan pushed himself away.

'Pull milk from the horse, and have it ready, Druid,' said Ruan. 'By sunset tomorrow you will have a hungry fawn to feed.'

Ruan did not catch Harkfast's reply; he had already swung away, heading eastwards.

Behind him Domgall tossed down the young man's breech-clout to give the slavering hounds his scent.

Harkfast did not dispatch Ruan to his fate without imparting all the aid that the principle of initiation would allow. A single clue assisted Ruan in the least dangerous but most difficult part of the blood rite. Deliberately Harkfast had told him that the white roe had been slain by hunters not of their faith. In all that quarter of Drumalban few men would slay a roe of any kind, let alone one with a milky skin. The only tribe which would commit such wanton sacrilege dwelled on the breast of the broad moor of Rannoch, a festering no-man's-land on the southern flange of the forest. Mountains blue as opals walled it in. Sluggish dung-brown rivers oozed through its ling, sourceless and without destination. Tarns and stunted ash, bog-rush and sphagnum, peat and heather crust were the rudiments of Rannoch. Seven tenths of the year it was the haunt of icy unchecked gales. Black bottomless bogs and sucking sands were threaded by tracks which vanished in the night sprinkled with lights said to be the lamps of undead things feared even by the men who made the moor their home.

Bands of hunters preyed on the multitudinous herds of red deer and on the giant deer with horns like open hands which Ruan had heard tell of but had never encountered. The Rannoch hunters lived in rude mud huts, holes and shallow caves. They had only one community, a raddled long-steading propped on slimy timbers over the lentic waters of Loch Toilbe. A better defended crannog did not exist in all of Erragail, for the stink of decay was stronger than a thousand spears to keep invaders at bay. Scattered over the wasteland, the Pictish savages lived without comfort and without gods, except dark forgotten ones which even prying Roman scribes had failed to unearth and whose cults lay buried like tubers under the detritus of more sophisticated religions. Wandering in couples or pairs of couples, the Rannoch Picts mated at will with any female of their clan. If the spawn of the mating did not please their eyes they flung the babes away to feed the kites and buzzards or lean wolves. White or russet, red deer or roe, buck or hind, the Rannoch hunters would kill what they could catch. At this warm season they were rumoured to stray out of the inhospitable fastness to snare the roes in the grassland at the very edge of the forest. Now, close to midsummer, the does were full with fawns and deserted their green coverts to lie up in more open country. Not all the families dispersed. But the bucks were spunky with fat feeding and the quiver of the coming rut, and the grazing out there was lush. Blond barley in a hot month would surely lure the roe from the trees.

Harkfast had given him the key to the mystery of where to begin his search. Success would depend on his own wits and the all-important will of Cailleach. Ruan ran with a loping stride, selecting the least congested paths through the thickets, chesting down whippy green boughs, steering wide of briar clumps and clinging thorns. The sun danced yellow through the leaves. Myriad insects drummed and droned like distant musicians, accompanying the steady hum of breath in the young man's nose, and the tune of facts, plans and speculations which played in his mind. About now, Domgall would be giving the hounds their heads. Gadarn would follow. The Pict would not release the dogs. In a pack of four, a runner would have no choice but to escape into the branches of a tree, out of which Gadarn would winkle him with fire or missiles and kill him as he fell. He would have to shake off the dogs before he could hope to evade Domgall or Gadarn. Speed did not mingle well with guile. He could not afford to loiter and lay false trails. His prime objective at this stage was to rescue the roe fawn. All he could do at present was put as many leagues as possible between himself and his pursuers.

The sun guided him. Changing contours told him he was aimed in the right direction. Indeed, the more he considered it the more certain he became that the fawn would be hidden somewhere on the moor's edge. A northerly tack would have taken him close to friendly settlements, a contact not fitting for an initiation test.

The river flowed broad and crystal in a pulling of the pines. Bordered by yellow flags and windflowers it ran shallowly over flat pebbles, but under the far bank the current gouged into the earth and the water was deep. Ruan took to it gladly, belly-high, chest-high, out from the tussocks, wading against the current. For several miles he touched nothing but the river bed and climbed through two sets of falls, keeping his scent dead; then the course narrowed and became rocky and water spouted white out of chutes and he was forced to abandon the waterway for dry ground again. At least he would have caused the Pictish packmaster some delay, though the dogs were too keen to lose him completely.

Following the climb of the river through larches, he came to the summit plateau of the broad hills. The forest was drowsy now, dawn-risers lazing in boles and burrows in the heat of the day. The sun's rays shimmered from a cloudless sky, piercing the thinning treetops. Ruan pushed himself on over the plateau and down into mixed woodland, scrambling through the undergrowth until, at long last, a clearing gave him a vista of the terrain ahead.

Crusted and caked, the moor lay baking in the heat. Scant clouds chalked the far horizon over the distant hills and to his right a stronghold of mountains blocked a gloomy glen. Bulky, hostile presences those summits were, even on a somnolent summer's afternoon. The moor was more menacing still, like a great supine beast slumbering on a gorse quilt, fir clumps like ticks upon its back, black tarns sweltering in the sweat of its hide. Gulping a dozen large breaths, he gathered himself and headed on down the slope, moving daintily and quietly now towards the swathe of rye-grass and knot-weed of the deer liggings.

An hour later he was belly-down in the tall lagg. Left and right, almost as far as his eyes could see, sand-tinted grazing filled the depression between wooded foothills and the hump of the moor. It all seemed smooth enough, but under the vegetation were many runnels and tripping dikes. A breeze ruffled the long-awned grass, nodded kingcups and crowfoot against his face. Crake of blackcock and moorfowl were all the sounds he could hear. But his inner ear was trained to pick up small vibrations in the air, and far, far off he could detect the black baying of the hounds.

The shadows of the mountains were melting into each other on the glen floor. The coolness of the evening could not be far away. Soon predators would come to feed on the grass-eaters who seized this hour to stuff themselves before the short summer and the shorter summer night ended. Ruan would have his diviners then.

Every instinct was keen. He drew strength from contact with this fine hunters' country. Stooped, he eased a route through the grass, using ruts to cut across the grazing range to the exposed flanks of the moor. There he found a suitable outcrop commanding views of the whole stretch of grass as far as the hook of Loch Patag. He settled to his watch.

He did not have long to wait.

Silent hawks climbed from their roosts, lifting on cooling spirals like flakes of bark. Buzzards, wind-hovers and fork-tailed kites discreetly tethered themselves over an arranged domain. Crouched against the outcrop, Ruan watched intently. A red kite finally caught his attention. Intrigued by something on the ground, it dipped and swam up again, carpal patches trembling with what seemed like eagerness, pale head cocked. Though it was far from Ruan's hide, he did not break cover, studying the patterns of the bird's flight as raptly as a scholar poring over script. When it dropped and cast back its angled wings, Ruan knew that the prey was dead. Casually the bird went down, vanished in the barley, and rose again with a tatter of meat hanging in its claws. It flew high and straight to a roost on the moor, there to spit pulp into its brood or, more probably, to gollop down the tidbit and beat back to the carrion for more. The red kite's station was filled by two carping buzzards, who circled and descended but did not rise again. They would fight and feed on the ground.

Wasting no more time, Ruan ran down a fold of heather-hag, sending startled hares scampering, spreading flocks of pretty day-moths behind him. He stopped once, knelt and listened, heard nothing, ran on, skirting bog-holes and peat-tarns until the tall grass gave him cover. He had to leap up like a fox to check the spot he had marked on the backdrop of the hill. Above him shoals of interested scavengers wheeled in interweaving circles, high and safe. At last he was close enough to force the ungorged buzzards to flap reluctantly into the air, mewing angrily at the intrusion. He approached the site from downwind, wary of stray wolves in the grass, after the big birds as much as the fly-blackened scraps of venison which dirtied the ground.

The Rannoch clan were all that the rumours said them to be, a filthy tribe who did not pole their kill to carry back intact to the steading. They ripped the carcass asunder on the spot, broiled and gorged the choicest parts and only then parcelled the remains to trot home piecemeal. The fire stain was obvious in the midst of the butchers' refuse. A skilled hunter would kill and flense and leave hardly a drop of blood or a sprinkle of hair to blaze his trail. But not the Rannoch Picts. Ruan doubted if the group would still be in the vicinity. More than likely they would be far off, snoring like sows in a snug heather covert, heads pillowed on sacks of deer stuff. They would hunt another area of the abundant range before dark, and again just after dawn, when the great feeding of wild things took place in weather as fair as this.

A cursory examination of the grass relieved his mind of doubt. White hairs adhered to the gristle of the four small hoofs which these hunters had wastefully cast aside. Disgust welled up in him. Only outcasts and savages lacked respect for the creatures which the gods sent to feed and clothe them. A good hunter, a true hunter, did not pillage the corpses of his craft. Ruan did not enter the circle of trodden grass. He fashioned the sign of the

76

thumbs, murmured an apology to Cailleach for the behaviour of all two-legged animals, then backed off downwind to seek the spoor.

The ways of wild deer were pitched to mislead predators. How would a white doe react? Nosing the hunting party, she would hide first of all. When her senses told her that danger was close, she would immediately sacrifice her own safety for that of her fawn. She would skulk low through the grass until well clear of the bed, then show herself in that graceful bounding flight which was so beautiful that it made men's hearts choke in their throats. Exposed, she would lead the chase as best she could. Only an ambush would take her, or a mean trip-leash stretched in the grass; perhaps, though rarely, a long-flighted arrow. However they brought her down, the Rannoch Picts would fall upon her and hack her apart, not pausing even to despatch her spirit first with a dirk slash across her silky throat.

Ruan soon found the slurred grass and the holes where the stakes of a trip-leash had been hammered into the ground. The deer had broken as she had fallen. A long splash of blood, heaving with flies, scored the barley stems. Casting right and left, he picked up signals of her passage and trailed them down the range close to the wood. The trees were so near that he could see the bars on the wings of the wood-pigeons which sallied forth to feed on the wild grains of the grassland. The fawn would be hidden nearby.

Crouching, Ruan cupped his palms to his mouth and imitated the doe's call—*whee-hoo, whee-huh, whee-hoo*.

The *eep-eep-eep* of the fawn came back at once, very soft and glad.

The tiny roebuck was well hidden in a bed of ochre grass. All roe fawns were spotted white at birth but this specimen was white all over, only its leggings and ear-tips showing red. By Ludnasada it would be just as milky as its mother had been. Its legs were folded, and it could barely lift its head to look up at him. He did not taunt it by giving it his thumb to suck. He lifted the frail creature in his arms. It would have been more comfortable to sling it round his shoulders as herders did with lambs, but he was afraid that he would break the delicate legs. Its tongue licked salt sweat from his chest, nuzzled and explored his features. With a day's beard on his cheeks, Ruan thought ruefully, he was almost as hairy as its mother.

He took stock of the situation. The sun was not yet down. He had discovered the deer more quickly than he had expected. Now he could head for any point on the horizons before swinging back towards the steading in the forest. Though he had eaten nothing all day, he felt fresh and not particularly weary. He stroked the fawn's ears, crooned to soothe it when it struggled against him. Burdened with the fawn, the return journey would take longer. Besides, as he had come out at speed so he would have to return in stealth.

The baying of the hounds was quite distinct. Obviously Domgall had handled the dogs well and had not been much delayed by the ruse of the river-walk. Though he could not see them on the hillside yet Ruan calculated that they must be within an hour's hard drive. Twilight was settling in. Gadarn would not be deterred by darkness. Holding the fawn tightly, Ruan struck out from the setting sun towards the forest, close to the shore of Loch Patag. The burden hindered his progress considerably. Before he had covered a mile, he realized that he could not escape by speed alone. Somehow he must devise a ruse to woo the dogs from his trail. In addition, he kept his eyes open for Rannoch Picts and skulking wolves.

Full dusk stuffed the groves with purple shadow. The loch was a flint dirk, chipped by night wind and greased with foam on its shingle beaches. A speck of colour, a fire, burned far off at the head of the long water. Ruan skirted the bog at the loch's tail and climbed out of the grassland into the firs. The going was difficult. The deer in his arms ruined his balance. A little way into the trees, he paused to rest and consider how best he could retard pursuit.

Below, the barley beds still held light and the moor was crowned with afterglow. He could not hear the hounds now but thought he could discern waving grass and an occasional glimpse of the Roman's head near to the killing ground. Behind Ruan owls hooted and brown bats dithered through the boughs. A swoop of feeding pigeons fled from the grass into the pines, marking the place, less than a mile away, where Domgall's dogs came strongly on.

Ruan was afraid now, less of death than of failure. He gripped his will as a warrior will grip a sword. Harkfast had taught him many things which lay below the level of language. He focussed his mind upon Cailleach, turning the prayer inward, making no formulation of it in words. The fawn in his arms was motionless, worn out by its journey, too weak to plaint. After a while, he climbed on. The slope eased, the trees thickening around him. Despair had passed, calmed by the mental contact with the well-springs of belief.

His nose told him when he entered the pig-run.

Cailleach had granted him the makings of a ruse.

Dung squished under his feet. Branches arched into a tunnel over his head. Suddenly he knew where he was. The trees had yielded up one of their many secrets. He was close to the oak-grove where Harkfast sent him to find acorns and special pal-mate leaves, the largest grove in the forest, defended by wild boars which the gods of the sanctuary put there to protect the spot against defilement.

Ruan walked jauntily on the balls of his feet, stooping and weaving through the narrowing arches. After a hard evening's rooting the boars would be resting up. A whole clan of them lived here, where food was nourishing and plentiful. Any one of the spoke-like runs might lead him to their sleeping ground in a clearing in the oaks. Pigs were dangerous but easy to hunt. Normally surly and quick-tempered, they would be sleepy now with the day's grubbing. Ruan was not afraid of them. He came upon the hog-steading suddenly, walking out of the tunnel straight into a stinking wallow. A dozen pigs sprawled on dry ground round the wallows, sows in farrow, boars and piglets lying on their sides, a few listlessly snuffling the tree roots. Before dawn they would be at their most active but at this hour he was safe, provided he made no abrupt noise or movement, and kept his nerve. They would have smelled him long since. He picked up the stamping, and curious guttural talk of the males as he emerged from the mouth of the run and, without slowing, strode purposefully across the clearing. The sounds would have sent panic through most men. Ruan recognized it as bluster, inquisitiveness rather than hostility. Piglets squealed questions. Sows grunted, hoisting themselves lethargically from scant straw nests to glare at him. Ruby eyes and white tusks showed quite clearly in the gloom. Knee-deep in slimy mud, he crossed the centre of the clearing. The turf shook as a couple of elder boars trotted after him, wagging their long-snouted heads incredulously at his insolence. Their bristle crests were calm along the dirk-backed spines, however, and there was no sign of hunching in the long legs.

It was difficult not to glance back.

The fawn's heart beat against his own, but the little roe was sensibly silent during the long, long walk across the pig-ring.

Finally he reached the far end of the clearing, dipped under the thatch of another run and, still without turning, walked on out of immediate danger. He did not halt until he set a mile of forest between himself and the pigs. Drenched in sweat, he felt drained by the tension of the experience. He hoped that Cailleach might bless the ruse with success.

Ruan did not have to wait long for Cailleach's answer. A howling, yelping, baying, snorting, grunting, squealing ball of noise rolled sudden as a thunderclap down the tunnel. Ruan chuckled. He hugged the fawn to him to keep it warm against the night airs, and jogged deeper into the forest, secure in the knowledge that the pigs would do for Domgall's dogs what he could not.

An hour before sunrise the surviving hounds picked up his scent once more. From the sounds which penetrated the din of the waking morning Ruan deduced that two of the dogs had dropped out—wounded, exhausted, or dead. He regretted that all four had not fallen to the boars' tusks. At least he had gained some time and in the cool night had made distance. As far as he could judge he was now half-way to Domgall's place and the Druid's wand. The night-long jog-trot had sapped him however, though he continued to walk briskly. The fawn slept in his arms.

80

Shoulders and back ached with the effort of carrying the creature, which now seemed as heavy as a stallion. The pines here were all tall and straight, the ground, free of undergrowth, dropping again. Before noon he would come into the Glen of the Marshes, at the head of the long, dog-legged sea-kyle of Struanmorm—not the shortest route home, but one which led over terrain favourable to a fugitive with hounds on his trail. How Gadarn had faced the pig-fight, Ruan could not surmise.

Following the river which flowed into the tidal marshes and out through the reed mace into the sea, he came down into the glen. The wind was from the sea, though the blue salt sight was hidden behind a hilly promontory. The lower slopes of the glen were gorse-blown and bright and he was tempted to lie there by the tumbling river and sleep. His eyes were gritty, every step pained him and weariness hung around him like iron fetters. He sniffed up the hot green odours of hill and shore. Herons, red-billed ormer-catchers and many kinds of gull infested the distant coasts. But the tall, rank reed-beds sheltered mostly ducks and geese, whose flesh was taboo to certain clans but whose feathers were prized as ornaments for masks and cloaks.

Ruan crossed the last stretch of grass, plunged into the warm, fetid water and took cover in the reeds. They were higher than his head and, with the tide out, he could have waded a full mile or more into the kyle before the black water cleared and chilled and covered his chest. In the reed mace he would cross and recross his tracks in the hope of confusing the dogs, thus allowing himself a chance to catch Domgall and Gadarn off guard. The Pict, however, was closer than Ruan had anticipated. Just as the young man took to the water, Domgall emerged from the trees, caught sight of him and came fast down the hillside, urging the hounds. The packmaster's excitement infected the dogs, making them howl and bell and race furiously for the reeds.

Ruan heard them. He tore off his breech-clout, ripped it into strips and tied up the fawn's legs with it. Next he placed the fawn on a bank of vegetable debris, and left it there. He had intended to use the marshes as an escape route, now, it seemed, they had become a prison. He waded towards the southern shore and veered left, bringing himself into line with the way Domgall would come. The hounds shouted, then were suddenly mouth-silent, though Ruan could now detect their movements in the rushes. A heron batted overhead, followed by a flock of chitter-ing moorhens. Knowledge and cunning had been his weapons last night. Today he must use strength. Lying low in the reed mace, he spread out his body, buoyed up in the brothy water. He tried not to think of himself but of the rare white fawn. His own life was less important than the life of the forest creature. He would protect and preserve it, uphold his responsibility to Cail-leach, no matter the cost. Domgall had not leashed the hounds. After a full day's trail and a battle with boars, the dogs too would be recalcitrant and careless.

Dirk in hand, Ruan hung in the water, waiting.

The stir of paws in the reeds was close now, coming closer. One hound, having lost the scent, was quartering the marshes, dabbing and dashing, seeking the quarry with its eyes not its nose.

Ruan sank back. Only the blade of his face was above water, the dirk held just below the scum.

The hound came into view.

It saw him. Wheeling, it paused, unsure of the evidence of its startled gaze and the strangeness of a face without a body. Then it decided that after all this was its prey and tore at Ruan, belling loudly, belly and legs churning the water. The liquid hampered it, robbed it of the thrust it would have had on solid ground. When it sprang at him, it had less than half its power of attack, giving Ruan the advantage. He swirled his body and offered his left hand to the champing jaws. The big head twisted, teeth snap-ping, gums bright red, tongue froth-fronded. But its hindquar-ters could not find purchase and it bit short by a handsbreadth, all the space that Ruan needed. He drove down with his calves, reared and snared the dog's collar with his forearm. Dragging the animal down on him, he drove the dirk deep into its chest, stabbing, withdrawing, stabbing again, his hand as fast as a viper's tongue. The hound thrashed and whined, paws raking his shoulders and chest. Ruan hauled it underwater, mounted it and pressed down, stabbing twice more behind its shoulder. Then it was dead, bled out or drowned, or both.

Oily scum thickened on the water. Flies, dizzy with excitement, began to congregate from all over the mace. Shivering and torn, Ruan faded back into the reeds. He had taken one hound, but had lost the edge of surprise. Domgall, Gadarn and the surviving animal would be cautious now, stalking him even as he stalked them. He followed his own trail to the raft where the fawn lay curled, eyes puffed, its bleating so weak that Ruan thought it might already be dying. His belly was full of urgency and rage. He felt swollen with it and rash. One hound and two men stood between him and the saving wand. The Pict was only half a hunter; the rest of him was warrior. Domgall would attack if he could. Even now Gadarn might be flanking him.

Wingless keds burrowed into the fawn's soft skin, and dribbleflies buzzed at its eye-corners. The sun beat down like a mallet. The rotting marshes fried. Ruan put the dirk in his teeth and paddled through the reeds like a natterjack. The last hound was quite near. He could make out its breathing as Domgall restrained it on the choke-leash. Wary of sending up a duck or nesting bittern to signal his position, Ruan headed away from the raft into shallower water and ankle-deep mud. The wind was still from the sea. He was behind it now, closer to the shore than the Pict. He would take them from the rear, stealthy and sudden. He swung seawards again. The reed mace was dense. He parted the blades cautiously with his fingertips and slid his body through the openings, until he came at last on Domgall's flank, and glimpsed the hunter through the stems. There was no sign of Gadarn, though. The Roman was too heavy to remain silent. Ruan had not settled in his heart whether he could bring himself to kill Domgall. The happiness of his boyhood was in part due to the affection of the man. But no rule said that he could not strike the Pict down. The risks inherent in the initiation were evenly divided. Domgall understood that. If it had been Gadarn there, Ruan would not have hesitated. Stepping over the water, he placed his feet down into it as a heron does, approaching Domgall gradually and soundlessly.

The Pict was intent on following the dog. The braided thong to the collar was as tight as a rod. The hound's ears and jowls drooped and its muzzle sipped the odour of its quarry from the water itself. The hound was all nose, not impetuous, other senses diminished. It was close to the raft where the fawn lay. Ruan watched the dog's hackles bristle, snout lift and brow wrinkle as it sighted the deer. The dog, the best of the pack, made no whimper, glancing up and back at its master. Undoubtedly Domgall suspected a trap. He did not yet realize that he was already within it.

Ruan gave his mentor no opportunity to fathom the error. He broke cover and, stepping high, plopped rapidly across the water. He did not reach for Domgall's throat, but grabbed the end of the bow which was slung crosswise over the man's shoulder, the draw-string notched tight for use. He pulled hard on the bow. The string gnawed into Domgall's neck and brought wide astonishment to his eyes. There was no way to counter the attack. Mercilessly Ruan rotated his wrist and looped the draw-string against the bow, snapping the wood against Domgall's gullet. The Pict emitted a gurgling cry, struggling to break the stranglehold. The dog-leash was still wrapped around his wrist and his spasmodic actions only served to drag the hound to its haunches. Ruan could have finished him with the dirk. Instead he clouted the Pict across the nape with the horn handle, clumsily seeking a prominent bone and, on the fourth blow, finding it. Mushroom-eyed, Domgall sprawled back against the young man, who pushed the unconscious body down across the hound. The dog swung, groping in the slime, and plunged through the leash-loop to its master's aid. The Pict's slumping form muffled its attack. It yelped and pranced back, sheets of mud exploding from its flanks. Still anchored to Domgall's wrist, it could find no stance out of which to attack the attacker and, in a welter of frustration, trammelled its forelegs in the leash, tripped, and sank, snarling and snapping at the binding as if that was now its enemy.

Ruan lifted the bow, plucked an arrow from Domgall's pack, fitted it to the string, drew and fired. The last of the four black hounds died instantly.

84

Ruan had no time to rest. Possibly Gadarn was still laid up in ambush, though he was beginning to suspect that the Pict and the Roman had not come into the marshes together. Ruan dirked Domgall from the leash, shouldered and carried him out of the reeds. He propped the unconscious man against a boulder above the tangle and bound his hands behind him with the leash. He did not tie his feet, however, in case a wolf strayed this way. After he had delivered the fawn he would return to the Pict's aid. He was sorely tempted to borrow the bow and arrows, but with the fawn in his arms they would prove an encumbrance. Besides, he did not know if it would be permitted within the terms of the initiation. Domgall's dirk was longer and sharper than his own. He fastened it into his sheath. Except for the belt he was quite naked now, the rags of his clout torn off.

Wading back into the reeds, he found the fawn, lifted it and carried it by a circular route out through the western edge of the marsh. There was no trace at all of Gadarn.

Relieved, Ruan followed the shore far down the kyle, then cut up into birch and elder scrub and set his course directly over the hills to the home-place.

He walked all that day, carrying the fawn in his arms. All feeling had gone out of his shoulders and pain gripped his neck. Specks and motes of red flurried across his vision, and there were moments when he thought he would swoon. It was clear, though, that Harkfast had not lied. The deer would die before nightfall. Responsibility to the little animal sustained Ruan. Thirty miles he trudged, dreaming of meat and mead and a soft blanket in a shady place. Navigation was simple. He could have travelled the paths in his sleep—round the kyle, up through the birch scrub, across the pass between the heels of the hills, down into troughs of oak, and steeply once more up into the towering pines. Though he crossed a couple of drove-roads, he encountered no man or woman. Around him insects chaffed, birds chirruped and cawed, and beasts wriggled discreetly out of his path. The sun slid past its zenith and dripped from the screen of the sky.

Now and again, he supped water from a stream and paused to bathe the fawn's mouth and eyes and cool its head. The creature's sides were barely pulsing and it languished in that sleep which could so quickly change to death. Toiling through the forest, Ruan muttered prayers to Cailleach and to Pasard, begging them to grant him determination and fan the tiny spark of life which still burned in the fawn's body.

The mountain shapes were flung low over the forest before Ruan reached the watering place, where the steading stream glanced and darted from grey stones under the beetle of the last hillock. Blaeberry shrubs wept tiny buds into the water and yellow-flags waved at the pool's edge. He drank again and laved the fawn, crossed the stream and dragged himself towards the clearing and the wand. He felt sure now that he would make his goal before sunlight deserted the pasture and the smoke from Harkfast's house lost all colour. Cushats crooned and crows flitted from their roosts to sup in the glades. Ruan extended the length of his stride. Pride filled him, as he crossed the narrowing stream and veered left to make the last half mile to the encampment.

A breeze shook the leaves and turned them like hands. The ash was frivolous, the oak pale. Shadows scattered in profusion over waning shafts of sunlight. In that cloud of light the Roman stood like the richest statue in the world. In the green woodland niche his body was pure gold, plump, muscular thighs straddling the pathway.

Behind Gadarn Ruan saw the avenue of the steading, leading to the Druid's wand, a silver stick before the weems.

Quite alone, Gadarn seemed as fresh and strong as he had been at yesterday's dawn, cat's eyes lazy and full of mirth. On the upper part of his left thigh, however, a bandage soaked up seepage from a wound, and he tilted his hips a little to favour his right leg. It was clear he had been wounded in the ruse of the boars and had doubled back alone through the forest to cut off the possibility of Ruan's arrival. No great cunning demonstrated itself in the plan. Probably it had been foisted on the Roman by necessity. Even so, he was still the appointed arm of fate, the kill-

86

master. He would not step back one pace to open the way to the wand. Those fifty yards of turf might have been fifty leagues.

'Give me the deer, Ruan, and you may live.'

'Nay,' said Ruan. 'You would still kill me.'

'Give me the deer and Harkfast will let you live.'

'I will not live in shame.'

'Give me the puling thing.'

'Take it, Gadarn; take it from me, if you dare.'

Night-wind dithered and was still, listening too, it seemed, to the impossible parley between stubborn men, one young and marrow-weary, the elder rested and fresh but wounded in the thigh.

'I think,' said Gadarn, 'that I will take your life instead.'

Twenty paces separated them. The growths round the path were thick. Only one route was possible to reach the wand. Ruan knelt and nestled the fawn safe in a thicket. It did not even mew now and its eyes were fast shut. Ruan touched its ribs and felt the pulse faint. It was not quite dark yet. Straightening, he stretched and shook loose the taut muscles across his back. Crimped flesh over his scars had opened and bled and sealed and split open again. He could not concentrate properly on the coming combat for dizziness and burning.

The grate of the sword brought his attention back to the Roman. Gadarn had advanced five paces, limping just a little. Plumpness contracted into power, naked chest smooth and dimpled with alert muscle. The sword blade was not inscribed. Grip and box-pommel were scrolled with golden wire, brazed to the tang with pimples of absorbent leather. Gadarn held it strangely, thumb and forefinger showing on the back of the guard, fingers tucked against the pommel. The hold seemed insecure and uncomfortable; Ruan could not see the purpose of it. Ruan held Domgall's long dirk in his left hand. His right was his fighting hand, but, swifter and surer, he needed it to wrestle with the Roman's sword arm. Shields, helms, armour and the lightness of swords made many a ringing contest. Here were none of these niceties of combat, only a broadsword and a Celtic dirk and two near naked men confronting each other in a quiet green grove.

'Come then, boy, if you are anxious to die over so trifling a matter as the life of a skinny fawn,' Gadarn murmured.

Ruan crouched as gamy old wrestlers in Culln's hold used to do in simulated contests with broad-horned rams.

'Come, come, strike me,' the Roman demanded.

So, Ruan thought, Gadarn was a defender. The style matched his idle nature. Ruan had intended to carry the fight, would have done so if the Roman had not urged him so impatiently. Now he would bide his time: he had no need to feign reluctance. He could not be sure how much of his strength remained after his gruelling ordeal. Bright blood webbed the cloth on Gadarn's thigh. Ruan worked on a strategy involving the injured limb. He would not attack that wing directly; a weakened thigh could be made to slacken and would surely suffer on the thrust. He would aim for the right side, the sword rib, under the blade. Gadarn's unusual grip still puzzled him.

'To make that flimsy dagger sting you must come at me,' said Gadarn, as if explaining a simple fact to a lumpkin. 'Now, come, attack.'

Ruan's throat ached. The sources of his cunning were arid, yet he remembered his lessons and would not be coaxed forward rashly, succumb, like a stupid lumpkin to the Roman's taunts.

Impatiently, Gadarn slapped his chest.

'Here, whelp. Strike here.'

Still Ruan held back. He weaved slightly, finding to his surprise that his mouth-muscles were drawn in a mocking grin. Surely Pasard was behind him, in him, all that old warrior's wry appreciation of irony flooding his veins like new sap in a spring larch. If he was doomed to die, what better place, what better hour, and what better cause would he ever find than this? The thought struck like a cold chisel and brazed the metal of his spirit.

If the cause was good enough, then time and place would always be ripe.

The roe fawn mewed behind him.

Involuntarily he glanced round.

Its head was slightly lifted, its eyes open. He could see its tongue vibrate. The *eep-eep-eep* echoed in his ears like the thunder of a drum or the loud clarion of a war-horn. In turning his head, he provoked the very act he needed at that moment.

Gadarn leapt forward to secure first thrust.

Momentarily confused, Ruan jerked back. He stepped with the right foot and then the left, shifting his weight from the waist, calves flexed, ready to change retreat into attack if the chance should present itself.

Gadarn's footwork was excellent, though a shade predictable. His handling of the sword compensated. The directions of the blade were baffling, a jab which was not a jab, a thrust transformed into a slice, a sweeping undercut which, in mid-flight, merged with the dragonfly dance of the point. Ruan did not even see the stroke which laid open his left shoulder, cut the padding to the bone. Neatly, ruthlessly, the Roman's sword did its work and flickered back into a bronze web of points and edges. Ruan cried out with the shock of the blow. Already the arm was totally numb as if the cords which carried the brain's charges had been cleft. Blood flowed thickly down his side, filling his armpit and trickling into his palm, sticky like a clay-sponge. Even so, Gadarn was in motion, not wholly comfortable leading the play. From that fact, Ruan culled what consolation he could. The injury even seemed to revive him slightly. He vented the cry as a bellow of rage, shook the dirk, saw the sword trace a flittery pattern in the air, chasing the illusion of the knife. Left toe to right instep, forward now, Ruan moved to attack. Swinging the lifeless arm like a strip of hog-meat, limp but full of weight, he struck the golden nose with it and, pivoting from the waist, smacked the smiling mouth on the back-stroke.

Warm, salt blood sprinkled the Roman's eyes. He thrust right, changed to a slice. Ruan slid left, felt the blade's panting but none of its bite, and sank his buttocks as if to slump into an invisible throne, holding unchanged the position of his feet. Blinded, Gadarn endeavoured to withdraw. He circled his sword and changed his grip on the handle, dexterity giving way to security. Ruan allowed the man no opportunity to regain the ascendancy. He projected himself after the Roman, rightwards, eyes fixed on the motion of the sword. As he had anticipated it rose and began to fall. Ruan rammed his hip into Gadarn's belly. The force of the blow lifted the man off his feet. The full weight of the skull-splitting sword-swipe was broken on Ruan's shoulder at the junction of the wrist. The weapon skittered harmlessly to the grass.

Reaching quickly, Ruan punched the dirk up the line of Gadarn's body, then heaved and flung him backwards and sent him crashing to the path.

Bleeding copiously from the belly-punctures, Gadarn lay on his back, staring up at Ruan, golden, narrow-irised eyes baffled, in anticipation of the slaughter-stroke.

Ruan tossed the dirk aside. He had no need to kill the Roman. Besides, he was probably too weak now to do it efficiently. He had lost much blood. It squirted out in a viscous cascade all down his side.

Scooping up the fawn, he tucked it under his right elbow, straightened and walked up the path towards the distant wand. With each step the density of the scarlet blizzard increased. He could hardly focus his vision on the silver rod or muster strength enough to plod one foot before the other, stringing out fifty paces across the compound to reach the Druid's marker.

Right hand under its belly, he lowered the fawn to the grass.

Crimson flakes swarmed in upon him. He knew he was falling. A last grain of sense prevailed; he slumped away from the little roebuck, and rolled on his wounded arm. There was much pain then, like furnace-heated arrows in his flesh. Moon and stars whirled in an amber firmament, receding like fragments of metal melting in a pot. Darkness bubbled over him and gave him peace.

The last thing he heard was the *eep-eep-eep* of the new-born animal, an assurance that Cailleach had given it back its life.

3

The Tongue of all Telling

There was almost no darkness now across the land of Drumalban, and in the north, where other gods were worshipped, the sun shone clear and constant and men slept in shelter from its light. The odours of heat and ripening summer filled the air at all hours and the little rain that fell came gently across the pine-tops like spindrift from a flax spindle. The Sambradh was as bountiful as the Geimredh had been cruel—but that was as it should be in the order of things. For eight days Ruan knew nothing of weather, north or south. He dwelled in isolated regions of fever, wandering the rank marshes of nightmare, until Harkfast's poultices drew the poisons from his wounds, and rhymes and cool infusions set him on the natural course of healing.

However, when he was recovered, and lay in the Druid's house under a light summer-night sheet, he continued to be troubled by a haunting sound. It came at the dimmest portion of the night, a deep humming note, like the mouthing of sorrowful women, only lower, hardly within the register of hearing. The fawn, which slept by Ruan in the steading, would tilt its head from its hoofs and listen too, blinking sloe-black eyes in wonderment as if it could discern profundities too deep for human ears to fathom.

The sound was both near and distant. It reminded Ruan in this of the enchanter's music which he had heard so long ago but could never completely banish from his memory. This note was not silvery, though, less musical than vocal and did not seem to be directed at him. He was still too weak to rise and search out its source. Even given strength, perhaps he would not have gone, sensing some Druid magic behind it. Even so, it disturbed him. When the tone had sounded its monotonous song and ceased, its vibrations lingered in the oak-tree tops, striving towards the mountains, to follow the winding rivers and pursue the albatross over the long cockscombs of the waves of the seas of the western coasts, plaintive and forlorn. Ruan could not find sleep because of it. The Druid told him nothing to soothe his awe.

Harkfast was too occupied with healing to talk with Ruan. First the fawn had to be coaxed to feed from a pap bag filled with curdled pony-milk, then Gadarn had to be brought back from the edge of death. All the Druid's skill was needed to coax the Roman from the other-world, from the idleness which made him content to loiter on the borders of the groves of the dead. Domgall had dragged himself into the clearing at noon on the following day, wrists rubbed raw in the bonds and his skull all weltered with blood. The Pict and the fawn mended quickly, but Ruan and Gadarn needed much nursing.

Ruan wondered if the Druid regretted having contrived such a difficult test. Still, as it was, at the cost of three dogs—one being only mauled not killed by the boars—Ruan had undoubtedly proved that he was ripe and ready for the manhood rite and to undertake the arduous regime for which Harkfast had trained him.

Ruan's first intelligent question when he wakened from feverish sleep was for the health of the white roebuck. Harkfast showed it to him, fattening, glossy and moist-muzzled on its reedy shanks. When Gadarn eventually decided to rejoin the living of the earth, and changed his skin from sickly yellow to pale gold again, he bore no grudge against his young adversary, for which Ruan was truly glad.

Five days before the midsummer ritual, Ruan was up and about and speedily recovering his strength with the fresh breath of the forest in his mouth. Though unable to leave his litter, Gadarn too was demonstrating a healthy appetite, not for pine-fragrant air, however, but for meat and wine in astonishing quantities.

The midsummer ritual began an hour before the day of the equinox. It went on in fits and starts throughout the morning and afternoon then, as dusk fell, became more serious.

Garbed in a simple shift of saffron wool, Ruan went alone

with his Druid to a secret sacred grove. Here oak, yew and rowan grew together and ivy twined through all the boughs and united the trees together into a sanctuary of enormous potency. The waning day was silent, Ruan silent in the circle's centre. His arms were raised, chin tilted towards the fork in the largest oak through which the first rays of the sun would break, shafted directly on him. He had been changed by his experience of late and felt the significance of the rite deeply, moved by the dignity of the ancient forms. In the finest of his surviving regalia, Harkfast stood among the roots of a large oak, facing his foster son. The Druid's arms were folded, his eyes closed. The litany began when the sky was as dim as it would become. Chanting in a loud, unwavering tone, Harkfast offered Ruan's future into the hands of the gods, and named all those gods and goddesses in strict order and in all the tongues and all the guises which the laws demanded. With each cadence, Harkfast stepped one short stiff pace forward, then began a fresh refrain.

On the twenty-fifth such pace, he tarried, composed himself and summoned his concentration to tell the gods of Ruan's lineage and to pray to them collectively for the future. He spoke of the possible glories of that future, making florid bargains on behalf of the young king, dinning the overlords into blessing the reign. When that prolonged chant was concluded, the quality of twilight had altered and clear spaces beyond the oak fork were shimmering with awakening day, the day of the pivot of the year. It dawned clear and cloudless and star-blest, encouraging omens. Harkfast's prayers were now more intimate, short injunctions, aphorisms, memorials of history; prayers more akin to curses, showering vituperation on the Romans who had slaughtered the priests and raped the priestesses and felled and burned the mighty trees which had stood as symbols of the gods and kings of old. Gripped by unusual passion, the Druid's voice rang loud in the cool silence. With obvious difficulty he kept this syllable of the ceremony to its proper length, caught himself in time and ended with a tearful blessing.

Ruan was stirred too. A last short personal prayer to Cailleach, Lugh and Danu wrung tears from the young man's eyes.

Every verse was accompanied by a pace, and the last of all brought Harkfast close to Ruan. Not until the old man knelt did the new sun of the new reign gild Ruan's brow.

Those beams were his crown.

The young king wept, but did not move or utter a word until light bathed all his body; then he stretched forth his hands and laid them on the Druid's shoulders and appointed Harkfast and commanded the priest to rise.

Thus the main part of the ritual ended, and Ruan became a man.

At noon on the day of midsummer, the Druid sacrificed a white bull-calf which Domgall had bought for the purpose, and formalities gave way to feasting. Gadarn even managed to struggle from Domgall's house to the Druid's to tuck away beef and corn cakes and washings of mead and jars of wine. Domgall gave Ruan a round hide targe on which was painted the outline of a white roebuck. Harkfast's present was a sheepskin parchment covered in printed Greek letters which noted the imposition of Ruan's taboos. They were not many and not demanding—the king must not kill or partake of the flesh of the roebuck; the king must not wear garments fashioned from the skin of the boar, though he was free to eat pork; the king must not whip or kill a dog in any land or circumstance. There were other disciplines too, but they were minor. Ruan thanked Harkfast for the parchment, promised to store it safe and study it from time to time, lest he forget and break the taboos and bring ill-fortune on himself and his dependents.

It was two days after midsummer before Harkfast satisfied the regal curiosity. Ruan was full of impatience to discover what his destiny would be.

Harkfast invited him to the steading.

Ruan seated himself on a pile of furs which the Druid had provided for his comfort.

'Now, Harkfast?' Ruan said.

The Druid nodded.

To Ruan's surprise, the man did not plunge into a long-winded explanation. He reached instead for the leather sack which had hung from the roofbeam peg for so many years that Ruan had almost forgotten its existence. Harkfast unthreaded the draw-strings and slid his fingers carefully into the mouth of the sack. Shedding leather as a day-moth sheds its birth-husk, the harp came slowly forth. Ruan had never seen a harp like that harp. It had a full-bowed forepillar and a graciously curved neck to bed the teats of the strings, thirty brass strings fine as summer rain, bright still and taut for all their long disuse. The sound-box was hollowed from a single piece of willow. Base-hoof and neck-boss were engraved with yew-wood medallions, intricate patterns worked in fronds and vines. The wood was blackish, except where harpers' hands had grained it down, forming lighter stains and even slight depressions, buffed by the pressures of a million notes and a hundred thousand songs.

Harpers had once been exclusive servants of kings and wealthy chieftans; ordinary men could not afford their valuable services. Lately, however, the revered tradition had degenerated. There were those who strummed the strings of crude triangles at marketings and festive gatherings, howled joy-songs and low satires and bragged of their long training in the musical arts. Even the hounds at heel could tell that such men were shams, that their only magic was an ability to make the teeth grate in the back of one's head. Only a true harper could have mastered the magnificent instrument which lay cradled in Harkfast's hands. 'This,' said Harkfast, 'is the Tongue of All Telling.'

Ruan sat up. The artifact of woods and wires had not been exposed just for his amusement. This harp was a prophet of the future, linked in some way with all the changes that had occurred throughout his life so far. Probably it was this harp which had foretold his summoning to the cold high valley eight summers ago.

'Is it your harp, Druid?'

'Would that it were,' said Harkfast. 'I am but its keeper, not its master. Do you take me for a fellow with three lives that I could learn to be Druid, Bard and Minstrel all in one? We have knowledge of each profession, of course, for history and incantation are not so far removed from each other. But, as you will have no doubt remarked, we are individual servants of the king.'

'So it seems that I have a harp—but no harper.'

'Patience! I mean . . .'

'You mean "patience," my Druid. Habits do not drop from one's mouth in a day. Besides, you may be my Druid but I would be no King without your conniving. Tell me, did you use this harp to call me to the valley when I was young in Culln's hold?'

'I cannot answer that question, Ruan,' said Harkfast. He lowered himself into his favourite position, legs out, spine against the posts of the wall, the harp cradled in his lap. 'However, I *will* tell you of this harp and of the one man who can draw the future from it. He told me of you, and of much that has happened.'

'What is his name?'

'Mungan.'

'He is dead?'

'Nay, he lives.'

'Without the consolation of the instrument?'

'Poor Mungan became enamoured of another religion; a harsh philosophy which sweeps from the east. It makes mean demands on its followers,' said Harkfast. 'A priest of this cult travelled among Mungan's tribe, the Damnonii, and wooed him from his ways and bribed him with promises of tranquillity and stuffed his head with the lore of this eastern prophet.'

'But Mungan was a prophet in his own right, was he not?'

'Mungan will always be a prophet. It was that which he was put on earth to be, and until this priest honeyed his ears . . . Ach, well, what does all this matter to you? To put it curtly, Mungan had already drifted from the Royal House. Prophecy is a heavy burden. He was weary of it. It soured his pleasure in life. Even in the music he could summon from the strings of his instrument he found no measure of enjoyment for himself.'

'Tell me more of Mungan.'

'Mungan was the last son of the last son of the famous Harpers of King Faind, overlord of the Damnonii prior to the Roman invasions. Faind was a Gaul by extraction. The ancestors of Mungan too were Gauls in the time when the groves still stood in the land of all origins, and secret doctrines were the province of men whose power was immeasurable. Mungan has told me that the sound-box of this harp was hewn from the bole of a living willow tree, that the tree was healed thereafter and did not wilt and rot. That was taken as a sign, and his grandsires, whose names are forgotten, found that one son in seven could pluck visions even sharper and more precise than the dreams of the beef-eating, thumb-sucking Druids who were, I hasten to add, great magi in the groves of Gaul.

'When the Roman Eagles occupied that faraway land, they burned and hewed and destroyed all the sacred trees. The Harpers took flight, as did the Druids, to protect their gifts. Mungan's ancestors sailed by various adventurous routes to seek refuge with Thormund, the sire of the sires of Faind, who had married a princess of Gaul and was thus kindly disposed to exiles. They were given portion, appointed as Harpers and won great honour in that court. They bred Bards as well as Harpers, even a Druid or two sprang from their stock, before great and bloody wars drained Thormund's line and the best of the nobles of all Celtic tribes. So the corruption of the Romans spread, and with it mistrust and suspicion and, worst of all, disrespect for the wordy professions.

'There was more to Mungan's desertion of the Royal House than that, however. There was a killing, a charge against the Harper which a jealous Druid caste judged harshly. Mungan fled. He wandered north. He met with me, stayed a season or two with Pasard and learned how to sing of the future to please the King's ear, and privately for my ear too.

'Mungan carried a weighty burden. He could no longer invent, only reiterate the truths which the strings of the willow murmured to him. After a time he returned to the court of the Damnonii, who, as you know, had adopted many of the Roman ways. He intended to return to us, bringing his wife and children with him. But he found that the woman had taken the false Druid to her bed, and would have no more to do with her first

97

husband. In wrath Mungan killed her.'

'How?'

'With the harp,' said Harkfast. 'He struck at her violently. The base-hoof broke her skull. She bled to death. Mungan fled at once, went south, met with this priest of the eastern prophet, and found "solace", as Mungan called it, in this person's teachings.'

'What of the harp?'

'Mute,' said Harkfast. 'It would no longer speak to Mungan. It is strange to me how Ninian, the name of this priest, professes a doctrine of love for all men, yet would not permit Mungan to keep the harp which, according to Ninian, was an evil and heretical object. Ninian even wanted Mungan to burn it as if the spirit of the wood was black with wickedness, which, of course, it is not.'

'How did it come into your hands, Harkfast?'

'Mungan deserted Ninian's sanctuary of white stones, sought me out and left the harp in my keeping. In spite of all my counsellings and pleas, he felt himself compelled to return to this Candida Casa, as Ninian called it, to the meditations and privations and denials which the priest said were good for him, and which Mungan believed would soothe the troubles which tortured his mind.'

'Have you heard aught of him since then?'

'Nay, I have not,' said Harkfast. 'But I have not forgotten to pray to our gods for his return.'

Ruan smiled, and pointed his forefinger. 'You wish him to return now and be my Harper.'

'Ay.'

'How will we find him?'

'The harp will find him.'

'Can you make music?'

'The harp is lonely. It no longer wishes to be mute,' said Harkfast. 'Reason and purpose are all that men need to shape their lives; it is the same with the spirit of the willow-barge.'

'If Mungan's ears are blocked with false philosophies, how will he hear it?'

'He will hear.'

'Have you sounded it?' said Ruan. 'Ay, you have pulled a note from it each morning since I passed through the ceremony of initiation.'

'In the morning air it is at its purest,' Harkfast said. 'I dare not *play* the instrument, but I touch a summoning note from the broadest strand. Mungan will hear that.'

'And he will journey here?'

'By Lugnasadh he will be at your door, Ruan.'

'And you strike that note each dawn to guide him?'

'It is better to keep him steered; unless the lies of Ninian and all that so-called "peace" have changed him. Mungan was always too sensitive and impulsive for his own good.'

'Harkfast, it seems that you have given me a kingship, a Druid and now a Harper. With Domgall as my Swordmaster—'

'And Gadarn.'

'Gadarn?'

'Your Regulus, Ruan. I did not bring him here just to kill or be killed, and I am heartily thankful that his life was spared. Gadarn is full of knowledge of the world—'

'Meat, mead and women, you mean.'

'And many, many other things as well,' said Harkfast. 'Besides, no king worthy of his portion ever sneezed at expert advice in the matter of eating, drinking and pandering.'

'Will he serve me?'

'He was prepared to die for you—though I do not imagine he thought it would come as close as it did.'

'Very well. Let Gadarn be my quartermaster,' said Ruan, magnanimously. 'Now that I have the beginnings of a king's entourage, and have been shaped and moulded with the proper education, it is fitting that you tell me what you intend me to do. Without subjects I can be no proper sort of king at all.'

'A king is a king in spirit, whether he rules over a nation or a quilt of fleas.'

'You did not fill me with the essence of Pasard simply to rule over fleas,' snapped Ruan.

'I found you through the word of the Tongue, and brought you to me to fill the gap left by the passing of the infant son of

Pasard. That infant was not Pasard's first child. He had four strong sons, all of whom died in the defence of the Royal Dun in the country of Gairesa on the long peninsula of Erragail in territory first purged by the Romans, and later seeded by the settlers of Hibernian clans. Pasard was defeated in battle; all his clan was slain.'

'All?'

'All but a handful,' said Harkfast. 'The few that were left—and none were warriors—fled far into the seven kingdoms. It was a day to make the gods weep, there on the Hill of Adders above the Swineherds' Loch.'

'With whom did Pasard battle?'

'The legions, of course.'

'But why did they attack the clan so forcefully?'

'They feared Pasard; ay, they feared him more than any other Pict in all of Drumalban, more than any man since Hannibal.'

'You could not prevent it?'

'I had been persuaded that there was no danger at that period. I had gone with all the Druid caste to a Beltane gathering in the selfsame grove where you discovered the boar's lair. It was a purposeful convention. Pasard had had much success against the Romans. It was in my mind to rouse the most powerful of the cult against the Eagles, and work that way towards another uprising. Ach, but the price of my conceit was high. Spies told the Romans. They attacked Gairesa while I was gone, and put all the knights, the nobles, the free men and women, the herders and settlers and even the bondsmen to death.

'Pasard would have died too. But the queen found him wounded and set him in a light chariot and drove through the looting hordes, screaming and half-naked in the fury of her grief for her four dead sons and her dying lord. She crashed and thundered the horses to the shore and through the storm waves and up again to a route she knew through an alder brake and back by a drove track to the hills. And when one beast died in the traces, she cut it loose and upheaved the chariot and flogged on the remaining animal until it died too and fell and spilled her out upon the ground.

100

'Varro, commander of the Roman flail, sent scouts to find her. There were many spies in the area, and she was in mortal danger, hidden with the king in a cave on the highest sea-cliff in the realm, living on berries and raw fish and things scraped from pools under cover of darkness.

'But I had word of it by then, and took the yew sticks and wrote on them and bent the will of the assembled Druids and dreamed a dream which showed me the queen in hiding. I went there alone, without murmuring even to my priestly brethren. I exhausted nine horses in my rapid flight. When I reached the cave, I healed the king and, under cover of a fog, brought him and his queen out and found a sanctuary north of Gairesa on a small isle of the sea, which we reached by curragh, and to which, with great stealth, I summoned the elder caste.

'That Beltane gathering was the last of the great assemblies of Druids in Drumalban, for many of the Pictish tribes had forsaken the kingship for female lineage, and all over the land the power of the Druids waned almost to dust.'

'How long ago, Harkfast, did this tragedy occur?'

'How long does it take for a rock to crack with frost. The snap of it and the run of the fissure is over instantly, but the stresses and all the inner wasting is so gradual that it cannot be marked in numbers or in seasons. I do not know, Ruan, how long it has taken for men to become confused and to forget all that was cherished and held in esteem in the sane and ardent days of our race. With the first stroke of the first axe in the oak groves of my fathers in the shadowy land of Gaul, perhaps, the process of decay began.'

'But you still had the king and queen and all the elder caste?'

'Ay, but no safe refuge.'

'What of the other tribes, those who had fought side by side with you in rebellion against Rome?'

'Afraid.'

'Afraid of retribution?'

'Nay,' the Druid said. 'Afraid of me.'

'I cannot believe it.'

'Ach, fosterling, you have seen but a pinch of the things of which I am capable. While others have degenerated into mere mortals, I have kept my faith and my arts sharp-whetted. Even as a king you have no right to ask me to tell you all that I am. Only mock-priests boast loudly of their strengths and accomplishments.'

'Tell me, then, of Pasard.'

'Much you already know. He was a great king and ruled fat subjects, and believed in the true faith and would have died for that faith. The hardest duty of his whole kingship was not to die but to live on after the extermination of his clan and the murder of his four fine handsome sons.'

'In secret, on an isle?'

'We left the island, and hid ourselves in abandoned brochs and caves, scuttling off like dormice when the seasons brought voyagers near our doors. We spent summers in the trees, making ceremonies to Cailleach, who was Pasard's first and last divine. The Romans pulled back. The Picts and the Scotians plundered the walls and sallied lengthily by sea-coast routes to loot and pillage all that their greedy hands could reach. It was the end of the true time of the sword. Matters material now count for more than sanctity. Ripeness in the nature of things is held less in countenance than swift gains of treasure, cattle, horses and the various bartering coins which are the pandering of luxury and false power.

'Even the forces of the minds of my Druids withered. They could not make the magic which would infuse the queen with fertility and germinate the seed of another child. The king was old, and she not much younger, and all those years we prayed and sacrificed and made ceremonies to assist a conception. Even my own skills and herb-craft could not contrive it, however, and when it came to pass that she believed herself with child, Mungan would not confirm from the Tongue that the infant would thrive.

'We had gone to the high valley, the location of which was shown to me in a series of induced dreams. Though there was wood and berry-bearing shrubs and game and the climate was benign, none of us were young enough to hunt well and the pickings were very lean indeed. Pasard had lost his power to provide. It happens to all kings who live into the late years. I knew that he would die, that the queen would die, and the infant would never live. So, I brought you to me, as had been rumoured in the voice of the harp.'

'But you have not yet explained why,' said Ruan. 'Though I begin to have a glimmering of reasons, I would be grateful if you would tell me all that fealty to your profession permits.'

'The tribes who fear me, do so because they deduce my intention.'

'And what is your intention, Harkfast?'

'We are at the beginning of a great period of change,' said the Druid. 'With the legions almost gone, we are open to attack from the raiders of the seas, those who were formerly our allies. From Hibernia, from the Fresian countries, the Frankish kingdoms, from the grounds of the Saxon-kith, and the realms beyond Thule, they will come to pillage Drumalban and all Britannia. Most of all, however, I fear the creeping invasions of the missionaries who bear the message of the eastern prophet to our shores. The Tongue has told of this too, and I have not been deaf to rumours from many parts of the many countries in which I still have friends. Ay, I fear the Christ priests most of all. They profess loyalty to one god—as the Druids did when their theology was unsullied, and to the Son of God, who *was* the eastern prophet and transformed himself into the Godhead. They preach a doctrine of peace and love—but peace and love will not hold an empire together. I predict that peace and love will soon become causes for a resharpening of swords and a polishing of bucklers. The blade and the torch will flash again, though the dignity of the ancient combats will be debased by the hypocrisy of fighting for *peace*.'

'And the Druid caste will be robbed of the last vestige of their power?' said Ruan.

'That power is but a tool, Ruan. It is the preservation of the kingship which is important, the continuity of the rich stores of knowledge which the profession holds in its keeping. Most important of all, however, is the protection of the Celtic race as one race and not a fly-cloud of warring clans.'

'It is no small wonder that the tribes fear you,' said Ruan. 'I understand now why you hid me away in the woodland and taught me the kingly crafts in secret.'

'It is no single clan which must survive,' Harkfast went on, 'but the cultus of an entire nation which is in danger of being erased from the stones of time itself.'

'You preach a mighty unity, Druid.'

'I do.'

'But unity means the imposition of one force over all other forces; bloodshed and conquest.'

'Ay, in the beginning.'

'I am your reborn warrior, the king set up for all to follow?'

'And I am your priest ordained. One station complements the other, and has done since the systems of men were formed. Given sufficient power we can impose unity on all the tribes of the Picts. Beneath the pettiness which spoils them, they are fine men and great warriors. This, Ruan, is how it is: to the south are Britons and Cymric peoples exhausted and made weak by long dependence on Roman authority. Up the coastal region are scattered the kinsmen of Erin, settlers, warrior bands, pirates. In Erin, or Hibernia if you prefer the Roman name, the old ways are still in fashion. They have strength behind them, but not enough I fear to withstand the inroads of the Christ priests, or the madness which is in all Hibernians to destroy themselves from vain pride. They have always been inclined to squander their strength in arguments and trivial feuds.'

Cradling his knees with his elbows, head cocked Ruan sat forward. 'You wish to begin with the Pictish clans, Harkfast, to band them together into a conquering army as you did once under Pasard?'

'But more, greater, supreme,' said Harkfast.

'Tell me then how I will assemble my army? I cannot buy the swords of the mercenaries, for I have no sword-lands to give away in return for their services, and no settlements to tithe and no conquered cantons from whom I can extract tributes. In the eyes of every dwarf ruler of every collection of wattle huts, I will be nothing but an impoverished upstart.'

'Ruan,' said the Druid. 'Do you believe that I have burdened myself with so much boredom and suffering without having a plan at the end of it?'

'Then tell me of it.'

'In good time,' said the Druid. 'Listen, fosterling, how do you train a whelp to do your bidding?'

'With patience, kindness and the whip.'

'Aught else?'

'Commands.'

'The word of command,' said Harkfast. 'That is the crux of all power. The word is the symbol of authority.'

'Do you propose that we conquer, like these Christ priests, with mere words?'

'Listen,' Harkfast said. 'Deep still within the tribes of all the races of men on this bulk of land lurk memories of ancient kings and buried gods. Some are still worshipped; others are forgotten by the mind, but remembered in the heart. I have often told you that a man will die to defend a belief if that belief is buried in his thinking, if he has been trained to respond to symbols which represent the ideal. In wild places, far from roads and forts and villas, in caves and forests, on the remoter islands of the seas, there are men who still uphold the most ancient faiths. The symbols, you see, are not yet destroyed, merely lost, disused.'

'Speak plainly: what symbols?'

'There are many from which to choose,' Harkfast replied. 'One will be enough for our purpose.'

'You will riddle me to death, old Druid.'

'I cannot make it clear to you yet awhile,' said Harkfast. 'All I can plainly tell you is that much will be required of you, but that the reward is the stewardship which Pasard failed to obtain, the rule of the kingdom of the whole land. Think of that, fosterling, when it seems to go hard with you; think of the extent of that power.'

'Ay,' said Ruan, wistfully, though he could not quite imagine it.

'You will be a legend. You will be the hero of songs, god on earth, saviour of our diverse peoples, greater than the greatest Emperor of Rome.'

'If I do not die first.'

'It is a minor risk to take for such immeasurable gain.'

'My life is quite precious, Druid, at least to myself.'

'You are a *king* now, Ruan.'

'Then tell me the shape this symbol will take?'

'It is better that you hear it from the mouth of the one man who has seen it with his naked eye and still lives to remember.'

'Who is this man?'

'A wonderworker.'

'A Druid?'

'No, a presser of fine weapons, a magician with metals, Slan the smith.'

'Where will we find him?'

'Mungan knows,' said Harkfast. 'We will go on our quest after we celebrate the Samhain festival.'

'In the *waning* of the year,' said Ruan. 'Is that an auspicious time to make such a beginning, Harkfast?'

'More than the waning of the year,' the Druid replied. 'It is the waning of an age. We will set out on the night of the waxing moon in the winter solstice, and travel under the cover of cold winds and snow. In the short light, the men we seek will burrow into the ground like badgers.'

'Slan, you mean?'

'There will be others,' said Harkfast. 'Mungan will know of them.'

Ruan looked again at the harp, then reached across to touch a finger to the willow-barge. It felt weird, warm and velvety and disturbingly vibrant like the flesh of a young woman. He did not have the audacity to touch the strings.

'This harp will bring Mungan?' he asked.

'It will,' said the Druid. 'And in turn Mungan will map and shape an appropriate journey for us.'

'For what purpose?'

'To visit Slan.'

'And what will he do?'

'Tell us how to raise an army.'

'An army of what race, Harkfast?'

A crooked smile wrinkled the corner of the Druid's mouth. The red underlip shaped.the words quietly. Ruan could hardly believe that he had heard him rightly.

'An army of the dead,' the Druid said.

Part 3

The island

The feast of the blood-smearers

Low on the cold horizon the broken heights of Sketis showed sullen through the mists. Though only a mile from the mainland at Alsh and the Rhea channel, the island was cut off from Drumalban as effectively as an anchored curragh. A chain of manned brochs protected the narrows. Winter seas and storm clouds served guard on the rest of the coast. In summer the kyles were dotted with Vinadia's boats. They plied the waters like ferrymen, but their occupation was much more sinister. Ruler of a southern branch of the Smertae, Vinadia had no foothold on Sketis—nor did he attempt to establish one. It was hardly a tempting province. He was content to cull profit from control of the shortest crossings. Trained mariners not only held the inner coasts against raiders but extracted tithes from any wanderers whose business might lead them to the mysterious, misty isle.

To Vinadia Ruan gave no thought as he first stared down from the track onto the shores of Sketis. Dark rumours invested the peaks and shrouded glens. The island held a peculiar terror for some men, and lured others as wayward moths are drawn to the destructive flickering of a lampwick. All the members of Harkfast's band were conscious of this unease. The horses chaffed fretfully and the remaining hounds, a dog and a bitch, slunk whining to cower under the cruppers at the limit of their leash.

It was an hour after noon. Winter was biting now for the first time since Domgall had smoored the Samhain fires in the camp in the forest three parts of a moon since. On the inland mountains snow had fallen, but the peaks of Sketis were bald, attracting as yet only mist and salty rain. A raw west wind smote Ruan. He huddled the cloak-hood about his ears, shivering as it filled with air like a sail. The excitement of adventure had gone out of him, out of his companions too to judge by their grim expressions. Even Gadarn had lost his idle smile and, smitten by the atmosphere of foreboding, gripped the mare's rein tightly.

Gravity was Mungan's normal mien. At the best of times the Harper was taciturn. Elongated and sorrowful, the man's face was incapable of registering pleasure. It seemed longer than three months since first Mungan had stumbled from the trees, groping his way into the clearing like a blind man. Weak with hunger, ragged-robed, he had spoken little of his arduous journey from Ninian's sanctuary by the Blue Bay. Harkfast did not press him. It was sufficient that Mungan was united again with the lonely harp, that his fingernails had lost none of their evocative skill and that his voice could still interpret the music which the strings muttered to his ear. Tall, stooped and spare, Mungan wore no beard. A coating of stubble, though he never shaved, remained miraculously at the same thickness on his jowls. So far, Ruan had not dared meet the Harper's eye, for the pupils, though not unusual in colour or formation, had an impenetrable quality, more daunting than challenging.

Mungan only really came alive when he sang. Surprisingly, he was not reluctant to play. Passing his nails across the strings he produced melodies which were secular and perfectly real, fragments of lyricism as gentle as a maiden's lips, and choruses which transported the listener into the barracks, tents and taverns of stalwart soldiers. Only when he joined his voice to that of the strings did the tone deepen and become otherworldly, beaded with portents and mysteries. On the night of Lugnasad, four days after his arrival, Mungan sang his first song. In it was all the bitterness of the bondserf, the relationship of masters and servants, the rudiments of love, red lust and the purifications of loathing and, as the night and the song lengthened together, hints of Ruan and revival, rebellion and resurrection. The second feast of music took place ten nights before the Samhain. Its patterns were just as complicated; an anthem to Harkfast, and, latterly, more of the martial strain which so moved Ruan that he wept. Towards the culmination, Mungan sang of ringing metals, and a solemn island, and of future time. Ruan gleaned images of giants and hags and beasts, though even Harkfast could not properly interpret the symbols. On a flourishing of chords which made the brass strings leap against the teats, Mungan abruptly clamped his forearms over the instrument and smothered its voice. He had released all that was to be told. He would provoke the harp no more.

Then there was a period of activity. Ruan and Domgall leashed the hounds, drove them to the Samhain market in Dun Ara and there traded for pack-ponies, provisions and coin. The gold and silver tokens were relics of the mint of Garotendium which a mad renegade Roman had founded in the fond belief that a man's head graven on metal would give him more authority than control of legions or an emperor's staff. Caledonian looters soon taught him otherwise, and much of the plunder was loose in the west even now. Domgall allocated Ruan an afternoon to ride out from Dun Ara and take farewell of the girl Rea. Though nobody told him so, Ruan had it in mind that he might not pass through this quarter of Erragail again.

In spite of the station of the moon, fair weather prevailed. Harkfast scattered veiling seeds around the camp and, leading the last two hounds, Domgall accompanied him towards the birch-brake, heading northwest. Mounted, armed and laden, Ruan, Mungan and Gadarn followed behind. That morning it had all seemed hale and adventurous. The good feeling had lasted in Ruan's breast for five whole days. But when the wind rose and clouds skirted the sun, pleasure melted into duty and duty into burden, until they came at length out of the forest and over the hill-track at whose end the isle of Sketis lay in wait.

Ruan reined and trotted his horse ahead to the point where Harkfast had halted. Through the narrows waves licked up foam, scudding from Hibernia or the tail of the long islands of the furthest horizons. In the whole extended view there was no sign of life.

Harkfast slumped low in the saddle, baggage strapped behind him to make a cushion for his spine.

'Where is Vinadia's Dun?' Ruan shouted against the wind.

113

'North, over the ridge,' said Harkfast.

'The track drops and ends at the water's edge.'

'A false track,' the Druid explained. 'Designed to entice travellers into tackling the crossing.'

'And then?'

'They are ambushed by Vinadia's curraghs, and—"tithes", shall we say, are extracted.'

'I am sure that you mean "extorted",' said Ruan. 'Vinadia is a pirate, is he not?'

'He calls himself Protector of the Coast.'

'Sketis is not under his control.'

'Sketis is under no man's control,' said Harkfast. 'Vinadia claims to hold off the forces of the misty isle.'

'And what do those peoples who dwell on Sketis have to say to that?'

'Who knows!' said Harkfast. 'You may ask them that question.'

'How will we make passage?'

'In a manner open, honest and humble. We will pay our dues in advance.'

'Dues?'

'We will present him with the black dog and the black bitch,' said Harkfast. 'Vinadia is rumoured to be a collector of fierce beasts.'

'We could make the crossing at night, secretly,' Ruan suggested.

'We have no suitable boat.'

'A curragh is easy to construct.'

'Nay, fosterling, we depend on Vinadia's friendship.'

'For what reason?'

'Lest we are obliged to leave Sketis quickly,' said Harkfast. 'In winter the isle can be a prison. It will be sufficient to have weather to contend with, without brawling with Vinadia's ferrymen as well.'

'I see the reason of it,' Ruan admitted. 'Where is the road to the Dun?'

'Hidden in the trees yonder.'

'Then I will lead the approach.'

'As King, you must,' said Harkfast. 'But cautiously, cautiously, fosterling. It is possible that we are already under scrutiny.'

Ruan raised himself in the saddle and scanned the surrounding land. He saw nothing to indicate that Vinadia's scouts had located them. Even so, the others were watching him, awaiting his command. He signalled direction with his sword-hand, steered the reluctant horse down the banking towards the pines. Though Ruan did not feel courageous, he would not shirk his responsibility as King and leader.

Within an hour they had traversed the ridge. Weems, stores and tall, stone-constructed brochs of Vinadia's Dun lay below them, seemingly peaceful under whey-coloured cloud.

Vinadia laughed, merriment bubbling out of his chest like scum from a freshly tapped mead tun. Every man in the feast-hall laughed too, clipping off the sound at precisely the same instant as their chieftain. Vinadia was a rotund little man, cheeks so puffed with fat that his eye-slits were almost invisible and his mouth like the puckered aperture in a bondmaid's needle-bag. The hair had fled from the front of his skull but he disguised the fact with a tonsorial rinsing so that hair and scalp were uniformly bannock-brown. A seagull-feather cap hung on a knob of the throne, which was set in a circular hollow in the earthen floor. The fringes of the depression were prettily ringed with polished boulders and pebbles and the ground strewn with straw and clean green boughs. Circles appealed to a quirk in Vinadia's nature. His antecedents, so his bard assured him, had been the original architects of the broch-form, the squat conical bee-hive towers which still protected not just the coastline of Smertean territories but most of Drumalban as well. Only in a furnished broch did Vinadia feel completely secure. Brochs were not large enough to feast a whole court, however, and so he had to content himself with a long hall like other chiefs and kings. The builders had done their best for him, adding mock rooftrees and

115

excavating the circular hollow to give him some measure of comfort when necessity dragged him from his privy chambers within the thick stone tower.

Anticipation rather than necessity had winkled him from his shell that morning. His beloved son Meglan had just returned from a five-month voyage, nosing into Rhea on a following tide like the spirit of dawn itself. Meglan was not Vinadia's only child. He had nineteen others by various acknowledged wives, but of that number only three were males and as yet mere infants. Meglan shared all his father's qualities, with the added boon to his nature that he relished voyaging. Now that he was of age and stature he relieved his thankful father of the onerous task of leading the fleet on its annual rampage south. Vinadia had tholed the exercise in his youth only because it was his bounden duty to the tribe, was profitable, and usually provided a satisfying slaughter or two to enliven the monotony of weeks in a slopping curragh.

On the lowest level of the Royal Broch were the trophies of that era in Vinadia's life; heads in jars, pickled hands, the flayed skin of a black barbarian, the private parts of a mincing Greek who had shrieked like a girl-child when the Smertean boarding-party captured the standing-rig in which he had been a passenger, and who had endured six long sessions of the edge, the iron and the whip before he finally succumbed. On the walls of the chamber were less perishable treasures; helms and shields and daggers, coronets and torques, and many other trinkets taken from the princesses and noble women who had filled Vinadia's nights with joy, before he bartered them for better, or they fell sick of their insignificant wounds and died.

Stacked at the rear of the feast-hall were the new treasures which Meglan had dredged up from far southern ports and intercepted vessels. Vinadia was too cunning to 'trade' with provinces north of the country of the Brigantes, some of whom might be sufficiently offended to make reprisals. Instead, Vinadia's ships ploughed seasonal furrows far to the south, even rounding the Dragon Rock at the hinge of the land of the Dumnonii to 'barter' with the fat craft which waddled over the short-seas to Gaul, loaded with gold and wine and many other rare cargoes.

By sneaking a sly glance at the surprises of the porters' bundles, Vinadia could tell that his son had fished far off. He would not spoil the fun by asking where the fleet had been or what special booty had been harvested. Waiting was all part of the game which he and Meglan had devised four years ago, when first the lad pinned his banner to the mast. The night of a fleet's return was marked by a great feasting. During the course of it Meglan would borrow the bardic stool and spin the spicy story of his adventures. Stories all told, the goods would be brought forth and laid out on a sail. Vinadia would walk round and over them and admire and be amazed and congratulate his son and the mariners and make fit and generous portion to them there and then—but only of the goods. Often there was more than mere cold treasure. There would be captives too for his entertainment, to provide diversion in the dark nights of the winter. It was the captives which Vinadia enjoyed most of all, and kept to himself.

As if the prospect of such a feast was not enough to fill a man's bowl with happiness, now a band of travellers had ridden into the Dun, offering to pay tribute for the use of his waters and the hire of a curragh to take them to Sketis.

Weird folk only would venture to Sketis in this miserable season, and weirder still to come gifts-in-hand to his hall. In truth, what with the drab weather and Meglan's return, it was likely that the strangers might have slipped undetected on to the isle if only they had paused to employ a little cunning. Had they not heard of his reputation? Perhaps they were so rich that they were willing to pay not to be delayed? Or had they dealings of such urgency on that cursed island that they could not afford the luxury of patience and risk an untithed crossing?

Vinadia was intrigued. Being a man who loved a mystery, he laughed again and signalled to the Knight of the Royal Flesh to admit the guests at once.

Preparations for the night's feast were far forward. Trestles were erected, benches slotted, fires and turf-ovens stoked. Serfs were trotting in and out with bowls and pots, mead tuns and jars of wine. Savoury odours tickled the chieftain's nostrils. Through the hubbub he could make out the appetizing hiss of crabs in the swell-pots and the groan of beeves on the roasting-spit. The sounds faded into silence as the strangers were ushered in. Vinadia was too shrewd a ruler to chide his people for their curiosity. Indeed, Meglan should be present to share the diversion, but the lad, like most of the mariners, was sleeping to revive his energies for the festivities. No matter, Vinadia decided, the strangers would still be here when Meglan woke.

The curtain at the hall's end parted. Two warrior kinsmen flanked the entrance. The Knight of the Royal Flesh made the gesture of announcement. Vinadia raised himself slightly on the throne and stared down the hall at the strangers. This was no brace of ore sellers, no solitary scholar, no nostalgic elder or student of war—none of the usual run who held Sketis in their eyes. Five men of differing castes and ages came singly through the narrow portal and gathered on the patch of welcome between the main rooftrees.

Vinadia studied them; a tall, gaunt elder in a grey robe, a handsome young man, a bronze smoothling who was probably of Roman birth, a stunted and scrofulous Pictish hunter, and a long, droop-featured person with a bristle jaw and a leather sack in his arms.

'What is in your bundle, friend?' Vinadia called.

'My harp.'

'Ah, you are a Bard?'

'I am.'

'Favourite of any particular king?'

The Harper did not answer.

Vinadia felt a prickle of suspicion.

'Will you play for me?' he asked.

'If it pleases you.'

Grey-robe, who had the cold eyes of a priest, stepped a pace into the aisle.

'Vinadia, Chieftain,' he said, 'we have heard much of you. We have heard that you are generous in giving of your time and energies, and the lives of your people to the protection of these coastal regions, holding back fierce raiders and all the other evils which waft from the horizon.'

'That is true,' said Vinadia, modestly.

'We wish to receive your blessing on a voyage to Sketis.'

'It is a short voyage,' said Vinadia. 'Hardly a voyage at all.'

'Even so, the blessing of Vinadia would keep us safe.'

'Are you the chief of this band?'

'Nay, I am it's spokesman.'

'Of what caste?'

'Of many mixed castes.'

'That is no answer.'

Grey-robe held his breath for a moment, then said, 'We are of the Votadini, Kerns of the Inner Court, the select of King Cleve.'

'Though I am but a nesting bird by the waters of Rhea,' said Vinadia, cautiously, 'yet I have heard tell that Cleve is inclined to uphold Roman ways.'

'In part,' said Grey-robe. 'King Cleve is the appointed guardian of the clans of the eastern seaboard, under a treaty made many years ago. As you will also have heard, he has no occasion to sally westward, for the peoples here are strong and able—'

'You do not have the appearances of warriors.'

'Warriors we are,' said Grey-robe. 'Except the Harper. Even he can wield a sword if the cause warrants it.'

'Kerns of the Inner Court,' murmured Vinadia thoughtfully. 'All of different origins by the tint of your skins.'

'Cleve is a gleaner,' said Grey-robe. 'Half the five hundred of the Inner Court once fought with the Attacotti, and the Attacotti, as you are aware, were the pick of all the sword-lands of the western world.'

'Ay, a whisper had brought that information to me,' said Vinadia. He smiled. 'Come forward. As Kerns of the Inner Court of Cleve I bid you welcome.'

So they came forward, all five, confident but respectful, and seated themselves on the straw cushions which the bondsmaids spread round the lip of the hollow-throne.

Vinadia slapped his hand on his thigh and the festive preparations started up again.

'Now,' said the chieftain, 'let us talk as friends.'

119

*　*　*

The sleeping chambers of the Royal Broch lay in the centre of the seven layers which piled up from the subterranean trophy-room to the guards' chilly barbican. A door of planks hung from weighted chains to keep out draughts which no curtains could stay. Woe to the man who rattled them when Vinadia slept, or pandered with his wives or concubines on the padded mattresses within. Meglan's wedge was narrower than his father's, though it too had wooden doors to give him privacy. The young man was surprised to be wakened from deep sleep by the cranking of the portal hatch. He struggled from the swaddle of fleeces and skins which smothered the floor, still dog-weary from his piloting of the shoals of the narrows' mouth. He blinked blearily into the flame of the rush lamp. Under the fleece his fingers closed on the two-edged dirk which was a more comforting companion in bed than the fairest virgin or the lithest whore in all the seaports of the west.

'Son, we have guests new-arrived,' said Vinadia.

Meglan sighed and slumped back against the bolsters of sweet-mart fur. Usually his wakening was a sign for the meats and cakes to be served. He could not imagine why his father had disturbed him with such paltry news. He could think of no living man who would cause his father to unfurl the cloth of gold or make him quite as agitated as he now appeared to be.

'Tell me of these guests, father,' he said, and, hands folded behind his head, listened to the chieftain's account of the strangers.

'You will allow them safe passage, of course?' Meglan said, when his father had finished.

'I have not yet decided.'

'If you will pardon the observation, father, I notice that you are somewhat distressed.'

'Their arrival spoils the feast.'

'Nonsense!' said Meglan. 'We have feasted guests before now.'

'I do not like to shelter them within my walls.'

'Why do you dislike them?'

'The tall one I spoke of, who calls himself Harkfast, I suspect

120

that he is a Druid.'

'Truly?' said Meglan. 'I have never yet met a genuine Druid. The others, what of them?'

'A motley assortment,' said Vinadia. 'A young man, a Roman, a Pict, and a Harper; a strange crew to seek passage to Sketis.'

'What is their business on the dreaded isle?'

'To buy swords for Cleve—they say.'

'The hags will not sell them magic metals.'

'What man can predict what the hags will do?' said Vinadia.

'Have the travellers offered tribute?'

'That they have.'

'In coin?'

'Dogs,' said Vinadia. 'Two fine black savage hunting dogs, a bitch and her mate.'

Meglan considered that the tithing price was not high enough for five men, but he could tell by the glint in his father's eye that the chieftain was much taken with the gift. Vinadia collected animals, housing them snugly in special stalls over by the cesspools on the seashore. Two serfs were devoted to the care and feeding of the brutes which included an assortment of wolves, wild cats and boars. From time to time there were foreign rarities too; a lion, a dragon, and a pretty-faced black-and-white creature which had proved itself the most savage of the lot but, like other hot-weather beasts, died soon after its imprisonment.

Meglan said, 'If you care for these dogs so much, accept the token and give the strangers free passage.'

'Even if they are not emissaries of King Cleve,' Vinadia mused, 'something about them indicates that it would be imprudent to rile them. I do wish I could fathom the business they have on Sketis.'

'Perhaps they speak the truth,' said Meglan. 'Perhaps they come only to purchase swords for the great Kerns of the Inner Court.'

'How could we unearth the truth?' said Vinadia.

'Heed your instincts, father,' Meglan said. 'Feed and entertain them, accept the tribute of the hounds, and allow them to go unimpeded on their way. That is the riskless policy.'

121

Vinadia nodded; he was not convinced.

Meat was portioned and mead flowed. Fat dancing wenches performed their ugly gyrations on the welcome patch. Two dwarves juggled conches to each other, more and more, faster and faster, until the long hall seemed filled with a blizzard of shells, and even the serfs stamped their appreciation of the skill of the miniature hands. Other entertainment included boisterous harpsongs, and Mungan was persuaded to render a saga of the repulsion of short-sea raiders by a courageous chieftain who might have been Vinadia—or then again might not. More mead flowed, and sour wine and floods of amber ale. Meglan's mariners had a place of honour near the round table at which Vinadia and three of his more vivacious wives sat, together with Meglan's mother, a portly chop-fallen woman who had long ago learned that, Pictish fashion notwithstanding, it was politic not to make herself heard in her husband's presence. Meglan was at the mariners' trestle, for he was truly one of them, friend as well as ruler.

Gadarn ate sparingly of the badly cooked foods and refrained from deluging himself with mead or wine. He needed no reminder from Harkfast that this was no time to fuddle the senses. Mungan watered his wine by measure half to half, and Domgall rationed himself to ale. Ruan and the Druid hardly drank at all though the meats were salty and nipped the palate. The guests were tabled to Vinadia's left hand, in station between the mariners and the warrior kinsmen. The babble in the hall was too constant to permit much conversation and the chieftain contented himself with occasional hospitable gestures with his drinking horn. So far Vinadia had not informed them that he would accept the gift of the hounds and bless the kyle and provide a curragh large enough to transport them across the narrow channel. Gadarn realized that the piggish little chieftain was deliberately making them wait, probably curious as to their purposes on Sketis.

The feasting continued far into the night. In due course,

Meglan took his seat on the bardic stool and spun the yarn of his adventures. The account—a tradition, Gadarn reckoned—raised wails of mirth from the Smerteans who fully understood all the hints and sly satires which were lost upon the strangers. Even so, only a fool would fail to recognize that Meglan did not talk of 'trading' but of piracy.

When the spinning was over, Vinadia commanded a sail spread on the floor, and goods were carried and spread out on it to be inspected. Courtesy required that the guests admire the trove. This they duly did, though without much enthusiasm. The booty was diverse but rich—amber and jade ornaments, sheets of beaten tin, nuggets of lead, bales of regal cloaks, furs and linens, and many other commodities. It was the wine jars which caught and held Gadarn's attention, however. He lingered long by them; six dozen man-tall, brick-coloured jars, each stippled with insignia of origin in coded letters.

The inspection ended with a congratulatory speech from Vinadia, an anthem by an ancient bard and the handing over to Meglan of seven-tenths of the treasure for distribution among the mariners according to their rank. The portioning was swiftly carried out, while the trestles were pushed back from the vicinity of the chieftain's table. When all was ready, Meglan and the Knight of the Royal Flesh, together with a complement of six of the strongest of the warrior kinsmen, left the hall to escort Meglan's captives from the grid-cells at the back of the hog wallows.

All true-born Smerteans, commoner, noble or bondsman, enjoyed this part of the proceedings best, for on the bodies of captives Vinadia wreaked that cruelty which most other monarchs expended on their serfs. Vinadia was considered a humane ruler, ruthless, slow to anger, fair in exercising tribal laws, careful to give no hint that he took pleasure in the punishments which his legal advisers meted out to offenders. Not even the tribal gods—all of which were male figures—were permitted to impose themselves above Vinadia in the minds of the clan. Relying not on crops and cattle-health but on the skills of its sailors and shipwrights, it followed that discipline rather than imagination governed the peoples' attitudes to its gods. Under Vinadia, the Smerteans were secure, comfortable almost to the point of luxury.

Fear, however, was a commitment of all free races, and needed an outlet in the communal mind. Sketis provided this outlet. Chieftain and subjects shared a terror of the cursed island whose peaks cast gloomy shadows over the Dun, made men shudder and women mutter ancient say-saws and rub the cream of boiled ormers into their bellies to ward off cramps and barrenness and the other hideous pestilences which the hags of Sketis might blow in their direction. The creatures of the isle were seldom seen. Mists hid the worst of their doings. Only brief glimpses of firelight or a column of kelp-smoke told the Smerteans that living things still inhabited the place. It was not known what exact shapes the entities had recently assumed. In memory was the story of how once a great school of warriorship had flourished there; how young knights and the sons of kings had travelled from the rim of the world to study and train with the hags, developing their skills by fighting wraiths until their swords were so subtle that they could shave the crest from a broody curlew without causing it to fly off in fright. But that was long ago. The school was derelict now, and only mines and sooty forges remained, hidden in caves far below the leaf-green sea-kyles where Vinadia's curraghs did not dare enter even to escape the fury of the winter's gales.

So the Smerteans claimed the channels, dwelled in the shadows of the misty mountains, and no man among them dared set foot on the island just across the water. In public spectacles, as well as in the casting of details of Vinadia's private sports, they found relief from the tensions which the nearness of Sketis imparted.

Gadarn knew little of all this—though Harkfast had given them all warning to treat Vinadia with the utmost caution. Intuition warned the Roman that hospitality was only a mask which might be removed at any moment. Besides, he had read the stippled code on the wine jars. The chieftain's son made no bones about the jars' origin. They had been taken from a trader's barge encountered in a bay east of Ocrinum. Thoroughly familiar with the Ocrinum traders, Gadarn knew that they would not bargain with an upstart northerner, not at any price. Obviously the barge had been pillaged, probably stripped and sunk. Though nobody in Vinadia's clan could decipher it, Gadarn's own name was scribed in code upon those jars. He still had a share in an import business which operated from the harbours of Dumnonii territory. It hurt him that barges in which he had a share should be plucked from the channel like feathers from a goose's breast. Interception, to give it the polite name, was a hazard of every dealer's business. But the loss of profit was less distressing than the thought of the friends and companions who might have been slain in the battle.

Gadarn moved closer to the rear of the hall, into the vicinity of hanging pinewood torches and the stoves' bubbling broth pans. Brands and scalding liquids were effective weapons if the situation should deteriorate into a brawl. Only kinsmen were permitted to carry blades in the feast-hall. But Gadarn, veteran of many tavern scraps, was confident that he could escape unscathed and take his chances in the darkness outside. The corn-coloured mare, stronger than any mount in this territory, could easily leap the rampart by the cesspool shore. Glancing across the throne-pit he caught Domgall's eye, gave a curt nod to confirm that he at least was ready should Harkfast's passive policy prove wrong.

The first of the line of nine captives entered the hall, a Frankish maiden of sixteen summers, tall and dark-haired, with a flat-featured face. Her feet were caked with the dung of the weems and a poultice of mud covered a wound in her arm. Even so, she could not disguise her breeding or her handsomeness, or the ripeness of thrusting breasts and full thighs under her shift-like garment.

Vinadia supped from his wine horn and got slowly to his feet, fat cheeks swollen with anticipation. He approached the prisoners at a leisurely gait. Immediately Gadarn recognized the response that the girl's temper roused in the Smertean ruler. She had no fear. She had not been broken. Consequently she would make a perfect victim for degrading tortures. In most lands south of the earth wall the prisoners would have been entered as serfs. But the Smerteans were jealous of their bloodline, down to the humblest dog-boy. Gadarn sensed that he was in the midst of a clan tainted by a kind of madness.

In all there were nine prisoners, fastened at the wrists, hobbled at the ankles and linked to the line by braided leather twists. Four, including the handsome Frank, were women, the rest adult males. Scrutinizing each prisoner in turn, Vinadia walked softly up the rank. If he was disappointed in the quality of the human booty he did not show it. They were, Gadarn thought, an unprepossessing bunch—except for the dark-haired maiden. The other women had already been reduced to a state below the level of despair, yet it was not to the Frank that Vinadia steered himself but to the least attractive of the four, a scrawny blonde whittled down by the hardships of capture and confinement. Even with the chieftain directly before her she continued to gawp vacantly at the floor. Gently Vinadia placed his knuckle-ring under her chin and tipped up her head, forcing her to look into his eyes.

The Smerteans were motionless now and silent, a silence pregnant with anticipation.

The perfunctory nature of the deed made it all the more nauseating to a civilized man like Gadarn. With three rapid strokes, Vinadia ripped open the woman's shift, snatched a knife from a kinsman's sheath, and slashed the captive's throat from ear to ear. Her garment slid down, revealing the flat, dry sacks of her breasts, pale flesh already freckled with blood. A spasmodic reaction caused her wrists to jerk against the manacles, twitching, and then she died.

Flinching and bucking like cattle, the remaining prisoners leapt back, the taut leather traces flinging the corpse into grotesque animation and sprinkling blood-drops all around. Hastily the Knight of the Royal Flesh caught a fistful of the victim's hair and clamped a small horn cup against her gashed throat. Exerting all his strength he dragged the line of captives straight again, while the cup filled. Pulling it away, the Knight handed it to Vinadia. Without hesitation the chieftain spilled it over his scalp. The steaming fluid trickled down his face. He rubbed it from his eyes and the corners of his mouth then, receiving a second portion, splashed it across his breast, staining his woollen robe to the waist. Thus anointed, Vinadia stood back.

The Knight cut the dead woman's bonds, dragged her from the line, hoisted her body on to his shoulder and carried her from the hall by the serfs' exit. The ceremony had taken only a moment and during it no man or woman had broken the silence. By its conclusion, however, the tension was feverishly palpable.

The Frankish maiden now stood alone, sullenness transformed into defiant courage. Vinadia waited until the Knight returned to his station behind the prisoner then, with the wet-bladed knife still in his fist, approached the maiden, bent slightly and touched the blade to the fork of her thighs.

Gadarn looked away.

Harkfast had pinned Ruan's wrist to the trestle top, preventing the young man from rushing furiously to the girl's aid. Seated, Mungan cradled his harp and peered at the spectacle through the strings. Domgall was on his feet behind the Harper, slack-armed, prepared. Harkfast's immobility held them all in check, however. The Druid would not be provoked by Vinadia's wanton cruelty. Harkfast's purpose was to reach Sketis. He would not imperil that aim for the life of any man or woman, freeborn or slave.

Stamping started, low at first, soon growing.

The knife point pricked the maiden's linen shift. She stiffened and lifted her chin, jutting out her breasts proudly, supposing that she was already as good as dead. But Vinadia did not kill her. It was not his way to waste handsome girls on sacrifice. Cocking his wrist he deftly cleft the shift from her navel to her ankles, then, to the accompaniment of a surge in the crowd's response, ripped it from the collar downwards and wrenched the seams apart, baring the girl's body.

At the sight of her heavy, dark-nippled breasts and the tangle of black hair at the meeting of her thighs, the mariners lost control. Bellowing, they sprawled over the trestles, big fingers grabbing greedily as if to haul the girl down among them. Grinning, Meglan held them back, letting them gaze their fill, dwell on the pleasure that body would give to their overlord in the snug, smothered layers of the broch. It was all that Harkfast could do to restrain Ruan now. If the girl's humiliation had lasted a moment longer the young man's fury would surely have boiled over.

Gadarn sighed. He could readily appreciate Ruan's frustration. After all, the maid was well worthy of 'rescue'. It would not be unalloyed chivalry which prompted Ruan to risk their lives. If the prisoner had been some raddled scarecrow, no doubt Ruan would have held his temper more readily. As it was, Meglan ended it, signalling to the Knight to remove the maiden, still naked, to the security of the Royal Broch.

Meglan was a smooth-limbed, crop-haired young man of twenty-three summers, even now inclined to resemble his father in the moon-like shape of his face, but not so round yet, and taller. It was unlikely that Meglan felt any sympathy for the Frank. He was merely being careful in case the mariners' lust became too explosive and spoiled the festivities. The danger seemed to have passed.

Jug-bearers toured the tables, pouring liberally. Men, and women too, cooled their cravings with wine and mead, and settled down to see what further amusements Vinadia had devised for them. Meglan, not Vinadia, was arena-master of this circus. The son showed a fine flair for drama. The air of the hall was so thick with smoke that at first Gadarn could not discern the reason for the crowd's excitement, or the retreat of the knights and the bondsmen from the entranceway. Shifting position, jostled by Smerteans, he moved closer to Domgall and peered through the forest of heads.

Then he saw it—a brown bear lumbering upright on hind paws. Seven or eight feet high it stood, clawing its way forward, muzzle flecked and snarling. It was more than fifteen years since last Gadarn had clapped eyes on a wild bruin. Travelling bears were common enough in the vicinity of barracks and forts, but they were cub-trained by packmen and lacked that innate viciousness which marked the breed in the wild state. Nobody had tamed this animal. Its hair was blackish-brown and thickly matted, except where the bindings had rubbed it bald. Its eyes blazed red with hatred. Even the keepers were afraid of it, though it was tethered safe enough to heavy logs and iron chains. Meglan himself led it by a nose-ring looped to a slender rope, a pretty deception, of course. The brute was not under the young man's control at all, but held back by the log-chains. Its keepers were armed with spears and spikes. Hammers and iron hooks were on hand to anchor the links to the ground should it prove necessary to protect the crowd.

A clamour rose from the onlookers. Dripping wine on to his blood-stained sark, Vinadia unwittingly retreated a step or two as Meglan led the bear to the centre of the hall. Forepaws weaving, it tried to rake him with its claws. Meglan showed no fear at all. Turning his back on the beast, he walked down the aisle to the round table.

'Vinadia, my honoured father, I have found you a special gift,' he said. 'No hand-fed pet, I assure you, but a bruin as fierce in heart as a Smertean chieftain. Will you accept?'

'Ay, Meglan.' Vinadia cleared his throat. 'Indeed, I will accept.'

'Take him then.' Meglan held out the knot of the long tether.

Vinadia swallowed, rubbed his bloody fingers on the rump of his breeks and took the rope.

'See, father,' said Meglan. 'I will demonstrate how to take the spleen out of him.'

Sprinting the length of the aisle, Meglan darted left and right, avoided the swing of the paws, and pummelled the wet black snout with his fist, nimbly leaping out of range as the claws swished past him. The bear snarled and hauled itself onto its hind legs again, the great weight of it rattling and dragging its chains, almost snatching Vinadia from his stance at the end of the rope.

The Smerteans cheered and stamped thunderously at Meglan's daring. In spite of his momentary loss of dignity, Vinadia laughed too. He put his arm around his son's neck. 'The bear will be the king of my menagerie.'

'Nay, father,' said Meglan. 'I have another, rarer animal to add to your collection.'

Vinadia's eyes widened. 'What can be more rare than a forest bruin?'

Turning, Meglan signalled to the kinsman by the door. The man went out into the darkness of the compound. Like the others in the feast hall, Gadarn heard the distant sound with trepidation. It had a pitch and timbre which churned fear in the belly, fluctuating from a low growling noise to a high chittering whine. Closer it came to the entranceway. Even the bear was disturbed, hunching its shoulders and hauling restlessly at its bonds. All eyes were fastened on the drapes.

Parting, they revealed a sight which made even Mungan gasp. The two dwarf jugglers came first, dancing and jigging backward on to the patch, tiny fists clasped round the stems of straw torches which they scythed and jabbed behind them. The object of their baiting shambled forward into the light.

The giant was taller than the bear, more stoutly shackled. His features were distorted by stark terror; even in repose they would have been grotesque enough. One bulbous eyeball protruded, the other was missing, its crater overgrown by a fungus from which oozed greasy tears. His teeth were broken stumps. His skull was hairless, except for one tuft which stood askew above the right ear and imparted a list to the whole mammoth head.

Two of Meglan's trusted mariners aided the kinsman, driving the giant with flaring brands, scorching his calves to make him prance and howl the louder, his coarse hairy muscles straining the chains. For all the giant knew of his place in the world, he might have been buried in the deepest corner of the fiery caverns of the dead. Each nerve and fibre concentrated on evading the burning things which hurt him less in the body than in deep cores of pain bored into his memory.

The giant, however, had no tongue with which to exorcise these experiences, or plead mercy from his tormentors.

In all that astonished throng, only two men knew the true source of his suffering.

130

One was the giant himself.

The other was Gadarn.

The portal was flung back. The crowd spilled across the compound. Though penned by eager Smerteans, Mungan could just make out the spear-carriers on the fringe of the mob. He reasoned that Vinadia had ordered a loose watch kept upon his guests. Hugging the harp to protect it, he followed close on Harkfast's heels. Just behind him Gadarn was desperately thrusting and shoving to reach the Druid's side. Mungan would have given way but, hemmed in tightly, he remained caught between the Roman and the Druid.

'You must stop it, Harkfast,' shouted Gadarn.

'I dare not,' said Harkfast.

'I know him. I know the giant,' Gadarn protested. 'He is named Bellerus and was the servant of my partner, Challo, in the territory of the Dumnonii.'

Caught under the flap of the Roman's cloak Mungan lost a portion of the shouted conversation, nudged on towards the weems by the horseman's knees. When he struggled free of the folds, Gadarn was saying, '——fire. Bellerus is deathly afraid of fire.'

Harkfast shrugged. 'A man must live with his fears.'

'It is not ordinary fear,' protested Gadarn. He snatched at the Druid's cloak-hood. 'Not fear as we understand it. Bellerus has the courage of a bull, believe me. In all the world he fears only fire.'

'What would you have me do?' Harkfast said.

'Redeem him.'

'He is Vinadia's prisoner,' Harkfast said. 'I cannot intervene.'

'Then I will.'

'Nay, Gadarn! I forbid it.'

'Let me tell you——' Gadarn's voice faded as the surging crowd drew him apart from the others.

Mungan felt a little sorry for the Roman. Fundamentally, though, he agreed with Harkfast, indifferent to the giant's fate.

131

Even now that he was back in the wilder north lands he could not quite shake off Ninian's influence, that diffidence which Ninian's philosophy confused with inner peace. He would go like a sheep where the flock took him, and at best experienced only mild curiosity as to what would happen next.

The weems was larger than the feast-hall. Cattle, sheep and horses had been driven into pens at the rear. Dung and straw droppings still lavered the floor. The weems had been dug latterly into the side of a hill. Dry stone walled and thatched, it formed a natural arena. A gallery ran round it. Fifteen feet from the floor, broad enough to carry six men chest to back, it was fronted by a waist-high railing of unbarked wood. Pine props held the decking steady, making alcoves round the space beneath. Eager Smerteans filed through the upper doorway to pack the best viewing areas. At the nether end Vinadia already occupied the royal stool on a deep balcony which overhung the weems. The queens and other women were relegated to inferior stalls against the outer wall. Armed knights pushed an avenue through to the balcony and led Ruan's band there one by one. It was all Mungan could do to prevent the harp from damage as he was sucked through the gallery rabble like a leaf in a torrent. As they breasted their way on towards the balcony where Ruan and Domgall waited, Harkfast and Gadarn were still engaged in argument.

Bracketed torches flanked the seats of honour, otherwise the upper tier was unlighted. Below, however, the arena was bright with flaring resin and the bulbous glow of big hanging bowls filled with fish-oil and fur wicks.

Time, thought Mungan, seems to have changed tempo. They were moving now with increasing urgency towards a confrontation. Domgall pulled him across the corner bridge safe onto the balcony. The Pict's swarthy features were puckered with anxiety.

He muttered into Mungan's ear, 'Did you mark where they tethered our mounts?'

'Ay, in the stable to the rear of the feast-hall.'

Now they were all present, Vinadia engaged Harkfast in

conversation.

'You enjoy sport at Fortreen, do you not?' Vinadia asked.

'We do,' answered the Druid.

'Cleve is noted for the giving of games.'

'But they are games of skill, man to man,' said Harkfast drily.

'Beasts are but forms of the parts of man,' said Vinadia, obviously quoting a tribal adage. 'It is but fair and fitting that a man should be pitted against embodiments of his baser nature.'

'I do not altogether agree.'

'Tell me what it is that you really seek on Sketis,' said Vinadia suddenly.

'Weapons.'

'Not martial instruction?'

'The Kerns of the Inner Court have no need of instruction,' retorted Harkfast.

'I understand.' Vinadia's fat face rested like a puff-ball on the quilt of sealskin where the hood of the cloak dropped to the collar.

Mungan listened, watched and said nothing.

'Great Vinadia,' said Harkfast. 'We are anxious to be on our way as soon as possible.'

Vinadia paused to peer down into the arena. 'Tomorrow,' he said, casually. 'Tomorrow you shall have your curraghs and guarantees of safe passage. I like the look of the black dogs, and thank you heartily for the gift.'

Before Harkfast could express his gratitude for the chieftain's sanction, the small man slapped his palm upon the railing, and shouted, 'Look, they are about to begin.'

For all his excitement, the ruler of the Smerteans maintained that underlying coolness which was the root of leadership. He would not allow the avid expectancy of his subjects to lessen. Chanting, hammering their heels on the decking, the crowd made the whole structure shake as if it had a pulse of its own. Vinadia's cheeks glistened with a lather of anticipation, globules of sweat beading his skin.

Unshackled now, the bear was driven into the arena. Swaying on all fours, it shambled from beneath the balcony. Wooden square-shields strapped to their forearms protected the goaders from mauling. Trained serfs, they were used to the handling of beasts, and very spry of foot. Cautiously they prodded the great animal into the centre of the arena, using whip-cracks, long needle-like spears and spluttering straw reams fastened to poles. They edged the bruin round the gallery so that the ardent Smerteans could jeer and spit upon its fur as if it was a hostage capable of suffering humiliation as well as bewilderment and pain.

The giant was brought from a trap on the opposite wall, stripped of his breech-clout, robbed of the one vestige of decency which the most despicable criminal of the southern courts was permitted to retain. His burned-out eye socket streamed brownish fluid, and his broken mouth was lathered with saliva. Brands crackled and scorched his buttocks, making him prance comically and scamper and beat at the flames with his hands. For all his ugliness and the apparent cowardice of his behaviour, the women were much taken with the size of his dangling parts, and giggled and whispered lewdly to each other and elbowed forward for a better view. The Dumnonian was more beast-like in his helplessness than the bruin against whom he would soon be pitted.

Mungan frowned.

The harp was warming in his hands.

Smoothly and without hostility, Gadarn took a pace towards the chieftain.

'Vinadia,' said the Roman. 'I will pay you fifty sesterces to reprieve that man.'

'What man?' Vinadia asked.

'The giant,' said Gadarn clearly. 'Stop the baiting and deliver him to me and I will pay you fifty golden nuggets.'

Vinadia's eyes glittered avariciously. But this was no time for bargaining in coin.

'Does he appeal to you?' said Vinadia. 'He is unusual . . . in more ways than one.'

'Sixty nuggets.'

Harkfast attempted to catch Gadarn's sleeve but the Roman thrust him away.

'Well, Vinadia?'

'You are a guest in my hall,' said Vinadia, spreading his palms. 'Fain would I grant your request. Alas, it is too late.'

'I *know* him,' Gadarn hissed.

Most of the crowd were watching the argument now. Having lost the attention of their chieftain, the ring-wardens steered bear and giant apart, circling them slowly round and round the arena.

'How could it be,' said Vinadia softly, 'that a kern of the Inner Court of Cleve is acquainted with a creature captured on a wine-trader's barge two full sail-months from Fortreen?'

'It is enough that I know him and count him my friend and thus wish to protect his life,' said Gadarn. 'And if that is not sufficient, then sixty golden nuggets will weight the balance.'

'Nay, sixty nuggets is not enough.' Vinadia slapped his fist impatiently on the railing. 'Sixty hundred nuggets would not persuade me to call off my evening's entertainment. But stay, Roman! If you know this man, you will be well placed to judge his prowess. I will not *sell* him to you, but I *will* strike a wager.'

'And how will you wager?'

'On the bruin, of course.'

Gadarn's fist rose and would have smitten the fat Smertean where he sat, if Ruan had not caught his wrist and, using all his strength, stayed the blow. Behind the stool the kinsmen stiffened, sword-arms tensed.

Vinadia stared into the stranger's cat-like pupils.

'Throw your life and the lives of your companions into the ring, if you wish,' he said. 'I am sure that my people would be glad to excuse you, or even aid your suicidal intent. We would all enjoy the spectacle of your body staked out below. Masena, my favourite little wife, might be persuaded to add glamour to your passing by thrusting your sixty golden nuggets, heated for ease of entrance, into your vulnerable orifices.'

Death hovered over chieftain and Roman alike, over them all in fact. Gadarn could kill the Smertean overlord with a single blow of his fist, but would instantly die too, hacked to pieces by the kinsmen's swords. They would all die.

Mungan frowned again.

Indifferent to his fate, he frowned only because the harp was promisingly flushed now and he wondered what the sign might mean.

Harkfast uttered a single word, not in any language that Mungan understood. Gadarn's arm slackened and fell to his side.

Strange, thought Mungan.

The Druid's eyes were closed.

Vinadia shoved himself to his feet, belly pressed against the balustrade.

'Meglan,' he shouted.

The entire weems was still, except for the wailing of the giant and the grunting of the bear.

'I am here, father,' the young man called, waving from his seat among the mariners in the centre area of the gallery.

'Meglan, one of our honoured guests wishes to wager sixty golden nuggets upon the outcome of this contest.'

'On which decision, father?'

'On the victory of the giant.'

'Take him on it quickly, father,' Meglan shouted. 'It is a profitable wager.'

'Is that your considered advice, my son?'

'Ay, the bear will surely win.'

Sweating, smiling and jovially acknowledging the cheers of his subjects, Vinadia seated himself on the stool once more.

Gadarn too was smiling.

Vinadia said, 'All Romans enjoy a wager, do they not?'

'They do,' said Gadarn. 'What is the stake on the Smertean side? What will you give me if the one-eyed giant should win?'

'I will spare your life.'

'Spare *his* life, you mean?'

'Nay, the giant is doomed whichever way it falls,' said Vinadia, pleasantly. 'It is *your* life you wager with, Roman. I hope that it proves more worth than your sixty precious nuggets.'

Wasting no more time, Vinadia raised his hand.

Whips cracked and torches wagged. The bear was steered inward towards the man.

Mungan hardly noticed.

In his hands the harp had come alive.

Before Ruan quite realized that his companions had taken a hand in the struggle of man with animal, it was all over. No sooner did the giant, whom Gadarn called Bellerus, become aware of the presence of the bear than a ripple of music drifted from the harp. Mungan's fingernails tipped the strings, forcing volume, so that the song stole from the balcony to mingle with the smoke from wicks and torches wafting low over the weems.

Bellerus had drawn himself up before the animal. Finally discovering an object upon which to vent its rage, the bear raised itself on its short hind legs and punched and scratched at the giant's head and body, then, upright and lumbering, bore down on him. Bellerus did not retreat. He seemed transfixed.

The crowd roared, and the harp-song swelled insistently.

Then Ruan understood that this was a sleep-song, a spell spun from threads of black dreams, endless nights and the unplumbable slumbers of dead things.

The bear sagged, red eyes losing the fierceness of wrath. The growling in its throat took on a softer tone. Seizing his chance, Bellerus lowered his head and drove at it. His bald crown struck it full on the belly, so that breath hooted hollowly out of its mouth. Even so, the paws did not have the power to retaliate, stole towards him so lethargically that a child could have evaded them. Bellerus crooked his arm under the fork of its thigh, lifted it and threw it over as Caledonian athletes did with pine trees in friendly domestic competitions. The bruin's spur-claw scraped a long scribble of blood down the giant's shoulder, but the wound was shallow and did not distract Bellerus from his purpose. His strength was remarkable. The whole weems shook with the weight of the beast's fall. The feat won gasps and murmurs of amazement from the Smerteans. The man's concern was not to conquer the bear, only to find an escape from the threat of the fire-brands. The bear lay where it fell, on its back, paws tucked dormantly to its chest, short legs splayed wide. Many of the watchers took it for dead. Ruan knew better. Over the changing rhythms of the harp he could hear its rumbling snores.

Toppling the stool, Vinadia leapt to his feet. Crimson with rage he shook his fist at the bland-eyed Harper.

'You have deceived me,' he screamed. 'I am educated enough to have heard tell of sleep-songs and similar magics. You are *not* warriors. *You are allies of the entities of Sketis sent to try us out!*'

Gadarn rammed the heel of his hand hard against the base of Vinadia's nose.

The ruler dropped like a pigeon arrowed on a branch. Gadarn caught the swooning body, swung it high above his head and hurled it backwards over the railing. The bundle, wrapped in the folds of the sealskin coat, made a compact and satisfyingly solid thump upon the arena floor.

Ruan had no need to look down to ascertain that Vinadia was dead. Gadarn's blow had been lethal.

Stunned silence descended on the Smerteans, disturbed only by the crackle of the brands, the bruin's snores and a slithering crescendo from Mungan's harp. He held the instrument high, in a position no other Harper would adopt, and let its summoning mix with the calling regimens of the Druid's brain.

So the gale came, sighing in its infancy, playfully fluttering the tapers and fine stuffs which scarfed the concubines' shoulders, teasing the mariners' beards and the braids of the bondserfs, licking the bear's fur and making brown shadows dance across the roof. Rapidly burgeoning, it tore at the shields of the guardsmen, plucked smoulders from the goaders' poles, and buffeted the dwarves who, sensitive to disaster, swam against it until the blast blew them hind over head and rolled them away like tumbling weed. The wind itself was noiseless. It did not whistle or skirl or howl derision at the puniness of men, though it brooked no barrier to its progress through the weems, and slammed and rattled the traps and shutters until their thongs frayed and flew apart and the overhead thatch decayed into a rain of chaff.

Slowly Harkfast lifted his arms and, with a winsome gesture, enticed the gale to greater passion still.

The Smerteans were confused.

Some were spurred by rage at the death of their chieftain, others crazed by fear. Thrust back by panic-stricken women and favoured serfs fighting to reach the doorway, Meglan and the mariners struggled to push through to the balcony.

Ruan caught the spear in the hands of the Knight of the Royal Flesh, twisted it free, shovelled it back and drove it up under the hem of the link-mail sark deep into the man's bowels. He withdrew the blade and with a second jabbing stroke holed the heart of the kinsman next in line.

Domgall too had found a spear, Gadarn a sword. Three in a row against the rail, the companions fought against the remaining warriors, defending the motionless figures of the Druid and the Harper, while the gale rose and battered down the big doors and spun the jagged planks into the heads of the crowd.

The shrieks of the women were mixed with cries of pain. In the arena the wardens were flying before the force, clamouring to find escape. In the centre of the wind-tide stood Bellerus. The magic did not trouble him. Indeed it filled him with delight. Jigging and laughing, he clapped his hands as the streaming flames of lamps guttered and torches were snuffed out and a fireless night enveloped the weems.

The harp-song ceased.

Harkfast returned to them.

Ruan heard the Druid shout, 'Over the railing.'

Shapes were active around him.

Holding the spear above his head, Ruan vaulted the railing and landed on the spongy dung of the ring below. Here the darkness was less than total. He could discern objects—the bear's hummocky bulk, the naked giant, the sheen of painted shields which the goaders had dropped. Then Harkfast had him by the arm, dragging him towards the exit under the balcony.

Anchored by a cross-split spear a guard clung tenaciously to his station in the funnel of the gale. Ruan could see him clearly, outlined against the grizzled hill. He lifted the stolen weapon to strike the man but Domgall reached him first. The guard cried out and fell away and was whisked off and sent dead and sprawling to the beaten grass round the butt of the building. Then Ruan was running again, the wind behind him dwindling as he put distance between himself and the weems.

Accompanied by ranks of cold grey cloud, dawn was coming over the mainland ridges, the sea smooth and calm and frost-rimmed, Sketis blanketed by mist. Only the weems was possessed by the storm, the thatch, ripped off now, spiralling upwards like the smuts of a bonfire. The babble of the trapped Smerteans carried far and loud into the empty shell of the morning.

In the compound and surrounds of the Dun serfs and lesser wardens, confused and full of dread, darted hither and thither for want of leadership, not yet knowing if the rumours of Vinadia's death were true or false. A bowman, posted on the crown of the broch, fired countless arrows at no particular targets, while a kinsman-at-arms endeavoured to herd his complement of spears into an orderly squadron. Without Vinadia, Meglan or any of the lesser chiefs, no man had the wit or initiative to set extra guards upon the stables or picket the route through the sea-gate to the jetties a half-mile north.

Ruan found the horses tethered under the stable roof, just as they had left them. As all the grooms and dog-boys had fled, there were no Smerteans to oppose them. Ruan stirruped Harkfast into the saddle. Mungan mounted more slowly, burdened by the uncased harp and anxious for its safety. Domgall and Gadarn came last, grinning and bloody-sarked, the Roman holding Bellerus by the hand, pulling him on. The giant had lost his terror and was not reluctant. Meek as a bullock, he allowed himself to be led by a man he dimly recognized as a kindly companion of his former master.

'You will follow us, Bellerus,' Gadarn told him. Swarming up on to the back of the golden mare, he reached down, grasped the tussock of hair which grew from the giant's skull and gave it a firm tug. 'We will protect you. Do you understand?'

Bellerus nodded vigorously, grinning all over his grotesque face.

Harkfast reared his horse and bounded it forward, ducking

140

under the eaves of the stables, urging the mount on, hitting a gallop long before he reached the unguarded gate. In a whirl of manes and tails the rest of the horses followed the Druid's lead, whinnying and snickering, yielding to the riders' urgency. Hanging in the saddle Ruan reined, watching how the naked giant sprang after Gadarn and set a stride as speedy as the gallop of the mare.

'My dogs,' said Domgall, craning back. 'Ruan, my hounds.'

It was not the thought of the dogs which took Ruan back into the main patch of the Dun, however, but the memory of the Frankish princess. Even that was faint yet and no fit excuse for his compulsion to commit one more act of aggression against the Smerteans. Perhaps he would have stormed the Royal Broch alone to prove courage to himself. But prudence mastered impulse. The sight of Meglan and five of his fittest sailors racing out of the lower door of the weems, caused him to change direction. Instead of riding for the broch, Ruan raced his horse hard towards the cesspool wall. The goaders and two terrified dwarves were beyond it, gathered in confusion round a kelp-fire in front of the grids. They watched Ruan as he spurred the horse towards them, then, as the animal leaped over the dike, scattered and fled howling in all directions.

Instinct told Ruan what lay behind those grids. Reining before the foremost gate, he hacked and hewed at the draw-rope and cut it through. Stone ballast sank and cracked upon the pebbles. The gate rose up, releasing the rank and acrid stink of the animals penned within. In the lightless cavern, Ruan could see eyes glittering, then the slinking shapes of wolves stealthily coming forth. He trotted on, cut the second draw-rope, then the third, and, at the last of all, discovered where the hounds were. Domgall's black dogs did not cower and hang back. They shot out into the light like otters into a pool, sleek-black, glossy and savage.

Calling to them, Ruan drove down across the rock-spits, splashed through the scummy pool and took the path beyond the wall. The dogs bayed behind him. Meglan and a knot of Smertean warriors swarmed over the wall to reach him. But the beasts were out, loose in their caves and, growing bolder, sneaking forth. Ruan did not know what they were, only recognizing wolves and striped cats, but the noises they made chilled him and he turned long enough to watch one piebald brute no larger than a whelp rush snapping at the throat of the nearest mariner. He saw the man go down, screaming in agony, and the others back and spread out, pursuit forgotten.

Flogging the stallion's flanks, he galloped along the track, then reined him down towards the shore where, in the distance, the others waited for their king.

The broch stood like a stalwart challenge. Ruan hung the horse on the crest of the path, pausing to gaze back. King or not, he could not command his companions to do as he would have wished them to do and ride back to release the Frankish maiden. His memory was teased by her arrogance and courage, the handsome promise of her body. No, he could not go back. The course was set for Sketis. But, he promised himself, if all went well on the island, he would return this way again, run the gamut of Smertean rage, find the maid and rescue her from bondage.

Tugging the bit, he heeled the horse's ribs and rode hard towards the channel harbours.

2

The dreamers of the forge

From where the golden eagle soared no living man was visible on the barren plain below; yet man there was, plastered flat to the steep grass slope which wrinkled up from the glen's edge to overlook the shore. Crog lay as motionless as moss, clad in a coat of goats-hair plaid loomed specially for him by the Mother Hag and dyed to blend with the lineaments of the land which he patrolled. Hair and beard, bleached from fiery red to rye, and wind-tanned flesh gave him the likeness of a tuft of weed or a fallen alder trunk rotted by rain. He could lie so still that dormice nested in his ear and fostered young before his watch was done and duty made a gentle detachment necessary.

Crog was thirty winters by the count, first child of nine whom Mother Hag had borne when her fighting days were done and men engaged her in combat of a different sort. His father, a common Scotian, had been washed ashore from a foundered curragh, aided by the Sketians, and nurtured for his wit and skill in ore-dowsing, until he died of ague at a natural age.

Raised as a runner, Crog could not recall a time when he had not known what would become of him. He was loved by all and loved all in return, particularly the Mother Hag who had been generous enough to give him birth. Mated with Cyprinida, he had bred two sons to run his portion of the coastline when his own calfs shrank and his lungs collapsed like punctured bellows. Last summer Cyprinida had been handed on to bed a final term with Leaman the Sea Master, hopefully to provide a sailor or two for the future of the loch fishings.

On clear days, which that day was not, Crog could lie on the screes below the old watchtower and count the inhabitants of Vinadia's Dun. He was so long in sight that he could even make out the knots in the rigging of the wind-curraghs which put out from the jetties to flirt with Rhea's currents. If that morning had not been drizzled with harr he might have wondered at the wind's havoc in the region of the weems. As it was, the first hint of disturbance that came to him was the paddle of oars.

Rowers were common enough, but these were not experienced oarsmen. No Smertean, man, woman or stripling, ever scraped the hull or smacked the sea with the blade. The craft was a mile up current, coming down on the ebb. Yesterday he had observed Vinadia's travelling fleet close to the headland. After five months or more on a voyage they came home with noisy triumph, sails cracking, oar-thongs creaking like sinews as the crews eagerly bent to drive the ship the last few miles. Even Leaman admired the Smertean mariners' skills. The occupants of the approaching curraghs were certainly not of Vinadia's clan.

Crog scanned the haar in the northern kyle and picked up the prows of the two curraghs as soon as they became visible. Square sail hoisted, one tacked to take advantage of a westerly. The other risked no sail at all and dithered errantly on two oars, lame as a snared cormorant. Crog recognized the complexion of the green-dyed, greasy Smertean curraghs, though clearly there were no Smerteans on board. As the craft ploughed gradually closer to shore, Crog quickly assimilated vital details. It seemed that the golden-skinned man and the grey-robed one of whom the mother had spoken had at last arrived.

Crog slithered backwards, somersaulted and came up on the downhill gradient already running. He did not run like a hare or a stag, did not lope, stride, sprint or jog. Instead he seemed to blow weightlessly across the plain like a withered leaf in the approximate direction of the foothills.

Behind Crog, far, far off on the cockscomb of the east range, a linking runner remarked his progress and immediately filled the unattended beat. The second runner had the curraghs in his eye before they spun sluggishly to the shingle. By then Crog was five miles along the track of the Glen of Arrows tumbling on towards the Loch of Slapping Waters and Cuchuillin's peaks.

By the time the occupants of the curraghs had splashed

ashore, unloaded their horses and accoutrement and mounted up, tall Crog had reached the Boreaig path from which the caves led down to the palace of the Mother Hag.

'I do not like this place,' Gadarn said.

'It is a place like any other,' Ruan said, though he did not truly believe his own statement. 'Look, grass, stones and sky.'

'It will rain before long,' Gadarn said, glumly.

'So we will be wet,' said Ruan. 'You have been wet before.'

'The clouds seem as if they will rain blood.'

'If it would rain kirtles,' said Ruan, 'we might cut cloth to keep your giant warm.'

The mare was walking now and Bellerus, one fist tangled in the animal's tail, had no trouble in keeping pace.

'If he stops,' said Ruan, riding by Gadarn's side, 'he will surely tear the rump from her without intention.'

'He will not stop,' said Gadarn. 'He can maintain a horse's speed for two days and nights without winding himself.'

'Yet he is afraid of fire?'

Gadarn scowled. 'You have pricked ears even in the height of danger, young King.'

'I harbour no malice towards your giant,' said Ruan, 'though his visage is ugly enough to curdle milk. Indeed, he is almost sufficiently ugly to be a Roman.'

Gadarn smiled; he never resented a well-turned insult.

He said, 'Only the gods know who fathered Bellerus. His mother—may her bones writhe in the mire—was the daughter of a minor priest in a subdued tribe of the Dumnonii, a simple people who have taken well to the infiltrations of civilized culture.'

'Roman ways, you mean?'

'What other ways can be considered civilized?'

'Ah, I am in no mood for argument today,' said Ruan. 'My mind aches with the memory of Smertean corruptions. In fact, I might even be inclined to agree with you. Continue the history of the giant.'

145

'When the woman lay down to deliver,' said Gadarn, 'a thundercloud passed over the place. The babes wriggled into the world to storm and lightning; a bad omen for any mother, doubly so in the mind of the pagan. Bellerus, you see, did not come out of the womb alone.'

'He had a twin?'

'He was one of two identical male infants,' Gadarn explained. 'Probably the mother suffered excesses of pain. In any case, she was filled with dread at the portents and, having no clear idea who the father might be, convinced herself that the babes were spawned by an evil spirit. Enlightened officials tried to dispel the notion, but the woman was deranged. For four years she waited, accumulating evidence to support her fanciful belief. Then, one midwinter afternoon, she took the little boys out on to the moor above the town and performed a rite on them.'

'The fire rite?'

'You are familiar with the theory that an evil spirit will not inhabit a maimed body?' Gadarn shook his head sadly. 'She scorched their tongues and burned an eye from the head of each of her children. The weaker of the two died. Bellerus survived. But now his mother could not bear the sight of him and cast him out on to the moors where he was found by my partner's father, taken into his protection, given succour and duly raised.'

'How did he acquire the body-scars?'

'Fighting,' said Gadarn. 'He takes pleasure in sportive fighting. Many a wager have Challo and I won on his prowess, especially in Gaul where they have greatly vaunted champions.'

Ruan studied the giant. He found that the man was staring at him as if he had taken in all that had been said, though he could not possibly understand the dialect. The burnt socket had dried now, a webby crust forming over it. The remaining pupil was as blue and tranquil as a spring pool. Ruan made a universal sign of friendship. Bellerus answered with a similar gesture and grinned widely, showing brown and broken teeth.

'We will keep him with us, will we not?' asked Gadarn.

'If you wish,' said Ruan. 'His strength may prove useful.'

'His presence reminds me of happier days in warmer climes,'

146

said the Roman, lifting his open palm to the sky.

The testing was superfluous.

Rain fell in large plopping drops, bending the leaves of the weeds by the fringe of the path, visibly spreading its rods across the ranges. Out in front Harkfast led. Domgall and Mungan brought up the rear. The path was barely broad enough to allow the horses to ride in column of route. It seemed to Ruan that they were riding on into nothingness, towards no specific destination. Domgall's black dogs were too weary to whine. Puffs of breath grunting out of the horses had become quite pale and cloudy as the air chilled. Rain drove down, increasing in volume, until the straggle of the path was totally lost and Harkfast a mere spectral shape. Rain streamed over the naked body of the giant. Only he refused to bend his brow to it, keeping his head high, not in defiance of the elements but welcomingly, as if the sheets of falling water washed out the memory of fire.

The jocularity with which Ruan had held gloom at bay would no longer yield a jibe with which to taunt Gadarn. Slouched over their saddle-horns the band rode slowly down the floor of the long glen into the hidden sources of the rain.

Under a canopy of thatched grass, four elder hags waited patiently in the grassy hollow beneath the rim of the hill. On the shore a squad of ormer-catchers paraded, quite unaware that humans stood near enough to sling them to death. Out in the grey twilight a bull-seal barked like a listless eructation of gas from a furnace. Fretted stones stood man-high about the secret cave mouth. Even in this winter month the grass was soft enough to hold the rain like dew in its velvet leaves. A stream ran freely from the ground, gurgling down to join the sea-loch's lapping waves. The canopy was planted on four stout staves fitted into holes usually hidden with boulders. Only the women were protected. Slan, Leaman and Crog waited bareheaded and patient by the standing stones.

The Mother Hag did not appear. She seldom ventured out now, except in the height of summer when simmering seas and baking hills reminded her of the seasons of her prime when she had conquered all manner of heroes. Defeat was not in her nature. But the years grew heavy over her head and it was all that she could do to support them cheerfully. So she sat by the kelp-fire, her swords by her side, in the great oak-root chair that a king had built for her with his own hands, and crooned old ballads and stirring sagas to stave off melancholy. Occasionally she would stroll down the tunnel to the forge and ride the bellows for an hour, a feat no other mortal could do and a sign that her blood had not quite turned to vinegar.

The elder hags, called Ochran, Machalla, Fidin and Weadla, were all that survived of the Mother Hag's ten sisters. Though the family was noted for longevity, accident and sword had done for the rest what the mere wasting plagues of age could not. The hags watched the rim of the hollow with keen interest, anxious to clap eyes on the strangers whom the Mother had conjured up in one of her better dreams, consolidating the nebulousness with images in Slan's fire.

Ochran was fat, with swollen breasts, a jowl like a torque-ring, and short legs. She wore a plaid of saffron, and a wig of albatross feathers. Machalla was fat too, but taller. She stressed her masculine build by squeezing her bosom into a plate of chequered leather and bright metal links, leaving her huge thighs bare under a lad's skirt. Fidin was hardly there at all, so stringy had her frame become since her last breeding eighteen years ago. Heather-plaid, neat-shaped, cloaked her, and a high collar and tip-hood hid most of her face, which had never been her best feature and tended to be whiskery like that of a seal-pup. Weadla was the youngest. Still prone to simpering fits, she tried to make her lank strands hang in ringlets like great Cuchuillin's, and dabbed her eyes with nightcoin to purple them again. Her garment was long and ribband-littered, a conch-shaped ornament of fur seated behind the nape upon which she could rest her head when weariness stole over her, as it often did these days.

It was the habit of the sisters now to compete in trivial things, to pit their jealousy against each other, not to spill it where it would do harm over the heads of the breeding maids, the nieces,

148

the daughters and god-daughters, or the grand-foundlings who were under their jurisdiction. The male inmates of the sisterly hold had learned well the tricky arts of discretion, mediation and diplomacy.

Thus it was that Crog said, 'Ladies, I am sure that you have noted the snorting.'

All four sisters nodded agreement, and tapped their ears to loosen wax.

And Crog said, 'Ladies, I am also sure that you have already detected the shaking of the soil.'

All four sisters modestly lowered their lashes and dug their heels a little more deeply into the grass.

And Crog said, softly, 'Ladies, why did you not tell me that strangers have appeared on the lip of the hill—to the south-west—just over the tussocks—there?'

All four sisters squinted, then gasped, giggled or grunted, according to their size and vision of how they had once been. Instantly composing themselves, they sharply instructed the menfolk to buckle their belts and try to appear at ease in spite of the excitement which must be coursing through them at the advent of strangers.

On the knoll to seaward of the hollow, the runner of that beat raised his hand. Crog returned the sign. The hags did not see the transfer of responsibility, though they knew the drills as well as anyone. They were peering through the curtain of water-dribbles from the canopy's eaves at five mounted men and an almost naked giant who slid and stumbled down the path and debouched without much dignity upon the sward.

'The golden one is mine,' Ochran growled.

'Nay; mine!' whispered Fidin.

'He would snap you like a razor-shell,' said Weadla. 'I care not, I will have the youngest, the dark one on the piebald.'

'Your eyes deceive you, sister,' Machalla hissed. 'He is ancient and warty and his horse is black. I will have him.'

'The giant is more your meat,' Weadla retorted. 'See, he is already stripped. Could you not make a wholesome meal of him?'

'Ay,' said Ochran, 'and nibble on the shrivelled little Pict to

149

fill the spaces.'

Crog and Leaman walked forward. They wore no ceremonial finery. Such niceties of custom had never held on Sketis. As he passed the shelter, Crog murmured, 'I am glad that you reminded me how seemly silence is, my aunts, otherwise I might have conversed beneath my breath with Slan.'

The sisters fell silent, watching, as Crog and Leaman crossed the sward and took the bridle of the leader's horse. Without doubt it was the one of whom the Mother Hag had spoken; tall, gaunt, grey-robed and priestly, with eyes like crystals in low strata rock. She had also spoken of the golden one, but had not elaborated on his handsomeness. It was many, many years since such a grand train of males had entered the community of the warrior women.

Crog bowed. 'Gentlemen, you have travelled far today?'

'Far, indeed,' said the priestly person.

'Is this the termination of your journey?'

'It is.'

'Do you seek council with Mother Hag?'

'Who would travel so far for any other purpose?' said the priest. 'It would be worth tenfold the miles and discomforts to converse with such a noble lady even for a moment.'

Crog bowed again in acknowledgement of the flattery.

'You came in Smertean curraghs?' he casually remarked.

'Stolen.'

'I guessed as much,' said Crog.

'The Smerteans are our enemies,' the priest added. 'We did what we could to cause them discomfort.'

'You are safe and welcome here,' said Crog. 'It will not be a luxurious billet, but it will be secure, that I will promise.'

The priest dismounted. None of the sisters coveted him or peeled the clothing from his hips in their imaginations. They sensed that he was beyond their reach. He ignored them as thoroughly as if the dribbling eaves had fallen and buried them under mash. Leaving horse and baggage in the care of Crog, the priest strode quickly over the sward to greet Slan. He offered the smith his hand and touched palm to palm.

150

'You are Slan, the smith of whom King Pasard spoke?'

'You have found me at last, Harkfast,' Slan said.

'You anticipated my coming?'

'The Mother Hag predicted it, but I think she may have skimmed it from my dreams.'

'Do you know what I want of you, Slan?'

'I have been ready for many years, Harkfast,' Slan said. 'It is not with me you must parley, however.'

'Pasard is dead,' said Harkfast. 'But his cause endures vigorously. I have brought another King.'

'The lad?'

'Aye.'

'A child of Pasard?'

'Nay, but he cherishes the essence.'

'It is meaning, not method which is relative now,' said Slan. 'How did you trace me?'

'I will tell you shortly,' Harkfast said. 'First I must bargain with the Mother Hag, lest she be offended.'

Slan laughed. 'Offended! She awaits your arrival eagerly. The beds have been prepared since Samhain. Come, Harkfast, I will take you below before this pestilential rain makes jellies of all us.'

The warrior-women followed no creed but that of the sword, and so had acquired no formal rituals with which to burden their guests. Their underground caves were partly natural but cracks and chambers in the porous rock had been extended and enlarged and linked by walls of pebble and daub. In spite of its half-domed hearth even the palace of the Mother Hag was comfortable rather than impressive.

Slan, who led the party underground, was a short, broad-shouldered man, with ruddy cheeks and a nose which, split at the bridge, spread impudently across his face. His hair was shaved close. A leather sark was clasped about his waist by an iron belt. There was nothing deep, secret or sinister about him that Ruan could detect.

On first sight, the Mother Hag too was little different from several seamed and weary elders whom Ruan had met. She was certainly larger, but unlike the crones who formed the welcome party, did not dress eccentrically. She wore a garment of warm wool, and a ram's fleece cloak complete with head and horns, the latter barked and broken and the worse for wear. She rose from the oak-root throne, and came briskly forward to embrace the Druid. Ruan noticed that none of the Sketians stood in awe of her. Even he, a stranger, felt her kindness and sagacity like the scent of dried myrtle in a kist. No paint or dye adorned her. She sported no jewellery of any kind, except two bright metal clasps to hold her grey hair back from her bony forehead.

Ruan thought how strange it was that Druid and Hag should greet each other with such warmth, hugging and crooning welcomes like long-lost comrades. The pair had never met before, of that he was sure, yet they had the rapport of kinsmen and affinities which Ruan could not begin to define.

Four saplings were strapped to form a rack beside the Mother's chair, a collection of fine swords mounted there, some forged from the bright metal which Ruan had heard called by many names and which was highly prized by experienced warriors. By the fire, a massive hound slept, jaw on paws. The animal did not waken throughout the long evening, though his snout twitched and his paws paddled as if memories of good hunting tempted him to pad outside to shiver short-sightedly in the rain.

Crog and Leaman introduced the company each to the other while they performed the social gestures which in other courts were left to bondserfs. They put out seal-skins for the guests, then brought a wholesome and appetizing feast of broth and ormers and fishes cooked in various herbs, and beakers of ale from a cool shelf. Ruan did not expect such easy hospitality. Sketis was supposed to be an evil isle, riddled with dreadful sprites—yet he sensed no atmosphere of corruption here, except in the way the four hags ogled Gadarn and murmured and chuckled to themselves, and that was mild and not threatening, and certainly did not distress the Roman. Pict, Harper and giant—the last now decently clothed—sat round the far arch of

152

the hearth, stuffing themselves with food and ale, relishing such hospitality after days of hardship.

The cave reminded Ruan a little of the lost valley of Pasard, though there was no decay here, rather a feeling of life quietly resting, like hounds in their stalls in the snows of midwinter. Above the smoke-crack in the roof the wind sloughed rain against the visible edges. Small spinners and rock-skippers played in and out of the fissures in the roots of the turf. White stains showed where gulls perched in cold weather to warm their wet webbed feet. Suddenly Ruan felt more at peace than he had done since that day when Gadarn appeared in the camp in the forest to aid Harkfast in the rite of initiation. But it was not a drowsy sort of peace, and held in it threads of excitement.

Harkfast and the Mother Hag were already deep in conversation. Ruan could not follow the dialect. He did manage to pick out enough words here and there, however, to realize that the pair had not yet fallen to the business of the quest but were discussing the calamities which had befallen the Smerteans, the death of Vinadia in particular. It occurred to him that he might be missing something material to his future. After all he was the King and the Druid his vassal—though he would not dare to press the finer points of that relationship.

He swallowed the tail of a baked fish, and washed it down with ale.

'Harkfast,' he said.

Druid, Hag and smith all turned to stare at him.

'I beg the Mother Hag's pardon,' said Ruan, 'but I am concerned.'

If the Druid was displeased at his fosterling's interruption he did not show it.

'Why are you concerned, young man?' the Mother Hag asked, speaking the language of the Caledones.

'Lest the talk pass into forgetfulness,' said Ruan, lamely.

When the woman spoke his excitement increased, similar to, though not matching, the anticipation he used to feel when hurrying through the glades towards the steading where Rea lived.

153

'Forgetfulness!' Harkfast's tone had an edge of reprimand.

Ruan wiped his hands on his breeks, and shuffled forward on the matting closer to where the ancient woman had seated herself on a hearth stone. Her knees, drawn up and slightly parted, made a hammock of her garment in which lay delicacies of fish and shell-food.

'Ach, Ruan, you are swimming with questions, as you always were,' said the Druid. 'Cannot you contain your inquisitiveness?'

'Mother Hag,' said Ruan. 'I have heard much of the schools which were here once and would consider it an honour to learn more of them.'

Mother Hag raised one wiry eyebrow, making the seams of her brow curl like vipers and the pins of her hair bob.

'This is no time for tales,' said Harkfast. 'If you must enter this round of talk, then you must do so as you wilt, as a King, not as a callow herd-lad.'

'Nay,' said Mother Hag. 'The tales that you would hear from me are mine and mine alone. Even my sisters share only a common pool. What is locked within me is the comfort of cold nights, not to be given away lightly. The stories are holy—all stories are—for they encase the deeds of the past and bear down upon the losses of the future. There are more purposes to the tongue than to wag out dusty chronicles for brief boyish amusement.'

'I regret my impetuosity, Mother Hag.' Ruan's contrition did not deceive Harkfast. 'Mention of Vinadia put it into my mind.'

'Vinadia is dead, I hear,' the woman said. 'None on this isle will grieve for his passing.'

'Have you fought with the Smerteans?' said Ruan.

'I have fought with representatives of every clan and every race,' said the old woman, modestly. 'But the old battles are over and new ones not yet enjoined. You must evade the son of the chieftain before you can make your way to the seat of your next destiny.'

'The sea is wide,' said Ruan.

'And your mouth wider,' Harkfast muttered.

The Mother Hag's eyes glinted, hazel no longer but coloured like the bright metal of her hairpins.

'Slan,' she said, 'has spoken of Pasard.'

Harkfast bit his lip.

'Too soon, this turn of talk?' the woman asked.

'I am a wordy man,' said Harkfast.

'And we are women of action.'

'What would you know, Mother?' the Druid said.

'You have informed me of your activities in the Smertean Dun; you have told me who the men are, but you have not mentioned the purpose of your journey.'

'I thought that tomorrow, in privacy, we might discuss it.'

'Let us talk of it now,' said the woman. 'The young man will be amused by our bargaining.'

'Why do you consider me a bargainer?' said Harkfast.

'You have come for Slan, have you not?'

'Aye,' said Harkfast. 'I have.'

'And you bring a king.'

'I do.'

'Do you think, good Druid, that I would set a smith to work the bellows of the Sketian forge without knowledge of his history?'

Slan laughed, a breathy sound like the stiff intake of his furnace flue. 'She knows all, Harkfast. She is not possessed of the gifts of seeing as are the priestesses of your cult, but she has lived long and met many fine men and has learned what to do with the ore of these experiences, how to forge it into prediction. Besides, I could not melt clean metal unless I dressed myself in truth and honesty. I told the Mother of my history. She in turn told me that you would one day come here. She did not know your name; I provided that. Pasard spoke of you often in the days immediately before the night of slaughter.'

'I meant to ask,' Harkfast said, 'if you fled, or were fortunate enough to have escaped?'

'Neither,' said Slan. 'My term on the mainland expired. I was required again on Sketis to stoke the forge as I had done when I was young and apprenticed to Vendon, who was smith for a hundred years and in his youth apprenticed to Sleight, who learned his craft from the man who dug the forge-cave out of the

155

rock with his bare hands and breathed fire into the loins of the grandmother of the warrior-women. I first came here from the horn-land when I was a boy because a priest assured me that I had the wonder of metal in my nails and would be a smith. The Mother was younger then, and still grew in her armour.'

'My question was of Pasard,' said the Druid.

'How you test me!' said Slan. 'Fain would I have waited to meet the Druid of the King. I did not *flee* and I did not *escape*. I left Gairesa two nights before the Roman raid and was on a craft for Sketis when it occurred.'

'The cause was lost.'

'I gathered so from the accounts of the battle which came down to us.'

'Yet you knew it was not over?'

'You are a preserver, as we are,' Slan said. 'But you move like the strength of the wind through the ages of present time, while we Sketians hang in time's caves like lime-spears, growing longer but frailer with the constant drip of days.' He lifted an ale horn from the hearth and sipped from it. The sinews of his throat swelled and the apple in his gullet bucked. 'Do you wish me to go with you, to show you the place where the Huntsman runs, and tell you how to catch him?'

'That is the crux of my mission,' Harkfast admitted.

'So men still have missions?' said the Mother Hag. 'Ach, I have heard the boasts of so many who would change the tilt of the world with their swords.' She held up one hand, finger pointed at Harkfast. 'In my dreams I saw you come with a golden-skinned man—he who sits yonder now. Is he not the King?'

'You have dreamed powerfully, Mother Hag, to view us at all,' said Harkfast. 'But Gadarn is of Roman stock. This young man is the King.'

'Born?'

'Reborn,' said Harkfast.

'Are you satisfied, Druid, that through him you can do all that Slan claims?'

'With the help of others of like mind,' said Harkfast, 'I deem it

156

possible.'

'You would rob me of my smith?'

'Only Slan can show me what I must find.'

'Ay, I was afraid that would be the way of it,' murmured the Mother Hag. She said nothing for some minutes, the ram's fleece drawn high on her shoulders as if the palace had been swept by a chilly draught. Then she pushed herself to her feet. Ruan, Slan and the Druid stood too, setting down their beakers. The four sisters were watching, greed and lust in their antique eyes again.

'It is cold here,' the Mother Hag said. 'In the forge I will be warm. Are you too weary to accompany me?'

Gadarn and Domgall also made to rise, but Harkfast signalled them to be still.

'Slan,' said Mother Hag. 'Let us show our guests the heart of the fire.'

Ruan hesitated. He was not sure if he was included in the invitation; then the woman held out her hand to him. He took it, felt a strength in her fingers which reminded him of how it had been in the high valley when first Harkfast touched him. Across the cavern the sisterly brood whispered and simpered, the rumbling chuckle of fat Ochran like the echo of a rock-fall. Their insinuations did not matter now. Holding the hand of the Mother Hag he would descend to the bowels of the earth itself if she chose to lead him there, walk down a tunnel to the space below the earth and fall out among the stars.

It did not take long to descend the worn steps to the forge door, or for Slan to turn the bolt and swing it wide. The forge was spacious and well-equipped with bellows, anvils, tongs and pincers, hammers, saturated crucibles, charcoal stacks, tripod racks, quenching troughs and, in bunkers round the walls, rust-red and bog-brown ingots and ore-sponges. In the mouth of the furnace the fire ebbed low and the stink of Slan's labours had thinned, leaving only remembrances of burning substances and acrid steam. Wood-and-leather puncheons hid the secret liquids which every prime-smith concocted to anneal his blades. In adjoining caves lesser impedimenta would be found, the braziers, rivets and scouring stones with which apprentices first made the errors out of which knowledge of the craft developed. Ruan imagined the forge to be deep below the loch, for the silence was like the silence of the sea, liquid and ear-filling.

Behind the huge four-lunged bellows a rude bench was perched above a pumping spar. Teams of boys would pedal the spar, forcing breath into the pipes, making the clapper-valves clack, controlling the blast as the smith required. Mother Hag went to this bench, girded up her skirts and sat down. Placing her naked feet on the spar, she rode air out into the furnace and fanned up the cinders to a bright glow. Slan fed in logs and fuel-cakes pressed from grass, kelp and bog-oils. The flames licked up gladly, well-caught.

Mother Hag sat back, shoulders against the wall, one hand raised to the cross-beam to steady herself. The fleece had slipped and Ruan could see a lattice of scars and puckered injuries upon her arms.

Slan straddled the anvil snout, arms folded. Ruan and the Druid remained in the centre of the room.

'There is a secret which Slan will not tell,' the Mother Hag said. 'It troubled him when he returned from his travels in the wake of the Pictish armies. How valueless were his journeys, though his swords and steel-tipped spears broke many a brittle Roman blade and ripped the tripes from Britannic mercenaries and paid men of Rhineland. Slan was our best smith. But I let him go, allowed him to break sanctuary to discover his own way in the terms of the new men. I warned him that he would find no chivalry, no mighty deeds, that slaughter would sicken him and victory would taste like sloe. But he was young, and strong, and his head had been turned by the tales of the fledgling warriors who came to be taught the glories of a dying art—until they too were caught and sucked into a maelstrom of conquest. It was too late for us, for the last of the warrior-women. We had no heart to sustain the line. Vendon was old; the forge blew only infrequently. My sisters grew lax, and I—I too slumped like burned dross in on myself. Though we bred men and girls like queens in a hive to train for the functions of our community, there were none to take our place. No more warriors. The need of schools for heroes had passed. A king could make himself hero by buying an army, laying waste to his enemies with no more skill than a flailer on a threshing floor. But Slan was hot for the Pictish rebellion. Besides, Pasard was known to us. We released our smith under bond to return when the deeds were done, or when Vendon passed to his rest. He was gone for a year, that is all: caught the tail of defeat, missed what there was of glory, and returned.'

'As I promised, Mother Hag,' Slan respectfully reminded her.

'Ay, when Vendon died. You returned full of grief for the last passing, yet not lacking a spark of hope that the sons of the heroes of our race would rise again. You spoke of Harkfast, a Druid whom Pasard had lauded. You spoke of many bad things which had happened, and how ill it was with our Pictish brethren and the substantial clans of the Celts. Everything we asked, Slan, you told to us—except the secret which made you start from your bed, sweating and screaming, and crying for release.'

'I told that only to Pasard,' said Slan. 'He swore me to an oath of silence.'

'We respected that promise,' said Mother Hag. 'And believed your assurance that Harkfast would come here in search of you, and bring with him the gift of a new kingship. For that gift we tolerated all. Tonight you have at last confessed the source of your fear, Slan. Already I have heard enough to indicate that no man, no army, can do what the Druid intends.'

'Yet we must try, Mother,' said Slan. 'There is no help for it.'

The woman smiled.

She said, 'The ambitious warriors of old were always doomed. Long or short, the centuries caught up with them, brought an end to glory and honour, to the vitality of struggles against the impossible. Ah, Druid! Ah, my beloved Slan! You two know well that all great combats are but wars against Time—or used to be, before greed for gain and temporal power sullied the hearts of the flower of the knights. And you, my impulsive young king, how gloriously do you devise your destiny?'

'As gloriously as I dare, Mother,' said Ruan.

'I needed no reply,' the woman said, without reprimand. 'I understand how the wise-man communicates his ambitions; how

159

Slan can be drawn to meet that which he most fears. It is a distillation of all failures that you contrive, Druid, the crystal of every sort of doom.'

'I do not believe that I will fail,' said Harkfast.

'Nay, or you would not begin at all,' Mother Hag said. 'However—to the practice of it. You will take my smith, and have him lead you to the places where the Huntsman rides. Could he not *tell* you where the territory lies?'

'It is any place,' said Harkfast. 'It is any battlefield where honour stands. You know of Nudd, I take it?'

'I know that Nudd is the Gatherer of Souls, the Captain of Great Heroes, that he carries knowledge of the histories of the brave, that he rides wild with his hounds over the bloodiest battlegrounds seeking worthy men to join his hallowed company in the Hall of the Warriors, in the preserves of the heroic dead.'

'And the Hand,' said Harkfast eagerly. 'You have heard of the Hand?'

'Ay, but little,' the Mother said.

'I have *seen* the Hand,' said Slan. 'I saw it during the battle of the Eagles with the Brigantes near Deva. No other man spied Nudd's approach. I do not know why I did. I did not wish for the privilege. But I *saw* the Hand of the Warrior Huntsman, big and gleaming gold, saw how he used it to pluck up the souls of those whom he judged fit to be his companions in eternal afterlife. Black-cloaked, riding a jet-black mare, with his hair streaming and his hounds, black too, baying, he came. I *saw* how he raised the Hand in summoning and how the souls of the heroes came to him, crying joyfully to be dead. I saw *all* this, and it made me deathly afraid.'

'The Hand is power,' said Harkfast. 'I would have that Hand.'

'Nudd too will fade,' said the Mother Hag. 'The Huntsman too will soon find his coverts bare of heroes. Men will die in droves, in thousands and tens of thousands, and their lovely, courageous deaths will become so meaningless that the death of a million will have less import, less relevance, than the passing of one brave prince. Then too Nudd will dwindle and lose his authority, and live like a wisp of cloud on his hill in the ruins of his

160

heroes' hall.'

'Slan will show us the Hand,' said Harkfast.

'Would you *dare* to command the dead?' the Mother Hag asked.

'I would dare to try,' said Harkfast. 'It is the only hope for all that we hold and cherish. I am sure that you are with me, Mother Hag.'

Now the woman changed her stance. She stretched out her feet and pumped two blasts upon the bellows-spar, lit the flame of the forge strenuously for a moment, then heaved herself up and moved away across the cave towards the shadows.

'I am with you, Druid,' she said quietly. 'I have always known that your coming would single out my destiny. But my sisters dream of men in their dry parts, and keep hope alive in that singularly silly way. They still have a little of their former doggedness left, however. In deference to them I must ask for barter.'

'What would you have?' said Harkfast.

'A dream.' Mother Hag turned now, arms folded over her breast. 'Once we were warrior-women; now we are only dreamers of the forge. I would borrow your dreaming power, old Druid, that is all. It is a season of many endings. But I do not yet know how it will fall for me, or if there will be glory in it. However, I do understand that I must use your sleeping power for one short night, to link with the power of the sisters.'

'You talk of an ending, Mother Hag,' said Slan. 'Is it not possible to give benediction to a new beginning?'

'Quite so!' the woman said. 'Quite so!'

Ruan was fixed on her. Inside he was full of awe and excitement. The Hand of the Lord of dead heroes was their objective; a brave, outrageous scheme. With the Hand he could indeed command all clans of all races. The woman's talk of doom and destiny did not allay his hunger for success.

She said, 'Druid, tonight we will all sleep. Tomorrow you will pick swords from Slan's collection. There is, alas, no time to forge blades patterned with cunning spells. Seven blades and seven helms of bright metal you shall have as a gift from the warrior-women. On the day after tomorrow Leaman the Sea Master will provide a vessel, and steer you a course wide of the Smerteans. I give you leave to take my smith. Slan, I release you from the bond of loving servitude. You may go with these men for whose coming we all have waited and who have brought not hope but the hopeless glory of ambition beyond reason.'

Her tall figure merged momentarily with the darkness. Ruan could see only the patch of grizzled fleece against the cave wall. He heard a bolt snatch back and the creak of hinges and watched night open up before him, depthless and clear and black, studded with a multitude of stars. Sea tang cleansed the forge. The lapping of tidal waters stole into the silence. The forge was not beneath the sea, but set along the kyle-side, great wooden doors opening out on it, so that the smith and his apprentices could cool themselves and gaze from the flames into landless distances.

Mother Hag stood in the doorway, arms upraised, fingers resting on the lintel, her body blotting out a wheen of stars.

'Harkfast, will you dream one final dream for me?' she asked.

'I will.'

Harkfast went forward to walk with the woman. They became quite small against the frosty winter sea, dark figures upon the shingle beyond the cavern arch; tall old woman and tall old man precariously balanced on the very edge of the sky's infinity, mere voices in the clarity of the night.

'See, there is motion in the stars tonight,' the Mother said. 'Do you read signs of destiny there?'

'I do not read them well.'

'Yet there are endings there, Harkfast.'

'There are endings everywhere.'

'How will our doom be sealed?'

'In heat and flame,' the Druid said. 'I have brought that too, alas, as I have brought the King.'

'No matter,' said the Mother. 'It is time to burn again.'

Their voices faded. The winter night was still. By Ruan's side the burly smith bowed down his head and wept.

* * *

Boud, mother of Meglan and eldest queen, did not shed one single tear during the funeral rites which attended the interment of her husband's bones. Vinadia was buried with a minimum of delay in the long barrow beyond the ridge of lamentation. No signals from the tribal gods indicated that they disapproved of the haste with which the Smertean ruler was put to earthly rest.

Dry-eyed, Boud scorned the wailing of the younger queens; a heavy-breasted, stout-thighed woman, sickened by their inability to realize that Vinadia's death would herald a new era of pride and prosperity for the clan. Even if she had plotted it, the passing of the self-indulgent chieftain could have come at no better time or in more propitious circumstances. Meglan was ripe to assume command. Twice the warrior his father had been, twice as ruthless, and ten-fold as strong in character: Meglan was only half Smertean, of course, the better part of him being linked by her bloodline to the Vacomi, a resourceful east coast clan who properly exalted women and were not burdened by ill-founded fears of mists and cloud-shapes and the contours of an offshore isle.

There were many funerals that afternoon, knights and bond-serfs and even women all put to ground. It was as if a battle had swept the camp, yet there was no revelling in deeds done or consolation in the litters. At first, raw fear numbed the brains of the warriors, robbed the decision-makers of their powers of recovery. Even Meglan would not send a group into the ruins of the weems to dispose of the bear and search for signs of how a five-man band had so thoroughly routed the whole of the Smertean court. Magic was no explanation. Belief in magic had held the tribe in thrall too long, weakened their defences in devious ways, which only she, Boud, could observe dispassionately. Outcast from the broch, object of neglect, scarred by Vinadia's nocturnal passions, she had no hold on any Smertean—save one. She could influence Meglan, and would command through him. So in the first hours of confusion Boud set herself above counsellors, impotent priests and upgraded kinsmen, ascertaining that there would be no mutters of mutiny or civil strife and that the links of rulership would hold fast until legal ceremony could be arranged. It was the queen who drove knights into the haunted weems to spear the bear, drag out the vulgar dead and cleanse the lingering evil with fire. It was the queen who marshalled troops and set the huntsmen to track and kill the roving beasts and fling them into the sea, in case their corpses contaminate the minds of the clan with more superstition. It was the queen who cornered the quartermaster and ordered him to break out the war-horns and shields, the dusty chariots and drays. It was the queen who supervised the sweeping of the feast hall, the securing of the treasure trove, posted guards on all the parts of the Dun, and flung them out to defend outer camps and towers and jetty-stations and all the remaining ships. It was the queen who dressed the loyal kinsmen in battle-garb and the majestic mariners in fighting mail and ranked them round the barrow, so that the priestly service paled and grief was given antagonistic point. It was the queen who, in the space of a day, stiffened the Smerteans to undertake that act which no orator, no overlord, could ever have provoked, using not ambition but response to put her purposes to the test.

The only task Boud did not oversee was that of laying out and ornamenting the corpse of her dead husband. That minor chore she left to the other queens; their knowledge of the parts of Vinadia's flesh was more recent than her own. Besides it was a role of no importance. In the hour before dusk, Vinadia was buried, slotted into his wedge of the barrow like his brother before him, only without the drab day-long incantations and dull chants. The fat chieftain's dirge was a snapping of vengeful banners on staves and the clink of swords in scabbards and, far off in the forest, the yelping of a wolf as the hunting detail ran it down and did it to death. By nightfall on the moonless coast, the ritual was performed and Vinadia gone. Then Boud split from her appointed stance with the other queens and gaggle of painted concubines, and joined her son at the head of the column. No authority was bold enough to stay her or instruct her to return to her allocated rank.

At the head of the banners, by Meglan's side, Boud led the mourning party back to the Dun, to eat the funeral feast she had prepared, and then to sleep to gather strength for war.

The clear weather of the night had gone. The day came shrouded in mist and sleet with a blustery beating of westerly winds. Sketis was closed in once more, shut off from contact with the mainland. In the inner kyles, so Crog informed them, the tides sucked fiercely and the voice of Volsas, the sink of the sea, was louder than he had heard it in many months.

In spite of the weather, Ruan did not shelter in the burrows of the palace. He went aloft into the whirling air and stared through the sleet at the foamy waves slashing the rocks around the loch. He no longer felt secure here, as Mungan, Domgall and Bellerus did. They would not leave the vicinity of the fire and luxuriated in the waiting time and the hospitality of the four sisterly hags who fussed over them and blethered to them as if the fact of their maleness made them royal and demanding of esteem. Gadarn, like Ruan, was disturbed by a feeling of impending doom. A practical man, the Roman no longer featured in the Mother Hag's plan; he was an accident of the sleeping mind, a mistaken figment of a destiny which Ruan did not yet understand. Gadarn held to his alcove, a tiny sleeping chamber in the wall of the tunnel which bored down from the palace room and, like a worm-cast, twisted back upon itself. Ruan doubted if he could have found the door to the forge, even if he had so wanted. In truth, he wanted nothing but to be out of the vicinity of Boreaig and sailing away from Sketis. Only when he was in the presence of the Mother Hag did these boilings in the soul cease to trouble him. Somehow, he realized that he stood now at the centre of things, that action had given way to meaning and that he would not, as in Vinadia's Dun, be singled out as a victim. Rather he would be incorporated into events over which he had no control at all. If the Druid knew what was brewing, he gave no comfort to the young man, and, indeed, kept himself well hidden during the course of that long and mainly idle day. Nor did Ruan see the Mother Hag. It was as if Harkfast and the crone had stepped into another plane of being, walking along the limb of the shore into the clouding sky to spend a night and a day examining the stars at close quarters. Fancies and fantasies nagged Ruan's mind. He could not be still as Gadarn was, for the Roman, though unsettled too, was content to lie on his back on the mattress in the snug rock-vault and wait for release. Ruan could only walk about on the grass of the patch by the cave mouths, circling like a pastured bull, struggling to control the strange turmoil in his breast.

It was late afternoon before Leaman persuaded him that he would be more comfortable below. Leaman was a bright-eyed elder, bald as a gull's egg, freckle-skinned, and stooped. He spoke in a dialect of the Caledones, but with a puzzling accent. He did not speak much, in fact, but had a softness of manner which was as persuasive as a poem. He came with the torch and took Ruan down by another flight of steps into the armoury where, to the young man's surprise, Harkfast and Mother Hag waited.

It was, he remembered, the Hag's promise that they should be equipped with all the finery that the Sketian stores could provide. The sight of the woman lifted Ruan's depression at once. He felt himself once more drawn keenly into interest in this ancient world. Any warrior, he supposed, would similarly respond to the treasures which graced the walls. Hung there were the harps of the warrior-kin, not stringed instruments, but bows of steel and well-wrought iron, bronze striped with twirled gold, silver chasing studded with valuable stones—the great swords which heroes had wielded and which had in them all the fibre of accomplished deeds, tempered with tales and damascened with histories. There were stocks of training swords, flexible and strong but not sharp, arrays of two-handed swords with fat hilts to offer good padding to the shock of strike. Swords ornate and swords plain, broad, short, long, flat-paddled and round, two-edged and saw-backed: also targes, shields, spears, gauntlets, helmets, breast-tunics, sarks of mail, thigh-guards and shin-protectors, shoulder-flanges, and many other samples of the armourer's art stored over from the days of the school.

From this trove Ruan was invited to select a suitable battery of weapons and protections, and was fitted out by Slan with all that a warrior would need. Wisely, he chose not for appearance or for weight but for the strength and pliant quality which made these Sketian implements so cherished where their work was known. The choice of a sword gave Ruan long delay. He browsed over many handsome blades, deciphering those which bore runic signs or inscriptions. He swished and struck and balanced them in his palm and held them up against the lamp-glow to read the boning of the whetstone and the closeness of the steel to the pommel cap. At length he picked out a curved-guard sword, the like of which he had never seen before. True, it was plain, and the hilt showed sweaty wear, but the ring of it was honest and the steel had the sheen of perfection. It thrilled him to cut the air with it. It was as if the weapon had been specially forged to fit into his hand.

'This shall be mine, Mother Hag,' Ruan said, 'if you are still inclined to offer it.'

The woman nodded, took the sword from his eager hand and turned it pommel-down. Below the angle of the guard were tiny runes cold-chiselled into the metal.

'Can you decipher them?' Mother Hag asked.

Ruan squinted.

'Ogham,' he said. 'Erish, I think.'

'Read it, young King,' the woman said. 'Read it aloud to me.'

Slowly, haltingly, Ruan read, 'Made by Falk—Swung by Tanglan—Dream-dealer is unsheathed.' He looked up, frowning. 'Dream-dealer?'

'Tanglan is dead a hundred summers gone,' Mother Hag said. 'The sword is very ancient.'

'Dream-dealer,' said Ruan again.

'The blade has chosen you,' said Mother Hag. 'There is no more to be done.'

'Harkfast,' said Ruan, 'what does it mean?'

'It is but a name that Tanglan picked, words that pleased him. He thought of the sword as the dealer of eternal slumber, the bringer of dreams of death,' the Druid explained. 'It is a splendid blade, is it not?'

'Who was Tanglan?' Ruan persisted.

167

'A young king,' said Mother Hag.

'How did he die?'

'In a fall from a cliff.'

'In performance of brave deeds?'

'Ay,' the woman said. 'He was a defender, a protector in the wake of Cuchuillin, a Red Branch knight, though young.'

'Yet you claim that his sword has chosen *me*?'

'I jest,' said Mother Hag.

Ruan knew that she did not jest. He held up the weapon, squinting at the minute script, pondering the significance of the name, wondering what affinity he might have with the king long dead.

'If you have finished,' said Slan, 'I must pack your armour for the crossing.'

'Are we leaving, Harkfast?'

'Tomorrow, if the climate favours us,' the Druid replied. 'The Mother Hag has been gracious and generous. We have what we came here to acquire.'

'Have you dreamed the dream yet?' Ruan asked.

'Not yet.'

Briskly, the Mother Hag intervened. 'Come, young King. Make way for your companions. They too must select their swords.'

Leaving the armoury, Ruan returned to the palace chamber. Food and ale were laid out on the hearth-stone, but the room was empty. He called out for Domgall and Mungan to keep him company at meat. Faint echoes were his only replies. Wandering down the tunnel a little way, he discovered that the Roman's alcove too was deserted.

He called out again.

The earth muffled and deadened his voice, and there was no response. In all the burrows of Boreaig, it seemed as if there was no other man but he.

The wind roared across the battlements of the Royal Broch. Draughts sucked out the torch flames and made the brands reek.

168

It was warm and snug within the chieftain's chambers where Boud had taken refuge from the clamour of the weather and the din of preparations. Every man and woman in the Dun was occupied. Mariners and wrights, packed off in parties to the jetties, toiled on by the light of bonfires, scraping curragh hulls, tarring the planks of the transport barges, replacing chaffed rigging. In the stores of the Dun, armourers were busy remembering old skills, and farriers and grooms, quartermasters and herders, slaughtermen and cooks, all laboured industriously, caught up in Boud's impetuous craving for revenge.

Hatred was a more natural emotion than grief. Well Boud understood that quirk of the popular mind. She had given them something to hate, an antidote to the poisonous apathy which could so easily follow the murder of a beloved ruler. While the Smerteans talked of Vinadia and remembered all the fine things he had done for them, slaved at their tasks and promised each other a slaughter to avenge the death, they remained unaware that Meglan would demand more than physical courage when the horns sounded assembly by the boats in tomorrow's dawn. Even Meglan did not really understand the purpose of the exercise. He was still too full of mourning, choked by the tensions of rage at the audacity of the five strangers who had so terrorized the stronghold and, in sight of all the people, assassinated the chieftain.

Boud read the confusion on her son's face, the knots of flesh and wrinkles which marred his youthfulness, and the sorrowful bewilderment which clouded his seaman's eyes.

She had chosen the wine carefully, mulled it with iron and spiced it with herbs and blobs of goats-milk cream and drips of honey from her personal hives. She had had the broch swept out and freshened with thyme and crushed pine needles, the fleeces changed and thick new blankets laid. She unearthed her cleanest scarlet robe, brushed it well, and put it on, braided her hair and touched up her cheeks and brows with juice, to welcome her weary son home from his chieftain's chores at the channel-side. He smelled of pitch and horse-leather and wet wool.

Boud greeted him, and sent away the serfs. She stripped him

to his clout, rubbed his body with warm cloths, gave him Vinadia's silk-lined tunic to put on, fed him wine and plover-meat, and talked quietly of the deeds of his father's youth. And when sweat ran again and beaded Meglan's chest, and colour flushed his unbearded cheeks, she said, 'You have made the preparations?'

'Ay, they are well in hand.'

'Have you summoned the spear-bearers and kerns from the outlying camps?'

'They will arrive soon,' said Meglan.

'How many to the muster?'

'Four hundred,' Meglan said. 'Every man, and many boys, will come to take revenge on those bloody murderers.'

'They were honoured guests under our roof,' said Boud, shaking her head, 'receivers of our hospitality, the best offerings of Vinadia's friendship.'

'My father will not go without recompense.'

'Did they sail far?'

'To Sketis,' said Meglan. 'They were seen on the black beach, unloading their pack-horses. We will wait for them.'

Boud raised her eyebrows. 'Wait?'

'I have guards on all the inner crossings.'

'The Druid will not be deterred by guards,' said Boud. 'You have seen evidence of their power.'

'Do you have a better strategy then?' Fatigue made him waspish.

'Attack the isle,' Boud said.

Meglan sat up. The queen wondered if she had misjudged the quality of his bloodline. He looked so like his father at that moment, hiding his fear, if fear it was.

'I cannot order an attack on Sketis,' Meglan said. '*Can I?*'

'The banners are lofted, the war-garb worn, and the horns vibrate with the calls of onslaught,' said the queen. 'Never have the Smerteans been more ready to wage honourable war.'

'But not on that dreaded island,' said Meglan. 'Sketis is taboo.'

'Not by the holy laws of the clan,' said Boud. 'A monstrous

extension of the mariners' tales has endowed that scab-land with its mystery. No priest has ever placed embargo on it; the chaste-books are empty on that score.'

'Ay, that is true,' said Meglan. 'Now that you raise the matter, Mother, I do believe that we are unworthily enthralled by the place.'

Boud shifted closer to her son. Her hand upon his chest pressed him comfortably back against the fleeces.

'The Smerteans are too bold a clan to cherish such un-reasonable fear a season longer,' she said. 'What evidence have we that there are goblins in the caves of Sketis?'

'Histories tell—'

'Histories tell us only of warrior schools, tutored by old women. Are the Smerteans afraid of old women?'

Meglan rubbed his nose with the heel of his hand, thoughtful but agitated.

'How far have our mariners travelled?' Boud went on. 'What strange sights have they seen? You have never flinched from any-thing, Meglan, nor have the Smertean seafarers.'

'The sea is our province.'

'And would not the harbours of Sketis be valuable to us?'

'Ay, that they would.'

'Would not the treasures buried in the ancient palaces—of which we have all heard—enrich your coffers, give you the gold to purchase sword-arms from our northern branch, to raise a conquering army?'

'We are mariners, I tell you.'

'Only because it is easier to be mariners,' said Boud. 'Only be-cause your father and his father did not wish to risk what they had against the Eagles. The Eagles have gone now. There is no conquering strength in all the land. Mariners and warriors yoked together could make you the wealthiest and most powerful ruler in all the provinces of Drumalban, and beyond. The Smerteans are the greatest fighters, the finest sailors, and the least fearful of all the clans written of in the histories. Yet, out of reverence for a dung-heap island, they squander their greatness and content themselves with piracy—'

'Trading.'

'We are *not* traders,' said Boud, vehemently. 'We are not so meek as the trading classes. The sword is the voice of our people, the sword and the grappling-hook and the pitch-brand.'

'Would they follow me to Sketis?' said Meglan.

'Tomorrow, they would,' said Boud. 'If you are bold enough to lead them and are not full of dribbling fear yourself for the black lies which are told of that place.'

'I have seen nothing to make me afraid,' said Meglan.

He sat up on his haunches. Sweat was flowing freely from him now. The spiced wine had brought it out like the breaking of a fever. Boud knew that the blood would be coursing in her son's veins, running red and hot.

'Make vengeance your tool,' she urged him. 'Make the Smerteans war against the wraiths which frighten them. Do you still think there are armies lurking in the mists? There are no armies—at best, a handful of withered hags and a stooped shepherd or two. We are not called the Blood-Smearers for no good reason, Meglan. But we have lost our pride to that place, to Sketis, and now we must regain it.'

Meglan was on his feet. The tunic was short for him, and tight. His muscles bulged against the material, swollen with warlust. Boud touched him, her hands upon his thighs.

'You are a better man than Vinadia,' she said. She *could* say it now, for the engorgement of his flesh made him prone to arrogance. 'You are better because you are all that he was and all that I am, and have the mariners at your back. They, those bearded seamen, they are afraid of nothing.'

'Bucks and stallions of the sea,' shouted Meglan. He smacked his fist into his palm. 'They *will* follow me.'

'Give them a living vivid sign that you are all that Vinadia claimed to be,' Boud prompted. 'Raise the hackles of your cockerels, the hair on the nape of your kinsmen; make the young queens shiver and the bondserfs cower.'

'How, Mother, how?'

'Blow on the trumpet of flesh, my son.'

'Now, tonight?'

172

Leaping to her feet, Boud caught Meglan's arm and led him to the wooden door which separated the wedges of that layer of the Dun. She worked the cross-bar, threw open the door, dragged the young man forward and thrust him into his chamber, his private quarters.

The iron racks which held the butts of the torches had been changed. The floor was strewn with fine white sand. Mattresses were piled up in a corner, the pelt of the prize bear, untanned and ticked with bloody skin, flung over them to make a rough and ready bed. A clay jar full of new wine cast squat shadows in the glow of the coal-cage. Meglan's gaze fastened on the naked body of the Frankish maid, slung by wrists and ankles from hooks on the outer wall. Shoulders stretched taut, her ripe breasts hung outward from her torso. Her ankles were strapped wide apart, and her body so inclined that she seemed to be striving to reach him, to nuzzle her heated flanks against him. Even her lips were peeled back by the tensions of the bonds, and her chin held up, so that a leering smile was stitched across her face.

Boud had arranged the victim well. Meglan grunted, the sound deepening into a growl of approval.

'Play on her, Meglan,' Boud murmured in his ear. 'Play on her nerves and sinews and her quailing flesh. Make her pipe like a curlew, and squawk like a gull. Break her in token of how you will break the shrivelled weird-hags of Sketis. She is an omen incarnate. You must destroy her will. Let the sentinels on the limits of the province hear how you crack the enemies of Vinadia. Let them revel in your pleasure and exalt with you tonight, and tomorrow you will rouse them, spur them on to invade the coasts of fear, conquer them as you will conquer the spirit of this sullen maiden now.'

The queen gave her son a push, propelling him across the threshold. It was not that he was reluctant to enter, merely that he savoured the anticipation almost as much as he would its fulfilment.

The girl writhed and choked against the collar. Her breasts quivered. Meglan stalked her as a wolf might stalk a tethered kid. Boud watched the tunic drop behind him, and then the

173

clout. Discreetly she closed the door so that her presence would not distract him from his work.

The ashes in the hearth burned low. Still no company arrived to turn Ruan's thoughts from dream-dealing swords and inner arguments. He longed to test the blade's sharpness on a Smertean neck, to rive the helmets of warriors with it, hew down the guardians of the broch in which the Frankish princess was imprisoned. The day would soon come, if he had his way, when he would rescue her from that corrupt tomb to ride with him on fresh adventures, to give him loving solace on the trek south in search of the Warrior Huntsman.

Dreaming idly, Ruan picked at the fish in the bowl and sipped the mild ale in his beaker. The dream deepened. His fingers slackened and the bowl fell and cracked on the flagstones. Ruan struggled, over-balanced and sprawled full-length upon the floor. He could not shake off the oppressive weight.

The sister hags crowded round him, Weadla, Fidin, Ochran and tall Machalla. Helplessly he watched them strip him of his cloak and sark. The memory of Harkfast's promise to the Mother Hag tormented him. When he was naked the sisters lifted him gravely and carried him as if he was as light as a stalk of barley down the steep tunnel and into the forge.

Roof rock, the stink of steel and iron, dissolving ingots and burning leather, the first low exhalation of the bellows seething life into the forge; Ruan, head hanging backward, could not see what awaited him. Not until the sisters lowered him to his feet and he found himself upright could he identify, with relief, the persons in the cave. Harkfast and the Mother Hag flanked Slan who, breeked and aproned, stood by the anvil. The Druid and the Hag had closed their eyes and folded their arms. They wore expressions of mutual serenity, youthful again and sublime.

Slan was bathed in the glow of the forge, ruddy with sweat, his smooth muscles veined and sleek as he lifted the hammer and the tongs. It was all a distortion, a figment of a dream, a sleeper's invention, a tale. The bellows breathed into the coals of their own accord, untended. Behind Ruan the sisters waited by the inner door, motionless and silent as stone. Before him the sea door stood wide, opening out to an opalescent sky. There was no evil here, only raw power loosed for eternal purposes. Slackly Ruan awaited to be alloted his part in the magic.

Slan grinned and winked at him as if it was all sport, then rang the hammer on the anvil, raised and struck again, and rang, and smote until the cavern was alive with the bell-like chimes of metal on metal, a lullaby for the Druid and the Mother Hag to push them down deep into the forgotten moments of their youth. The hammer beat, squatting and bending, black iron blurred almost into invisibility as Slan rained blows on the anvil. The forge blazed bright with yellow and vermilion flames. Sweat flew from the smith's brow, his eyes gleamed. Noiseless laughter poured from his throat as the flames leapt higher and sheeted him, drenching him in flurries of sparks.

Pivoting, Slan dragged a white-hot ingot from the forge and pincered it across the anvil's snout. The hammer clanged, changing timbre until it sang low and resonant as a drumskin, giving a pulse to the flowing flames which rose slender but substantial, flawed with scarlet and aureoles of gold. They appeared to gather round an unseen trunk, a vague shape which had risen from the heart of the forge. It stood tall, massing into the image of the Frankish maiden, dark tresses fluttering like smoke, her eyes blemishes of heat, her bright lips parted in a cry of ecstasy as Ruan stretched his arms to gather and draw her to his breast.

The vision warped, changed.

Fire caressed him, painlessly forming the likeness of a woman he had loved once and long forgotten; then his mother's plump and comfortable image flickered and died down, altering even as his memory snatched at it and he cried out heartbreakingly to bring her back.

Gone.

Instead Ruan was confronted by the visage of the Mother Hag, young, beautiful and full of life's yellow fire. Her hair streamed in russet waves, her features as fine and sharp as an eagle's. She beckoned him into the heart of the forge, breasts, arms, torso swimming in livid flame, hovering, a projection of the wasted wraith who stood behind, melted by the power of her fabulous changeling.

Ruan was both dreamer and dream, unable to measure the difference between that which he was and that which he wished to be, shaping the vision of himself from past and future, travelling between the compass points of love and terror which polarized in the fire-figure's eyes. The magnitude of her energy was overwhelming, a mingling of goodness and mischief, of bright, joyous passion and impenetrable darkness.

Impulsively Ruan flung himself against her, joined with her, the touch of her skin light and rough, licking his body like a cat's tongue. When he encircled her with his thighs it was like mounting on the wind, riding the sea tides, coupling with the sun.

How long he joined with the entity he could not calculate, moments, hours, years even spinning past, through exulation into searing pain, and down, cleanly cauterized of lust until he tossed back his head and shouted out and the seed spurted hot from his loins and his flesh was suddenly all devoured.

Shouting still, he clung to the scarlet image and sought to draw himself deeper into the heart of the fire. The fire-figure's eyes were celestial, as remote as the distances beyond the stars, brimful of the nebulous mysteries of realms forgotten or not yet found.

Ruan could hold her no longer.

The bellows' pipe sucked her away, disintegrating the form into random flecks and motes of colour, cooling instantly into charred ash.

Slowly, soberly, the hammer clapped iron, and was still.

In utter desolation, Ruan cried out. The dream had died away, leaving him no man-to-be but man accomplished, resolute, inflexible, and forever alone.

3

The ribbon of ice

Horses and teams of women manned the ropes by which the transport craft of the Smerteans' invasion fleet were dragged north to the head of Rhea. The gale had reduced itself to bluster, squalled with sleet. The mid-morning sun blinked angrily through cloud and made the leaping sea seem red, a bloody omen which, such was the temper of the clan, the royal priest elected to read as a favourable sign. Ten high-prowed boats were packed with the best of the mariners and the cream of the crop of kinsmen, all armed. A multitude of graceless, twelve-oared curraghs, ferries of the kyle, ploughed across the troughs and kept the broadside tide from swamping low, ponderous barges laden with stores and pack animals. Few sails were in sight. The masts were mostly down, for wind and tide romped in accord, and rudderless, unkeeled craft were better disciplined by oars alone. Rhea would give them all the speed they wished, the plume of the ebb directing them from the tail of the mainland shore, outward and across the kyle towards the shingle beach close to the place where Vinadia's assassins had landed.

It would have been better to attack in mist, with muffled oars and muzzled ponies, swords silently leathered. But the climate called for different tactics and Meglan could not wait. If their preparations were marked, it made no matter. Before long the serpent current would have the heavy boats in its grasp and the crafts of the main war-band would be strung out and rushing swiftly to the beach. Hunchbacked crones could not marshal a counterforce on such short order. Even the sprites, if sprites there were, would not operate well at noon in this mobile weather. Besides, the priest had promised conquest. There would be no danger in the landing, except from Rhea herself, and she was wild but not malignant and could be handled by any worthy Smertean.

Relaxed, Meglan drew his buckle tight and swept his sword-sheath to the rear. He stood high in the prow of the leading curragh, shouting out at the women to thrust harder on the weed-slippery shore. Behind him were all the mighty forces of the clan, enshipped and ready to be unleashed. It would have made Vinadia proud; though, now that he thought of it, his father would probably have appointed him as master of the fleet, and stood where Boud stood up on the headland, watching from a safe distance. Boud would have ridden into the attack at his side if Meglan had not forbidden it. It was difficult enough to keep the clan at fever pitch and persuade them to expend their fury on the haunted isle without allowing a woman to share the rulership in war. For the time being his mother had done enough.

The armour hung heavy on his body. As a seaman he was accustomed to wear only light leather plates. The elderly bronze pieces gave him the feeling of being a warrior of true stock. There lay Sketis, bruised by cloud and bloodied by the sun; no longer a repository of fear but the sanctuary of his father's attackers. He would have them all. Aye, even the giant. He would bring them back alive to the Dun and do slow and patient things to them, let Masena amuse herself in the long gloomy evenings, turn them over to the other young queens for diversion. And when they died, he would dismember what was left and prop the parts all about the corners of his broch to attest the thoroughness of Meglan's revenge. But it was not only for that purpose that he ordered the casting of the tow-rope, and commanded the leaward bank of oars to dip. Sketis too was his objective. It would be a fine start to his reign to release his people from that age-old tyranny.

The prow of the curragh swung as the current pulled it south. Proudly Meglan raised his sword and cut the trailing rope which linked him symbolically to the safe homeland. A cheer went up from mariners in adjacent boats, rattling on through the ferries and the barges, until the anthem to his popularity swelled from every male Smertean throat. Only the women on the shore were silent, full of fear still as to what their men would find there on that sullen isle.

High on the hill, her blue cloak billowing, Queen Boud stood erect, showing the gilded scabbard and the belt which Meglan had given her to signify that she was commander of the guardians, those womenfolk, girls and shivery elders who had remained behind.

Meglan, new ruler of the Smertean horde, saluted her with his naked sword. The queen replied in kind. Then with a lurch the banner-ship was caught by wind and tide and rushed with all speed towards the Sketian shore.

Ruan opened one eye. His hip ached. His arm was stiff because of how he lay upon the hard flagstones of the hearth-palace. Small, fresh logs, recently placed on embers, were igniting now, resin seeping from their veins, fragrant smoke wisping up towards the vault. Ruan groaned and turned on to his back. A large cloak and a sleek sealskin blanket covered him. It was not cold which made him miserable but the stiffness in his bones and the ache in his groin and the thick clotted feeling in his skull. It was as if he had supped an unripe tun of mead, or carelessly poured a horn of sloe-wine on top of barley ale. Yet he had done none of these things. He remembered eating fish, and drinking a beaker of mild ale. For the moment, not much else came into his mind. He propped himself on all fours and dragged his body to the hearth, using the wall to haul himself upright. He rubbed his eyes and tried to take stock. Dressed and whole he certainly was. But he did not feel quite the same as he had done last night. Sickness had nothing to do with it. Even as his first nausea began to pass off, the other sensation increased.

Glancing round the chamber he saw that all the band, except Harkfast, slept there, huddled head to head on the far side of the hearth, happed in cloaks and blankets as he had been. Bellerus lay on his back, knees lifted like a camp-pole under the wool, snoring like seven sows at rutting time. Mungan had drawn the wrappings over his head. Only the base-hoof of the harp showed above them, like a concubine's head. Domgall slept snug between the two black dogs, no larger than his mattress-mates and much the same colour. Only Gadarn was awake, though his bleary eyes indicated that he had not long emerged from sleep.

Ruan found a water jar, drank from it, and splashed handfuls across his face.

'Here,' groaned Gadarn. 'Before I die.'

Ruan fed him water from a beaker.

Gadarn groaned again. 'I have drunk more mead as a lad of ten and suffered less for it. Black Annis crawls about my gut, and Nemon besoms my throat. More water, Ruan, for the sake of life itself.'

'Were we together in our revelry?' Ruan kneaded his temples to restore his memory.

'No,' said Gadarn. 'I do not recall seeing a hair of any head at all after I left the forge.' The Roman rolled, complaining, on to his belly and surveyed the palace. 'All here?'

'All save Harkfast,' Ruan answered. 'I too was alone last night. On that I will stake an oath to Cailleach.'

'And I to Juno's paps.'

'I *cannot* remember,' Ruan said, working his forehead with his thumbs now. '*I cannot.*'

'Even Domgall's hounds have been slain by mead, it seems.' Gadarn wallowed under the blanket again. 'How strange it is to have the rind of revelry without the jollity.'

'Strange!' Ruan said. 'Too strange to be natural.'

Stiffening in his mind were many tiny memories, touched like the blood-red sea-flowers in the rock pools of the shore, groping softly to coax knowledge into his brain. His body lamented the indulgences of the night, yet his mind rejected the thought of them. Nothing tangible came to him then. He reeled towards the entrance where the tunnel dropped and led downward to the forge. The blankness of his mind tormented him.

He called out, 'Harkfast!'

The Druid did not respond. Now he thought of it, where was Mother Hag, and Crog, and the Sketian Sea-master, or those four sisters who never strayed far from the hearth? How stood

180

the sun in the world above? He stumbled down the tunnel.

Dream-dealer!

He remembered the sword of Tanglan, a king as young as he, dead long ages since. Grains of recollection drifted through his head like snowflakes. Before he reached the wooden barrier which shut off the forge, inklings of his dream were within his head.

The door creaked open at his first touch.

Ruan entered the forge.

The dream came flooding back, livid as silver, pouring through him. Shaken, he stopped in his tracks and clung to the lintel for support.

The furnace lay stone cold, ashes pale as chalk. The anvil was where it had been in the dream, not quite perfect to the block.

Full knowledge struck him like a blow. He was suddenly aware that he had not dreamed at all, that the mysteries which, for an instant, when eye to eye with that flame-born figure, he had almost grasped, still eluded him.

In a corner of the cavern Harkfast lay wrapped in his grey robe and sucking the tip of his left thumb, like some large babe which had cried itself to sleep. Try as he would Ruan could not rouse the Druid to consciousness. Desperately he shook Harkfast's shoulder, calling to him, commanding him to waken, but the priest was too exhausted to respond.

The Mother Hag touched Ruan's arm. He whirled. She placed a finger across her lips to silence him. She looked today as she had looked yesterday. All her nocturnal youthfulness had seeped away again, leaving wrinkled, leathery age. Ruan was embarrassed. Had he joined with this woman? This ancient? Had he performed an act of love with her? Or was it not her, but some daughter or granddaughter-thing which had been conjured up for the sake of ritual? The dream was fast becoming a nightmare.

'Mother Hag?' he asked, not meeting her eye.

'Do not question,' the woman said, firmly.

'Was it true, or did I stray into the Druid's dream? Tell me that, at least.'

She shook her head. 'The luxury of understanding cannot be

181

yours, Ruan. Even now the Smerteans are mounting an invasion on the eastern shore. Come, we have much to do.'

'But Vinadia is dead. I saw his corpse.'

'His son has defied Smertean tradition,' said the Mother Hag. 'Obviously he seeks revenge.'

'How many in the boats?'

'Four hundred.'

'How many can we muster?' said Ruan.

'Fifty.'

'Then we must hide,' said Ruan.

'It is not in us to hide,' said the Mother Hag. 'We have no excuse for hiding like frightened mice.'

'Then I will pledge my men and—myself.'

'You will leave with all haste,' said Mother Hag. 'It is not your battle, Ruan.'

'Our folly spurred Meglan to attack Sketis,' Ruan cried. 'It is my band that the Smerteans seek. They have no quarrel with you, Mother Hag.'

'Ah, you fail in understanding, young King,' Mother Hag said. 'A whole generation comes against us, new blood springing from old.'

'At least we can stand shoulder to shoulder with your people.'

She gripped him by the throat, her iron thumb pressing against his windpipe. '*Leave. I order it.* There is no point to this battle unless you, your companions, and the smith escape. Your mission, hopeless though it may be, is our mission too. Even now Leaman is preparing a raft. You may carry only such baggage as the raft will bear. The Sea Master will set you right on the drift, so that you will not land where Meglan's lookouts will discover you.'

'I *cannot* flinch from a fight,' Ruan said stubbornly.

'Your fight will be a long one,' said the Mother Hag. 'But it does not begin here.'

'Fifty against four hundred?'

The woman smiled. 'Odds are for star-worshippers,' she said. 'We are creatures of fire and earth. You have done all that we required of you. Now you must go.'

'Harkfast?'

'Harkfast is weary,' said the Mother Hag. 'He will waken soon. Crog will help him to the craft. Fear not, I will not let you leave without your Druid.'

'Mother Hag,' said Ruan, '*did* I dream?'

'You dreamed,' said Mother Hag, kindly. 'And the dream will endure.'

'In you?'

'Quickly, come. The Smerteans will soon be upon us and I must prepare my welcomes.'

She shifted her hold from throat to shoulder and spun him round. In spite of her age, there was much strength in her arm yet.

'My sword,' he called back as she hurried him into the tunnel. 'Where is Dream-dealer?'

'On the raft.'

Ruan hurried back into the hearth-palace to find that the men were up now, roused from drugged stupor, already buckling swords and dirks and making ready to depart. Cooks brought in meat and watered wine and set it round the hearth, though no one paused to eat. There were many strangers about. Girls and men whom Ruan had not seen before, each performed allotted tasks, stacking arms and armour, or dressing themselves in light mail culled from the store below. The preparations stimulated Ruan. Once more he pleaded with Mother Hag to allow him to fight. But she was adamant and had no more precious minutes to waste in argument. Signalling to Slan, she stalked out of the palace, leaving the smith to calm the young King. Ruan was finally obedient to the warrior-woman's command. She had assumed the major share of the enterprise, taken it from him, from Harkfast too, freed him as she had freed Slan.

'The Sea-master is waiting,' Slan said. 'We must go now.'

Ruan looked round; Gadarn, Domgall, Mungan and Bellerus all hung on his word.

'We will go,' he said, 'if that is how the Mother wills it.'

Slan hurried him up into the cold winds of the morning where, on the sward of the tall stones, more Sketians assembled under

183

the sisters' command.

The army was scant in numbers and in strength. It was comprised of maidens, with soft blonde hair chopped short to make them look like boys, and a few boys, garbed like men in leather and link mail all clutching short swords, and several women in the prime of their lives, sallow as the sisters and sharing the eagle-look which his vision of the Mother Hag had shown him. For all the haste with which they were marshalled there was a dreadful air of calmness, of control, almost of serenity to the host. Had they drilled in this manoeuvre, or was it a quality of the sheltered clan to meet battle and outrageous odds with such aplomb?

Along the rim of the basin, outlined against scudding wintry cloud, the chariots came, small, shag-haired horses linked in pairs between the shafts, a maiden in each box-bed holding the reins in her left hand and the frisks in her right. This would be no sly defensive action, no Pictish-style erosion of swift attack and swifter retreat. Clearly the Mother Hag would fight as she had always fought, openly, honestly, horn to horn with her opponent, leading the phalanx.

With all his heart Ruan longed to join her in this hopeless battle. He knew there could be no victory for the Sketians. Come nightfall the Smerteans would engulf the island. Even so, his rash and kingly character made him hunger to be part of this heroic defeat. Only a compunction to fulfil that larger destiny which the Druid and the Mother Hag had framed caused him to obey against his will.

While the Sketians instructed their ranks and set their chariots to stand upon the sloping plain above the track, Ruan and his companions were led along the shore. Laden with his sack of tools, Slan drove quickly from the sward, his big face solemn, almost lachrymose, at such a cowardly parting.

Leaman waited by a short pier fashioned from boulders and lashed timbers. The raft too was made of pine trunks, bound with ropes, the upper tier pinned by long rivets to a flotation base which rode high enough above the waves to prevent swamping. There was no mast. A stout rudder was racked to one side, four single oars axled to iron hoops to provide a steering aid. This clumsy vessel, it seemed, was the limit of the Sketians' seamanship. Leaman was a fisher, not a journeying sailor. Two lads were occupied in lashing loads to the raft. On Ruan's instructions, Bellerus, Domgall and Mungan fell to helping them. The pack horses were not to be seen, nor were Domgall's black dogs. Only Gadarn's corn-gold mare stood tethered nearby, waiting to be led on to the unsteady platform. From the baggage Ruan unearthed his sword and the targe which Domgall had given him. The bearing of the warrior's harness served to emphasize how ill it was for a king to fly before an evil foe. Ruan might even then have gone back to join the sisters, if at that moment Harkfast had not been brought out of the rocks of the harbour's edge.

Hardly able to walk unaided, the Druid leaned heavily on Crog's arm and on the shoulder of the red-haired woman who accompanied them. Under her arm the woman, Cyprinida, mother of Crog's children and wife of Leaman, carried the Druid's bundle.

'Harkfast,' Ruan shouted. 'Why are we fleeing from this fight?'

'It is not . . .' Harkfast's head hung slackly. It cost him effort to mouth the words. '. . . not our battle, fosterling.'

'All battles are our battle.'

'Board the raft,' said Harkfast. 'Here, give me your hand.'

In shallow water the raft's movement was barely perceptible. Experienced in trading, Gadarn would have some knowledge of seamanship. The Roman, however, was at that moment concerned with the welfare of his mare. Ruan studied the wave-race questioningly. Beyond the immediate protection of the harbour the bay was swollen, dark and brisk with foam. The first point round which they must stand was dashed by spray. Ruan felt apprehension at the prospect of the voyage.

'You will be well, young man,' Leaman assured him. 'See, how the water cools on the long stream out from the land. Yonder is the kyle, emptied by Volsas.'

'We cannot broach Volsas in a raft,' said Ruan.

'Nay, you have oars and a rudder for just that purpose,' said

Leaman gently. 'The golden man tells me he knows how to steer, and that the giant too is used to the feel of the sea beneath his feet. Aye, he could stand as a mast for all the height of him.'

'Where does Volsas lie?'

'Put all thought of Volsas from your mind,' said Leaman. 'You must hurry, though, for the minutes of the tide are vital. The kyle current will carry you south round Cold Point and the wind will then direct you into the Broad Sound far below Rhea. Volsas lies northwest. If you drive with the oars and harden the rudder against the horizon, she will not draw you much. You will spin like a cup off the edge of her drainage-trough and catch the shift of the tide and the stiff breeze of evening, which will combine to carry you to land far below the hem of Smertean territory.'

'Have you instructed Gadarn?' asked Ruan. Maritime details confused him. 'He will be our helmsman.'

'I have done so,' said Leaman. 'Take care of Slan.'

Ruan gave Leaman the salute of the sword and cautiously followed Mungan on to the raft.

Already he could feel the urgent gurgle of the sea beneath his heels as if he was perched directly upon the waves. By the rudder shaft, Harkfast sprawled on a roll of blankets. Domgall had wisely fastened a length of line about the Druid's waist and attached it to the high fretting. The mare shied and kicked her hoofs in rebellion. Gadarn calmed her with kindly words, making fast a fork of reign to each of the oar spars as he did so. Slan was last to board. He paused on shore for a moment, not to say farewell to Leaman, but to stare up from the bay at the hill where already the sparse ranks of the Sketian forces were assembled. Ruan also looked, saw Ochran and Machalla, in fine full armour and silly no longer, seated on small stallions and, in the distance, Fidin and Weadla, shining too, in chariots behind their shields. Along the horizon the sky was dark and grave but over the warrior-women an opening of brave blue showed in the lowering cloud.

Leaman waded into the water. With the aid of Crog and the two young boys, he cast off the mooring lines and pushed the raft until the big oars sucked in deeper water and the south-flowing

186

current tugged at the rudder. Gadarn leaned into it. The raft whirled and drew quickly out into the main stream of the loch. The coastline of the island opened, laying out vistas of its ridges and glens to the sailing men. As the raft bucked and swept past the point of the little bay, Slan raised his hand and directed their attention to the most prominent glen.

'There,' he shouted. 'There are the Smerteans.'

Shoulder to shoulder with Bellerus, Ruan shoved the oar-shaft furiously, staring in horror at the train of men who galloped to engage the pitiful company of the Mother Hag in a battle to the death.

'There, Meglan,' the kinsman cried, 'see where the raft goes, flying with the tide.'

Meglan reined and brought the leading riders to a confused and jostling halt. He saw the craft clearly and recognized the mare. Even at this distance, he could make out the men at the tiller and the oars.

'The grey-one, can you spy him?'

'By the rudder, sir,' the kinsman told him. 'He is lying low.'

'I have him,' said Meglan. 'He cannot escape us so easily.'

He gripped the bridle of the kinsman's horse and drew the man as close as the shoulders of the animals would allow.

'Ride hard to Rhea,' Meglan shouted at him. 'Take a fresh mount from the middle quartering, or any other that you can find, and ride like a thundercloud to the guard vessels. With luck, they will not have pulled far from the landing sites.'

The kinsman nodded. 'I am to instruct the ships to sail down channel?'

'Far down to the thumb of Cold Point,' said Meglan. 'That raft will emerge . . .' He studied the sky and the direction of the wind. '. . . shortly before dusk. We have an edge on them. I want them taken—alive if possible.'

'How many ships, Meglan?'

'As many as are left. Draw a complement of mariners from the rear-guard unit to supplement the crews. We will surely catch the cowards.' He slapped the horse's rump. '*Now, ride.*'

The kinsman was gone, mounting the track-side to avoid the clusters of horsed warriors.

Behind the vanguard, spread out along the glen floor, came foot-soldiers, kerns and pack-beasts, a long lean file stretching almost as far as the eye could see. Meglan had driven them hard, forcing them to march at the double. He did not want to camp without a conquest to stimulate the army's appetite. Drifting on the wind he could hear the songs of the mariners' unit, still strong in spite of the miles they had trudged since noon. Only four quarters of daylight remained. Still he had seen no signs of Sketians. Perhaps they *were* spirits who could vanish into the earth. On the other hand, they might be consolidating for a night attack. He did not relish that prospect. He would build a camp so tight and strong that a serpent could not infiltrate the watch undetected. Horsemen milled round him. He was uncomfortable in the saddle. He would have preferred to lead his sea-hounds in pursuit of the raft. It could not be, however. He was the chieftain now and a chieftain's place was at the head of his army. He studied the raft, noted its rate of travel down the inner arm of the sea-loch, and how smoothly it rode the waves. Within a minute it was out of sight.

Before him the track wandered on. It could not be far now to some form of habitation. Even a steading or a wattle-hut would give him something to destroy. It had not occurred to him that he might find nothing upon which to unleash his forces, that the crones who dwelled on the isle might seek refuge in the cloudy mountains or on the bogs. It would be like struggling with that fearsome magical wind which had destroyed Vinadia's weems again. Dread and frustration took hold of him. He tried to draw strength from the sight of his forces but their colours were not courageous and coppery cloud made everything sombre. The impetus of his mother's encouragement waned suddenly. He realized how desperate and ridiculous his plight might be if mists and sleet caught him thus dispersed, prey to every slimy evil which the black hills disgorged. This accursed and obvious track seemed to straggle on forever. For all his gloom he had a premonition that he was drawing close to *some* form of habitation. The raft was a clue. It had not sprung out of the loch by magic—not even Druid spells were that potent.

Meglan steeled himself to push on. Drawing forward of the warriors again, a horse-length ahead of them, he sat upright in the saddle, none of his uncertainty on show. Sea-winds buffeted him, blowing from the north, bringing the brine smell, libation to all mariners: bringing too—he sniffed—a faint reek of burning, and another muted odour which reminded him partly of a pig-wallow and partly of the stench of the House of Queens. He checked, then rode on towards the place where the track backed from the cliff-top and scrawled its yellowish line over the shoulder of the headland. Beyond it the sky was very dark and streaked with stains like chalk.

Meglan heeled the belly of his horse, trotting on towards the drop.

They came in line of four with no warning clank of metal or drumming of hoofs. One moment the land was empty, the horizon bleak. Next it was shadowed by the chariots, as if they had surged up from a crack in the earth's crust. Divots flung from the wheels, and the power of their steeds was supernatural. Small, swart, shaggy, bull-haunched horses yoked between shafts that curved like stags' horns, they rose and leapt from the rim of nothingness, seemed to soar like hawks, free in the sour air, until the horses discovered step and pawed down in unison and swept the chariots to the ground again.

In each chariot was a woman.

Though he had travelled far through the world, Meglan had never seen such manifestations of the ferocity of womankind before. The accumulated cruelty of Masena, the authority of Boud, the peevish spite of the several whores he had hauled from slave ships between Ocrinum and Gaul could not match the barbarous aspect of the charioteers. They were not of bestial mien, but *women*—women fairly blown by battle-lust, taller than giants, more magnificent that sea-eagles, swelled up by the justice of their cause. Clouded in thunder, they came at the Smertean horsemen full abreast, yard upon yard devoured and gone before

Meglan could control his fear enough to grope for his sword and shout an incoherent command.

The mounted kinsmen wheeled and enmeshed, startled horses rearing under jerked bits. Meglan saw how it was and what the strategy had been and how he must match that mad courage with his own. No nibblings, no wolfish skirmishing, no pitfalls or nocturnal knives, this was battle waged by bold warriors from the front. And he had buckled under it like a flawed shield!

The sword was in his fist. Slavers of rage spat from his mouth as he crouched low over the mane and drove full at them. He thought of himself now not as a man but as a high-prowed ship filled with the fury of the sea, dashing on into the eye of the storm. He lifted the sword as the noise came on him, deafeningly abrupt, the whole discharge of chariots and the cold bellowing of the women-things. He lifted the sword to strike. But there was no impediment to the edge. The chariots had split, two to each flank, rolling and pounding down the sides of the track, so that Meglan and those kinsmen who had followed him were trapped. He tried to turn the horse's head, but its fetlocks were sawn by the dirks of maidens who sprang out of the grass like hares. The animal crashed and skidded forward. He had barely enough wit to fall clear before it plunged out and over the cliff, screaming in pain.

The maidens were armed like warriors, leathered and mailed like men. Though young, they had a sinewy strength and all the control of veterans. Dazed, Meglan staggered to his feet. His helmet hung from his ear, strap knotted in his hair. He tried to adjust it, to calm his whirling vision, to grasp the sword in his fingers tightly enough to defend himself until the kinsmen could beat back the foe and rescue their chieftain. His teeth had bitten through his cheek. It bled copiously. Spitting out the blood which filled his mouth, he propped the sword, hoisted himself upright and swung round and round flailing aimlessly in all directions. The ranks of the vanguard were in confusion, riding out from the circle which a few, more sensible than the rest, had tried to form. He could not see beyond the mass of horses to learn how the kerns had coped. The girls were strung out along the hillside, above and below the track. Using the slope to advantage, they darted among the horsemen, crippling mounts and unseating riders. The chariots had vanished, though the grinding of their wheels was still audible above the din of slaughter. On the crest of the depression out of which the chariots had roared, a dozen boys spread out sparsely across the grass. Some lugged swords large enough to tax the strength of a full-fledged warrior, others carried only dirks. Quietly awaiting word of command, they did not approach the group-fighting.

Vainly Meglan cast round to make a target of their leader, found nobody in charge of the striplings. He spat out more blood. His dizziness had gone, and much of his terror. The worst had happened: he had been engulfed in a trap and separated from his main force. His prime objective now must be to win through to the unmarked units in the middle of the glen. He broke left, and headed uphill away from the forefront of the battle. He climbed unchallenged, high enough to bring into focus the cleverness of Sketian strategy. The whole of his army, it seemed, had been plunged into panic by the appearance of the charioteers and their female train. All along the glen floor Smerteans milled in utter confusion. The meagreness of the Sketian raiding party added to the humiliation. Four warrior-women led the charge, covering a beat of a mile or less, flanking the track-bound column. When the kerns fanned out to engage in combat, the lurking girls easily picked them off. The maidens seemed to be invisible, to spring from nowhere, vanishing again as soon as their kill was complete. Three or four had been smitten by the kerns' blades. The remainder continued to skip in and out of striking range with the wary alacrity of crows feeding on a corpse. All round the track lay dead and wounded kerns. The leading ranks had rammed back into the following groups, struggling against them, some retreating, some endeavouring to group into a defensive wall, a movement in which they had little training and no experience. Bravery and cowardice, intelligence and crass stupidity, all served to increase the chaos.

Veering east along the shoulder of the ridge, Meglan peered down the length of the glen. He saw that where the packmen and

191

drays lagged there was also disarray. Too distant to make out clearly, it appeared that the nether end of the column had come under a similar attack, a few fast chariots clearing out for skirmishing forces. Four overturned drays blocked the avenue of retreat. Spread out, the rearguard patrol was easy prey for Sketian marauders. Only at centre did the invasion column retain a semblance of military order. Here some kerns had managed to regroup round the mariners' unit. Seven or eight score of the best fighting men were pinned down in the middle reaches of the glen. Though unmolested as yet, they were stricken into inactivity by the confusion of their brethren. Meglan supposed that they were packed together in anticipation of the onslaught of the bulk counterforce. A strong, well-disciplined band of adult soldiers could murder them now like wolves in a sheep-weems.

Behind him, at the loop of the track, the Sketian boys trooped slowly forward. Working in threes, they killed all crippled animals and wounded kinsmen in the wake of the maidens' advance. Showing no enthusiasm for their task, the youngsters dispatched their victims cleanly, slitting throats or stabbing big-bladed swords into Smertean hearts. They collected no trophies of flesh or metal but evinced a ruthless efficiency which even Vinadia would have found more cruel than a welter of blood-lust and wild slaughter. Meglan almost tumbled to his knees to call upon his father's spirit to aid him, to drop curses on his mother's head for having promulgated this mad action. Instead he fixed his aim upon the mariners and steered a careful curve down the hillside to join up with them. He did not get far.

Without warning, a girl-child leapt from the grass and flung herself against his thigh. Chattering with fright, Meglan slashed his sword at her. But she hugged close against him and he could not shape an energetic blow. Her fingers groped, grabbed at his testicles, and a dirk drove deep into the hard flesh of his buttocks. Desperately, Meglan battered off the girl's helmet with the pommel, and flayed her skull with the hilt. Struck, she sagged away from him, her fist still clamped round his private parts, drawing an agonized scream from him. He raised his sword to sheer off her arm but the blow was throttled in mid-air. Behind him a second girl caught his sword-wrist and bent it back like a bough. Pain racked him. He dropped the sword and collapsed, dragging the maidens on top of him. Thrashing frantically at their sinuous arms and legs, he waited for a dirk to finish him—then heard the *thunk* of a blade in flesh and felt blood squirt hot over his throat and chest.

The kinsman, a cousin of Masena's, made short work of the Sketian girls, killing them with four swift strokes. Their bodies twitched on Meglan, coating him with thick, sticky trails of blood. For a moment he could not stir. He lay limp under chains of agony. Only when the kinsman tossed aside the maidens' corpses did the chieftain rise shakily to his feet. He felt as if he had been ripped asunder. Blood seeped from the puncture wound in his buttock. His leg was already stiffening like wood.

'Help me,' he moaned.

The kinsman supported him, and quickly placed a sword in his right hand. Meglan would have preferred to remain unburdened by the weapon, but knew that a chieftain's function was to lead, no matter how foul his wounds or how rapidly the life-blood pumped out of him. Gripping the hilt against his chest, he bit down on the pommel to check his sobs.

'I will escort you, sir.' The kinsman seemed eager to make him a hero. 'I will guide you safe to the mariners, who await you anxiously.'

'The—the Sketian army,' mumbled Meglan. 'Has it attacked yet?'

'I have seen no signs of a *real* army, sir,' kinsman replied. 'Only those accursed virgins.'

Meglan glanced at the children who sprawled at his feet, their long, slender legs entwined, cropped hair capped with blood. He kicked out at them viciously, then jumped with the stabbing pain in his buttock. Groaning and gasping, he propped himself on the kinsman's shoulder once more. 'Can . . . we . . . can we possibly fight our way through?'

'Ay, sir, if you can hobble.' The fool glowed with nobility and courage. 'I will chop a path for us.'

Meglan nodded. He crabbed after the cousin, who navigated a

prudent route well wide of the chariots, the maiden-herd and the remnants of the Smertean vanguard, and brought his chieftain down unchallenged to lead his mariners in a counter attack.

It seemed the battle was not over. It had only just begun.

Leaman lay across the wheel of a toppled dray. Body slanted, a spear stuck upright from his breast so that the first fine breath of snow rimed the shaft and gave it shape against the dark earth. Cyprinida's younger son was huddled like a pup at the Sea-master's feet, ribs and spine welted with blood where fleeing Smerteans had vented their despair on him in lieu of a living warrior. Four other Sketian youths and two grown maids were bundled dead with the venison and hog-meat, sheaves of dried hake and crumbled corncake which the dray had borne. A score or more of dead and dying storemen were strewn around, and seven of the armoured guardians whose insufficient skills had laid the butt of Meglan's column open to attack. Gusts of snow delayed twilight, brought a final whiteness to the cloud, enough to show Crog the melancholy details of the scene.

Drawing back, the runner hurried to the spot where he had left Cyprinida and his elder son crouched over a sulphur pot and a tub of seal blubber. Nodules of blue and yellow fire glowed in the pot which the lad had carefully nurtured throughout the late hours of the afternoon. They could see the four-wheeled chariot no longer. The slope was too steep and rock-pitted and they were too close to the targets. Crog knelt and put his cloak over Cyprinida and the boy, enclosing the sharp stink of the sulphur and a little of its warmth within the makeshift tent. He did not have to tell the pair that Leaman and the brother were dead. He nodded sorrowfully, biting his lip. They consoled him, and each other, with a touching of hands.

'There is freak light,' Crog murmured. 'We must make best use of it.'

'How many craft are there, father?' the boy asked.

'Four sails left early, and some of the smaller curraghs may have gone since,' said Crog. 'But there will be enough left for you to draw upon without possibility of missing.'

'Crog,' the woman said. 'How did they die?'

'Quickly and bravely,' Crog said. 'Some of the store guardians have gone on to join the main column, others have retreated to the lading shore, where we will find them out.'

'Will it be dangerous?' the woman asked.

'Ay,' Crog admitted. 'It will be no easy matter to evade their spears. On the other hand, we are few and free and they are many and enclosed. That will be greatly to our advantage.'

'Father, the sulphur will not burn forever,' the boy reminded him. 'Besides, it will soon be too dark to sight properly.'

'You are right, son,' said Crog. 'We will go at once.'

Rising he took his wife's hand and she in turn took the hand of her son. The arrow sacks were snugly laced and would not rattle, and the boy slung the pots on separate thongs so that they would not accidentally knock together and ignite. Though the pot-lid was tied down to a knob on the clay, the health of the flame gave the boy concern.

Snow blasted from west and northwest, shifting its axis constantly, so that the flakes weaved a net around them, and faintly defined the hummock of the hill above the bay. The boy and the woman moved across the land as silently as Crog himself and he was as quiet as a single snowflake falling on soft lag. There was no need to keep the wind ahead of them. It would sweep out over the sheltered sands and carry any hint of their coming far across the rushing waters of the kyle.

Crog had barely glimpsed the four fat sails spinning down out of Rhea into the Broad Sound but his intelligence told him why they had left with such alacrity, using wind and tide to speed them to the mouth of Cold Point. He prayed that Leaman had given the strangers an alternative plan to keep their raft from capture or from the harm of the hungry waters. He could do nothing now; that matter was out of his hands. His mission, given him by the Mother Hag, was simple of itself but difficult to accomplish. Waving down his son and Cyprinida, he crawled the last few feet to the base of the ruined watchtower and took his scout from behind its stones.

195

Rhea's waters were very dark, accentuated by a pale drift of snow building up on the hills of the mainland. The sky there was black and only the ground held light, barely sufficient for Crog to count the heads packed into the cove below. Two high-prows were moored long, standing out from the sand, probably anchored to snout into the current as the tide fed back. Curraghs and tiny coracles were beached on the sand like jellies and sprats. The multitude of men who crammed the cove created a great babble with their arguments. No doubt they were engaged in hot debate as to their fealty, staunch loyalists and quarrelling cowards going at each other with careless vehemence. Apparently, no Smertean had had enough wit to set a hill watch.

Cheered, Crog returned to the woman and boy and guided them stealthily up to the root of the tower. The base-circle, though only knee-high now, would give the lad shelter for his sulphur pot. The boy had hardly come to rest before he cowered over his materials, working with the arrows, straw-babes and linen strips. His dexterity was a credit to his teacher, Weadla. Crog and Cyprinida had no need to assist.

'Can you see the masts of the two big curraghs?' Crog whispered.

The boy glanced up.

'Ay.'

'Aim left of each mast, at the shadowy patch. Do you see it?'

'Ay, father.'

'That is the unprotected part where the sails are stored. The wood will not catch, but the sheets will. Two arrows into the heart of each shadow will spread the flame effectively.'

'I know that,' said the boy. His nervousness made him disrespectful. Crog could forgive the error at this hour. 'Weadla has drawn many sand pictures for us. I must hit the far craft very accurately, that will give the shore-men something to divert their attention from the flight of the arrows. Next, I must put a rain of steel-tips into their midst to scatter them to cover, then I must put as many blubber-guts as I can manage into each of the smaller boats.'

Crog slid his hand behind his son's ear and tweaked the lobe delightedly. 'I appoint you commander.'

Cyprinida said, 'Give me the short-bow and the steel-tips and I will baffle them.'

'That is sound strategy,' said Crog, who had had it in mind all along. 'I will go yonder to the lower point and spike a few Smertean fish on my own account.'

The boy had finished his work. He laid the fire-arrows out upon the ground, all wrapped and blubber-daubed, ready to be dipped into the sulphur pot. He slipped the yew bow from its shroud, strung it, tested the tautness of the thong and ran his finger and thumb down it to check for flaws. A snapped thong on such an occasion could burn a man's hand beyond repair, and cost him the whole exercise. Weadla had emphasized that lesson with the aid of a horse frisk. He would never forget it.

'I am ready, father. May I begin?'

'Is all ready?' said Crog.

'It is.'

'And the shifting winds?'

'I will allow for them as best I can.'

Crog kissed him on the brow, and Cyprinida too. Carrying the least tractable of the short bows and an elbowful of old bone-tipped arrows, he slithered off to take his stance as close as he dared to the Smerteans. The boy was proficient and could work on his own, though the squall made luck an unwelcome factor. Crog knew how his son would blow upon the sulphur scum, lightly disturb it with an iron pin, then dip in the arrows until the fat caught and spluttered. Then he would hold it up to catch the draught and burgeon into an unquenchable little torch, notch it to the bow and fire. From where he lay on the scree, Crog watched the beauty of the fire-blob's arch. How perfectly it climbed and caught the wind just as its impetus died. How neatly the blast turned it into a long descending curve that ended where the shadow of the sail-hatch cut across the deck. Such perfection, such expertise, brought joy to Crog. He laughed in sheer delight at the skill of his elder son, and cried too in remembrance of the loss of the younger. He took up his own bow, laced it and streamed arrows down into the crowd, until the last was gone.

Above him the blubber-guts wheeled like the discarded stars the gods once lobbed through the skies for sport. The arrows jetted down and stabbed clean on their targets, set the high-prows burning, the curraghs and the coracles, engendering flames to illuminate the beach and give the woman solid aim. Crog could hear the snarl of curragh hides and sappy sounds of the wood of the far-travellers' upper structures as they caught and flared. He could hear the yelps and bellows of the Smerteans as his flock of old arrows struck randomly into their midst, shouts and pig-like squeals as steel-tips shot from Cyprinida's bow nailed the scurriers square, spearing life from them like tiny lightning bolts.

For once amiable coolness deserted Crog and his habits dropped like hair from the head of an elder. He pranced up and down on the scree, lifted rocks and hurled them carelessly on to the skulls below, shrieking in rage and grief. He scooped up slag and snow and scattered it together with wounding missiles, on and on, until the first javelin, hurtling past his shins, restored his reason. Then he ran with all fleetness for the tower-root, found the boy, found the woman, took them by the hands and ran again, cold wind filling his cloak, and ran and ran away from the red stain in the sky, away from the beauty, the glory and the madness, saving himself and his family to fight again in tomorrow's dawn.

Spray-drenched and chilled, Ruan hauled upon the oar. Resistance was greater now, the raft's progress sluggish.

'Gadarn, why are we losing speed?'

'The tide is backing,' the Roman answered.

'But tides are never early.'

'I fear the Sea-master miscalculated,' Gadarn said. 'Maybe he estimated distances on the fleetness of a curragh. A raft is more ponderous. Whatever the reason, we have not rounded Cold Point when we should have done.'

'Rouse Harkfast,' said Ruan.

'I dare not leave this lively rudder.'

Ruan slapped the giant's ribs, indicating that he should

shoulder the full weight of the raft. Bellerus nodded and tucked the oar between elbows and chest. The tide was against them. The shaft flexed as the giant exerted his strength to bury it in the sea. The raft heaved under Ruan's feet. White water lashed back from the stalks, causing the mare to shy and struggle repeatedly against her bindings. Mungan and Domgall shipped the seaward oars. Slan and Bellerus pulled and Gadarn planted a rudder-line which would hopefully still carry them round Cold Point and drift them across the Broad Kyle to the mainland.

Tied to the rudder-stave, Harkfast had hardly changed position since boarding, though he was soaked by the fans of brine that pumped up through the spars. Kneeling, Ruan took the Druid's face in his hands and shook it vigorously. Under drooping lids Harkfast's pupils were like dull slivers of copper.

'Harkfast, you must waken.'

The Druid grunted.

'I order you to waken,' Ruan said.

'Have we reached—?'

'We have missed the proper tide, Harkfast.' Ruan held himself close to the old man. 'The Sketian mistook our rate of speed. Now you must do something, conjure up a wind or a following sea—something.'

The Druid opened his eyes but they were blank and virtually sightless. 'I have no power left in me. I am drained. Besides, I am no acolyte of Manannan.'

'Leave him,' said Gadarn. 'We will round the point shortly, and perhaps find a favourable stream, as the Sketian promised.'

Ruan hesitated, then, supported by the post, pushed himself to his feet. The tip of Sketis was dark now. Behind it the Broad Kyle waited, protected by a band of foaming water which girded the main branch all the way down from Rhea. The ropes sang a stiff formal song. The wind had unfurled a ribband of saffron light and painted on it the frieze of a blizzard sweeping across from the west.

'Will we have snow here too, Slan?'

'The tail might catch us before dusk,' the smith replied.

Ruan had just released the rudder-post when Domgall's shout

199

made him glance ahead. He staggered, reeled past the mare's flanks and fell against the rear oar, immune to the bruising it inflicted. Cold Point was close on his left. Nosing from behind it was a solid, oak-prowed war-boat painted in Smertean colours.

'Back us off, Gadarn.'

'This is a raft, not a coracle,' the Roman retorted.

Twelve pairs of oars and a cocked sail on her mast indicated the war-boat's potential. With sea-anchors spread, she hovered almost motionless in the merging currents. Obviously Meglan *had* been astute enough to set a watch for them. Ruan had no opportunity to study the vessel. Rushing at the rocky headland, combers caught the raft in a fierce grip. Instructed by Gadarn, the four rowers worked frantically to steer on to an open course again. Due to the confluence of tides, their speed had increased once more.

'How can we evade them?' Ruan shouted. 'What would a Gaulish trader do?'

Gadarn was too occupied with the recalcitrant rudder to think clearly.

'Run,' he shouted.

A second war-boat, sister to the first, crept into sight, further out from the mainland. Behind it, the bow of a third was visible. At this hour of dusk the green-hued hulls were clear upon the black waters, waves brittle white like bone-shards under the bows. The raft was almost off the Point, the leading war-boat adjacent to them. Ruan was no mariner. He could not devise an evasive ruse, or plot an attack upon three fully-manned war-boats. Smertean warriors craned over the waists, wagging spears and blades in gleeful anticipation of a capture. In the wide kyle the sleek craft would soon hound down the raft. A fourth hull hung at the back of the pack—four ships, all crewed by expert seamen.

'They will try to block us,' Gadarn said. 'Drop stones on us, sweep us into the sea with their long oars, then fish us out like kelp.'

'Or leave us to drown,' said Mungan.

'Meglan will want us alive,' Domgall said.

200

'I *must* rouse Harkfast now,' said Ruan.

'Nay, it is our fight,' said Gadarn. 'We can ask no more of the old man. Listen, the short-seas' traders do have one tactic which might be effective here.'

'We must try,' said Ruan. 'We cannot meekly surrender.'

'Though unkeeled, the war-boats are heavy-laden and carry a great draught of water under them, much more than we do. If I swivel the raft close to the rocks, then I might avoid contact with the ships and gain the inner passage of the kyle.'

'It will soon be night. Can you navigate in darkness?' Slan asked.

'Not well,' said Gadarn. 'No more can the Smerteans, however, even if they are familiar with the waters. They *may* hoist lights.'

'Which would expose their positions,' said Ruan.

'Once inside the Broad Kyle, we might use the first shift of the next tide to pull us through them in the darkness.'

'It will be very dangerous,' Slan warned.

'There is no other choice,' said Ruan. 'Do it if you can.'

Hugging the rudder, Gadarn bellowed instructions to the rowers. Inclining the raft landward he steadied her in the troughs of the waves just off the rocks. Shelves and steep reefs groped out to claim them. The eddies of the point brought slackness and swift rushes of motion and loss of all control. Then the backing of the sea received them and swung them out and round the tip of the promontory, and the whole straight of the Broad Kyle was revealed.

Ruan was relieved to note that the four war-boats were not the vanguard of a larger fleet.

Releasing anchors, the oars of the nearest vessel clapped into the sea, squaring bows against the squall. Mariners were rife upon its upper structures. But the manoeuvre was too tardy. The raft danced out of range along the coast of the Broad Kyle on the Sketis side.

Night was not far distant now. The ships were already fading against the monotonous hills. Daring had paid its tithes, it seemed. Ruan whooped in triumph at the success of the ruse.

This contest of nautical skills was almost as stimulating as warfare. Though the raft was picking up speed, carrying north towards Smertean territory, Ruan was unperturbed. Jubilantly he shook his fist at the sailors. Domgall and Mungan chanted obscene choruses. Resistance on the oars was once more light. The raft skimmed under the brows of Sketis.

The two leading war-boats came round in unison. The third and fourth were deeper in the current and wallowed clumsily, oarsmen sweating, commanders bawling. Once the war-boats were hard round and running true, however, Ruan's jubilation quickly dwindled. He recognized that their speed was greater, that their bulk gave them stability, and that by exercising skill and experience, the pirates might check and hold abreast of them, even force them onto the rocks. Now it was clear that they had not escaped at all, merely altered the inevitable order of events. Sooner or later a reef or shoal would drive them out into the kyle and carry them within range of Smertean javelins. Night might protect them. But darkness was too hazardous for a craft so close to an unknown, rugged shore. Ruan hung, panting, on the oar-shaft, then dipped the blade. It did not strike full, skating and skidding as if the sea rejected its intrusion. The pace of the raft had increased. The flat ponderous frame was no longer restrained, as if it had found malignant life of its own, wilful and self-destructive.

'Gadarn?' Ruan asked. 'What is happening?'

'Volsas.'

'But Volsas is not by Sketis,' said Ruan. 'It lies on the mainland coast.'

'True, it hides like a monster under the sheers of the bay on the mainland shore,' Slan said. 'But its attraction summons everything which ventures past. It drains the whole of the kyle.'

'The war-boats passed it.'

'They are large,' said Gadarn. 'And wisely chose the flood-tide to make their run. It was for that reason Leaman advised us to pull wide of the point.'

That too, Ruan realized, was why the Smerteans had shown patience. They were well aware what would happen when the

202

raft approached the whip of the maelstrom, where its submarine tentacles extended far, far out across the kyle. They were trapped now not by high-prows but by the ravenous watery creature which lurked in the bay.

Rocked by coils of foam and the curl of waves, the raft was extracted from the coast's shelter and hurled across open water. The Smertean craft crept down on them with restraint, drag-anchors reined against the persuasion of the current. The raft had no anchors, no chains, nothing with which to check its flight across the channel.

The mainland shore loomed closer. Ruan could discern the ribbed fringe of the whirlpool in the arms of the crescent cove, and hear its thunder, a roaring like the hunger-cry of a caged beast. In the aeons of its existence Volsas had swallowed more curraghs than had ever forged through Rhea's narrows. It had drowned more sailors than the three clans of the Smerteans could muster in a moon. Night did not hide it. Frothy ghost-light brimmed from it, and defined its surfaces, rough as bark, then glass-smooth and hideously polished close to its empty heart.

The wind brought the jeers of the mariners to Ruan's ears. It galled him that Smerteans should spectate at such an ignoble death. Dirks, spears, swords would avail him nothing against the water-cone. Reluctant to allow their victims an opportunity of escape from Volsas' clutches, the Smerteans followed as closely as they dared, discharging a volley of javelins to accompany the raft to its grave on the sea-bed. If only there had been less light, Ruan might have drowned in peace. But evil Smertean faces were visible in the twilight, watching eagerly as the raft's oars broke and the rudder cast its ropes and the iron hoops buckled under the enormous pressures of the sea.

The raft was spinning so violently that Ruan was forced to his knees, grabbing Gadarn's ankles with one hand and the stump of the rudder post with the other. Lolling in the traces, the mare was on her side, screaming in terror while the cant of the raft washed solid white water over her crupper. Around them the sea was no longer scarred by interacting currents. The sole source of power was Volsas.

Abandoning the snapped oars, Domgall and Mungan climbed painfully up the slope of the deck and held fast to the crook of Slan's knees. Only Bellerus seemed to have no fear. He clung to the security of the oar-hook as the raft breasted the casts of the outer ring. Here a swollen crest of water held a mass of debris. Within the dross-gutter, the substance of the water changed again, its cadences altering to a fearsome hiss, a sustained sigh magnified a thousandfold. Ruan stared down into the hub of the vortex where the sea lost contact with itself and droned into a column of air, a thick, groaning throat which, for all Ruan knew, bored straight through the sea into the earth beneath.

Harkfast stirred. It meant nothing. No Druid could wield power over such power as this. Only Manannan himself might plug the monster's mouth. No man there could pray to that alien god with hope of being heard. They were all devotees of the verdant, glowing gods of fields and forests, disciples of sun and moon, the rulers of the firmament, not of the waters of the earth. The sea-god had no reason to pity them. But Harkfast struggled, crouched, sprawled head-foremost down the steepness of the raft and might have been torn away but for Ruan's fist knotted into his robe.

The Druid's wallet was tied to other cargoes. The mare had rolled on it, hoofs gouging chunks from the bark, veined belly heaving. Harkfast's fingers teased at the fastenings, jerked the wallet loose. The mare kicked out, hoof narrowly missing the old man's skull. The slope steepened. Dragging on the robe, Ruan brought Harkfast higher, until the old man sprawled again upon his back. He seemed to be pressed against the logs by a huge weight. His arm flopped. His hand trailed close to the water.

In his fist was the bloodstone wand.

The red stone which topped the rod brushed the water-wall, skimming spray from it like sparks, stringing out a wriggling ribbon of silver.

The raft completed another circle. Harkfast uttered no incantations, fashioned no signs. Only the wrist which supported the wand had strength to it. Dipping the wand deeper into the hard liquid, he linked the groove's beginning to its end. Threads

204

merged, broadened, trailed deep wavering loops far down into the gullet of the pool.

Suddenly the spray, no longer water, grouped, gathered, and changed colour, tinting the whole cone with silvery iridescence and steely hardness. The howl of the vortex quietened. The dizzying speed of the raft's descent eased. More loops and ribbons flung from the apex of the staff, fluttering and expanding into dense sheets which rapidly coated the maelstrom's inner core.

Ice.

Ruan shouted: '*Ice*!'

Soon the raft came winding to a gradual halt. Surrounded by ice, it dug at an acute angle into the hard, green wall. No one spoke. Even the stricken corn-gold mare was silent, ears pricked, listening to the blizzard which, in the absence of Volsas' tumultuous roar, seemed as gentle as a summer breeze.

From across the kyle the noises of the Smertean ships drifted, sharp in the icy stillness, the crush of scum against the hulls, the bewildered shouts of the mariners.

'Ruan, what do they—cry?' Harkfast whispered.

'That they must pursue us,' Ruan said. 'They argue.'

In a voice less feeble than before, the Druid said, 'Pull me to shore with the baggage.'

'Will the ice bear our weight, Druid?'

'Ay, but not for long.'

One slip would project them down into the tunnel, into the jade-green pit, plummet them down to fathomless depths. With the utmost care Ruan and his companions abandoned the raft.

Clawing up the rudder bar and over the ice, all limbs spread, like a water-skipper on mud, Ruan led. Tied round his waist was a length of plaited rope. On the plain of the sea the ice was roughened by pustules of froth and brittle craters. It remained as hard as oak, however, all fifty roods to the shore. Seated on level ice, Ruan pulled in the necessary bundles one by one. The mare gave much trouble. Gadarn and Slan crawled at her sides, steadying her, cajoling her, keeping the bit tight against her soft mouth. Bellerus joined Ruan on the hauling-line to assist in restraining the animal when it scraped for purchase and endeavoured to lift itself upright. At length it was clear of the rim, and calmer, and Gadarn led it cautiously shorewards. Next came Harkfast, slack and burdensome as a motley of fleeces. He lay by Ruan's side while the young man brought up Mungan and his harp and, lastly, Domgall. During the activity, Ruan had no time to spare for the Smerteans. He was filled with an urgency which did not mate well with the need for delicacy and care. Only when Domgall crept past and started for the land, did Ruan give attention to their pursuers.

The mariners had nosed the high-prows deep into the brash-ice which padded the area of the bay and thinned out like a blubber smear well into the channel. The four craft were ranked round now, forty roods away. He could audibly identify the quarrelsome commanders, goading their men to disembark and carry the chase across the ice-floe.

Ruan loitered, listening. Intuition told him that the seamen would ignore their better judgement. It was all a portion of the design which Harkfast had released. The magic of a Druid's staff was nothing if not total. With much grumbling, mariners and warriors dropped over the warboats' waists. After all, they were Meglan's men and boasted that they feared nothing on earth or on the sea. Perhaps, having forsaken all belief in the properties of religion, they could not acknowledge the potent magic which had stilled the maelstrom, and put it down to a freak of the season. Cursing quietly, swords clinking, they clambered from the ships and formed the double crescent which was their customary mode of attack.

Domgall was safe on shore but Ruan lingered on the ice fascinated by the unimaginative behaviour of the mariners. They were treading now where previously they would not have dared to steer a ship, approaching Volsas' gullet as if it held no more terrors than a rabbit burrow. If ignorance supplanted courage, eventually all the magical elements in life would rot and decay. Perhaps *that* would be the dark age of Mungan's prophecies.

The Smertean formation was twenty roods away, stepping over the debris-mound where roots and branches protruded from the ice. In the crude tongue of a northern sept, one voluble seaman demanded to know where the sons of wart-pigs were hiding so he could hack off their dangling parts with his dirk. Ruan rose and ran for shore. The sailors spotted him at once, and followed like a swarm of wasps, buzzing with anger. All latent sense of wonder in them was instantly throttled by the sight of human prey.

Ruan did not look back. He headed straight for the mare which was grazing on sparse grass above the shingle of the cove. The Druid was propped against a boulder close to the edge of the ice.

By now the Smerteans would have circumvented the cone. They would have assembled into columns and would be jog-trotting after him, convinced of their indefatigable skill as hunters. Ruan ran faster, fell, slithered a yard or two on his rump, scrambled up and ran on. He was ten yards from the shingle when the Druid staggered out towards him. Harkfast walked like an uprooted tree, frosty garments brushing the ice, stiff in all his limbs. In his hand he held the rod.

Ruan slithered to a halt.

'Harkfast, the Smerteans . . .'

Harkfast caught at Ruan's shoulder for support, stooped and swung his arm. He released the wand. Propelled by the weight of metal and its stone capping, the staff whirred away across the ice. Spinning, then straightening, it vanished over the lip of the crater.

Ruan heard its fall—or thought he did—a whistle from the depths, diminishing into soundlessness, a pause of such intensity that he found it almost unendurable and clapped his hands over his ears to end it. At the throwing of the rod, the puzzled Smerteans halted, then they came on again, somewhat confused and out of rhythm, passing the outer rondure. A few struck up a battle cry, to stimulate the hatred which was the coin-mark of their rank. But the song lacked conviction and was soon smothered by the roar which spiralled up out of Volsas' depths.

Watching, Harkfast hung on Ruan's arm. Beneath the young man's feet the kelp was already spongy. The Druid toppled.

Ruan lifted the old man in his arms and carried him to the shore then, still cradling Harkfast, stood riveted, staring out to sea.

The Smerteans were sinking into melting ice like cattle into straw. They tried to run, but firm support was gone. The ice had assumed the consistency of salted oil. They sank through it—up to their knees, to their waists, armpits. Slashing at the liquid scum, they swam desperately towards the rocks. But Volsas was unlocked. Like a mammoth bull-roarer whirling below their feet, it unwound a deafening chord.

The current quickly picked them off. Those closest to the core were sucked perfunctorily down, others suffered moments of blind dread before the rotating vortex whipped out its coils, snatched at their hips and dragged them, shrieking, into its mouth. Mariners clung to the water-wall, clawing at it, briefly thrusting out an arm, a head, a foot, a leg with no more human shape to it now than a briar-root, dislodging not one drop from that steely spout until the water flew round clean and smooth again and all the infantry were gone.

But that was not the end of it.

The power of the sea was thorough and the coupling alchemy of the Druid's wand increased its energies fourfold. It snared the high-prowed ships as well, towed them into its province, to be champed and crushed by its outer rings, swamped and consumed piecemeal by its monstrous throat. Masts snapped like corn-stalks, oak-structures split into a thousand parts, frames disintegrated, and three thicknesses of hide spewed into scraggy strings and vanished with the rest. So clotted was the wreckage that Ruan could not make out the corpses of the crews. But they were there, embroiled like ships' fitments, scoured and smashed and lost, until not one head or hair, or spar, or knotted rope remained. And once more Volsas carved a circle pure as milk, the kyle was scuffed by little waves, and the wind blew unimpeded over the empty sea as it had done one hour before.

4

The battle and the broch

All the children were gone to their appointed posts. Only Crog and his wife remained within the hearth-palace while the Mother Hag took meat. Throughout the evening and the night, units had gone out in turn, eight at a time, their departures marked by notches on the tallow which Fidin lit before she left with the first foray. It was quiet in the cave now that the wind had dropped. Snow fell stealthily in fine soft particles upon the roof, silence made manifest. The entrances were sealed, walled up with stones outside, barricaded with wood and iron from within. Only the tunnel to the sward remained open. Meat bones, the dregs of ormer soup, horns of ale and unfermented mead cluttered hearth and ledges. Blankets and fleeces lined the places by the fire where young warriors had rested. But they were all gone out now and the big grizzled hound slept peacefully at last by the legs of the Mother's chair.

Only one blade remained in the sapling rack, a double-handed, two-edged weapon, pommel and guard entwined in the likeness of tusked seals. It was already unsheathed. Mother Hag would sport it in the old style, draped from a flimsy cord which a drawing stroke would part, so that, once bared, the sword would have no nest to hide in until its bloody duty was discharged. Mother Hag wore her most comfortable armour. A link-mail kirtle slung low over her flanks hid her shrunken calves. Helmet and leather gauntlet waited with the sword, while she picked at a rib of beef and drank sparingly from a mead horn. She seated herself on her chair, taking rest as she took sustenance because she would need all her stamina to fight bravely and well in the hours to come.

'I have allotted you no post, Crog.'

'No, Mother.'

'Nor you, Cyprinida.'

'We are ready, Mother.'

'You will do as I ask?'

'Ay, Mother,' said Crog. 'Our son is already at his station.'

'The younger is dead?'

'He died with Leaman at the fight of the drays.'

'In whose corps is the elder?'

'With the bowmen, under the command of my brother from the northern steadings.'

'Bowmen are always vulnerable.' Mother Hag bit off a strip of meat, but found she had no appetite and spat it into the fire, tossing the rib after it. 'You have another son, Cyprinida.'

'Nay, only two.'

'The third is but a seed in your belly,' Mother Hag said. 'Leaman's child.'

'I have noticed no moon-signs yet,' Cyprinida said.

'Nonetheless you are with child again.'

Crog and Cyprinida glanced at each other in bewilderment. They did not understand why the Mother Hag should reveal this to them now. Cyprinida would not be hampered by it. She could still wield a bow or a spear.

The Mother Hag said, 'You will not go to the battle.'

'But—'

'Listen,' the old woman said. 'Listen, and be still. I cannot talk long now and have much to say. You will not go to the battle, because I have another duty for you to perform. When I have ridden away in the chariot, you will bolt and barricade the last door to the palace. You will sprinkle the hearth-fire and snuff out the lamps and tapers. You will wait here in the palace for one day. At this hour tomorrow, and not before, you, Crog, will go alone into the air. Do you understand?'

'I understand,' said Crog.

'If there are Smerteans, evade them. Do not engage them in combat. I question if the invaders will loiter here. They will be uncomfortable without ferries at their backs. They will spend their time on the eastern coast trying to cross Rhea—those that are left alive, that is.'

'What must I do then, Mother?' asked Crog.

'Search the battle trails. If you find Sketians wounded, bring them here, tend them and keep them hidden. You will be ultimate commander of all survivors.'

'But what of you, Mother; of Machalla, Fidin and . . .?'

'We will be dead.'

'*Nay!*'

'Ay, children, this is our last call to war, a fine battle against long odds. In spite of the maidens and the night-hunting patrols, two hundred Smertean fighting men are gathered in the middle glen. We have thirty-seven swords.'

'Cyprinida and I can fight.'

'You are not warriors now, but keepers,' said Mother Hag. 'When you have tended all our wounded, you will search for my cadaver on the field. Bring it here, hew off my head—if it is still stuck where it should be—and hew off my limbs. Bury these parts in the long barrow together with my sisters' corpses. You will wrap my torso in linen and take it to the forge. There, you will scour the furnace, set it fresh with natural kindling, and place my body in its midst. Seal the furnace, seal the forge, and leave it untampered until the evening of the day on which the last of the greylags leaves our shores for distant Thule. When it grows dark, open the forge again, open the furnace and ignite the fuel. You, Crog, will ride the bellows. You, Cyprinida, will tend the fire. It will burn loud and rapid, with little smoke. When it dies it will do so swiftly, and you will not be able to revive it. Look carefully among the ashes. There you will find a babe, a living child of flesh and bone. Take that child, Cyprinida, and feed it milk from your breast, and when your own babe is born raise the fire-child and the lad together until they are grown.'

'And when they are grown,' asked Cyprinida, 'what then?'

Mother Hag shrugged. 'The Druid dreamed only one dream, a difficult dream in which he travelled deep.'

'Will he escape Meglan's war-boats?' Crog asked. 'Will he, perhaps, come here again?'

'He is more powerful than you imagine,' said the Mother. 'But

211

I do not think he will travel here again. It is of no matter. Now, Crog, have you understood all that I have told you?'

'I do not understand it, Mother, but I know what I must do.'

'Obey me this last time, my son, and you too, my daughter, and all will go well with you until it is time for thankful partings.'

The old woman slapped her hands upon her thighs, pushing herself up from the oak-root throne. The hound whimpered. She stooped and fondled his tattered ears and, though he did not wake, he was consoled and snored contentedly once more.

'Look after him, too,' she said.

Picking sword, gauntlet and helmet from the rack, she clasped them to her breast. Straightening her shoulders, she strode quickly across the flagstones and into the tunnel-mouth without another word.

Crog barricaded the tunnel door. He dampened the fire until it spluttered out, and extinguished all lamps and tapers in the cave. In total darkness, he huddled by the cooling hearth, holding his wife in his arms. The old dog snored and whined a little, but there was no other sound.

About noon, or so Crog reckoned, the snoring ceased. He laid his hand on the hound's flanks and felt how still they were, and knew that the beast had passed on quietly in its sleep.

The detail despatched to fetch food from the drays at the head of the glen did not return. Meglan could not find it in his heart to order out another squad. By then night was far advanced and every man in the square knew what the shadows and odd noises indicated. Though little experienced in this manner of warfare, even the mariners understood that their wounded compatriots were being efficiently slaughtered by the Sketian maidens.

Cold and hunger sapped them less than the nervous strain of staying alert for the onslaught of the full Sketian army. When the wind dropped, snow fell in tiny hard grains which veiled the middle distances and gave rise to imagined shapes and signs so that many false warnings and startled shouts disturbed the darkness. Meglan could not even doze for the wound in his buttock. It bled hardly at all, yet the ache constricted his leg, stiffening the whole limb like a sack full of sand. During the long cramped watch, he had time to ponder on their predicament, to realize how arrogant the mariners had become through seasons of piracy when prey was invariably weaker than themselves. That fact, coupled with his father's policy of long-range trading, had partially eroded the clan's pride. Boud had some sanity in her obsession. Only her impetuous demand that he act at once had brought him to this parlous circumstance. He cowered, shivering, under a cowled hood, blowing on his knuckles to keep his sword-hand supple, adjusting his weight from foot to foot to retain some flexibility in his knees. He had no inclination to devise strategies. How could he predict what the warrior-women would do next? Surely, adversity would steel his troops. The weaker elements—kerns, grazers and impressed blades—had been weeded out last evening. What was left was the meat of the herd, bull-like kinsmen and fearless mariners. They had been taken by surprise yesterday. But now they had had time to collect their wits they would fight bravely to the breaking of the very last shield. He was certain of their courage and loyalty, if only they could come to grips with the enemy. He doubted, however, if the Sketians would elect to tackle them bold-fronted.

Dawn nipped the air keenly before the war-horn sounded. It was not a brassy bleating, but a deep, resonant conch-note which passed from bank to bank, from ridge to ridge until it seemed to come from every quarter at once. Meglan tore the hood down, clapped a bronze helmet onto his head, unsheathed his sword and plucked up his round targe. Iron clattered. Men murmured and grunted. The walls of the square tightened. Nervousness spread like a plague through the Smerteans. Meglan raised his voice and shouted down the muttering, shouted down the lowing horns. No orator, he did not attempt a speech. He settled instead for a tuneless rendering of a song entitled *The Whales' Mating*, which every mariner knew by heart. The chorus gathered before he uttered the second stanza. Soon the swell of singing smothered the conches. As intended, the song gave his men unity and whetted their purpose. Cold, hunger, discomfort were not new to them. Only the method of fighting and the youthfulness of the attackers. Now they had faced the worst and were not cast down. Now they would fight and destroy those hags and their sly spawn with customary Smertean fervour.

The song rolled into the snow-cloud.

The war-horns abruptly ceased.

Out of pale distances the chariots came again.

Shoving his way to the edge of the square, Meglan peered into the mist. Hoisted on willing shoulders, chest, belly and back covered by shields, he scouted the snow curtain in all directions but discerned no activity except the patient approach of the chariots. The horses picked neatly over blankets of powdery snow. The wheels made no audible sound. The mariners continued to shout out their song.

Even a flight of arrows scything down from behind the line of chariots did not quell the mariners' choruses. Three volleys fell, a scattering of small, black arrows, easily diverted by the targes. Only four or five of nine-score Smerteans caught wounds. One was killed outright, struck in the throat before he could hoist his shield. Meglan reasoned that the chariots would not break line and endanger the archers. He perceived virtues in a defensive stance, began to suspect that the Sketians *had* no large army, and would be content to pick and pluck at the edges of the square, vanishing with the coming of light. Indeed, he could move the whole complement east, if he so decided, to regroup and revictual. The sounding of the conches was a deception. Any girl could hoot out a martial tune. It took a man to wield a sword in honest combat. He chuckled at the simplicity of it all. Since the Sketians could not split the square, he could draw back to more suitable terrain and design a double crescent or a palmate formation with which to penetrate their squalid ranks.

Piddling arrows fell once more. The song swelled fearlessly as the chariots passed gradually out of striking range. Already, early for the month, dawn brightened the slope, the glint of it on the snow. The sky was overcast, and snow sifted. But the gleam of sunrise surely lit the cloud and made the grains dance like gadflies against its reddening blush.

Five carts jutted shafts over the ridge. They appeared gradually, sprouting from the earth-shafts, then links, then wicker baskets through which flames already spurted and smoke poured in a shapeless haze. Five four-wheeled carts, saddled with baskets of burning stuff, hove over the summit and hung balanced above the glen.

Meglan shouted a warning. But his command was lost in the din as the Smertean square seethed, broke and scattered.

The fire-carts trundled down the crest. Gathering momentum, they spewed smoulders on the snow and tossed char into the air. Fanned, their fuel-masses burst into life, glowing red, then yellow, then white. The carts hurtled down hill, leapt the rutted shoulder of the track and smashed into the horde who milled there, compressed by the outer ranks.

One cart foundered on a rock, canted and drenched a knot of struggling mariners with blue-burning blubber fat. Two other carts met and locked wheels, cracking axles, bowing and shaking fiery wicker and kelp over helpless kinsmen. Sledding on a drift, the last cart ploughed a curved furrow at no great pace and blocked the hill itself. Though its course was unplotted, the archers were quick to seize its cover, knelt behind it and shot bone-barbs and steel-tips straight into the crowd. Smerteans who ran before the carts, though saved from roasting, immediately found themselves in combat with a maidens' brigade which had somehow infiltrated the tussocks just below the track. It was no rout now, though. The Smerteans were all too ready for battle. They fought the maidens with swords, dirks and spears, flinging aside their targes the better to grapple with their sinuous foes, and slew many. Sweeping the glen floor, the chariots returned from the east.

The warrior-women held the reins as lightly as they might hold feather-caps, slicing their swords to left and right, cleaving Smerteans in a bloody swath as far as the dismembered square extended. One horse stumbled, righted, then went pitching to the snow, screaming. The chariot lifted and decanted its driver, a giantess, fat as a sow, who somehow landed on her shoulders as

215

nimbly as a tumbling dwarf and sprang upright, sword in hand, curses spitting from her lips like wildcat's venom.

Meglan ran, not alone and not in cowardly crouch. Leading forty men, he chose neither the up-slope nor the down, but raced along the track towards the end of the glen from which the cunning attacks seemed to originate. On the western quadrant of the square he had been safe from the fire-carts and he saw no sense in returning to add flux to confusion. By accident, he had acquired a fighting force of thirty kinsmen trained in arms, salted with a dozen seasoned mariners. They flanked him gladly, free at last, and out of habit formed the crescent. They would not break now for maids or boys or blubber-baths.

They came upon seven men, took them unaware and hewed them down without losing step or shedding a single drop of Smertean blood. They trampled on in search of more. Forgetful of his wound, Meglan ran, dragging his leg after him like an empty scabbard. Two grown men who had loomed unexpectedly out of the mist had fallen to his sword. His blade had tasted blood again. The point reeked where it had stabbed clean through the leather-plate of one bearded rogue, who had died suitably astonished. He ran on, at once cool and fevered, beginning now to feel the draw of destiny, half-aware of what he would find at the road's eventual end.

The chariot was square to the track. The horses were quite motionless, snow sprinkling their rough pelts and the thick fleece which cloaked the shoulders of the charioteer.

Meglan had never seen anything so primitive or majestic as the tall warrior-woman who barred his path. She had more than her share of Boud's proud bearing, something of the proud Pictish style, but she was greater than Boud, and older by many seasons. Honed and weathered, her face was like that of an old sea-eagle, ruffed by grizzled strands of hair. Left arm cocked, the reins lay slack across her gauntlet palm and in her bare right fist her massive sword was held point-downward. Her spear jutted from its slot in the chariot prow like a banner without a ribband. A small, round, wood-rimmed targe, slung over the weave, displayed her personal emblem—a sourceless tongue of flame

216

wreathed by flowers of purple nightcoin.

Meglan could smell the sea close by, snow-veiled though it was. The ground here was flat and shallow and the snow cloaked it evenly. He knew then that the woman had intentionally chosen this spot for her battle, that her victory would determine the outcome for Sketis *and* for Smertae. How cunningly had she trimmed the odds to suit? Were forty warriors then her estimate of what one ancient hag was worth?

Behind her three chariots appeared in line; the horses were slavered and sweaty, sawing stoutly in their chests. One cage bore two women—a stringy, whiskered female in blue armour, and the mannish giantess who had toppled from the chariot in the field. Tallest of all, she wore plates of chequered leather inset with mail. The remaining sisters controlled a chariot apiece; a short, rotund woman, plump as a ptarmigan, the other brilliant-eyed, silly ringlets bouncing from her helmet's brow. No soldiers or maidens accompanied them. Their polished mail was freckled with blood. They halted the wheels ten roods away.

It was light enough across the invisible kyle to shed a pallid gleam upon the snow field now.

Meglan stood forth.

'I am Meglan, son of Vinadia, chieftain of the Smerteans,' he declared.

'Speak, Meglan,' eagle-beak told him.

'I come as conqueror of your place and your peoples,' Meglan announced. 'I demand your submission.'

'I am the Mother Hag, Queen of all Sketis.' The woman's lips hardly seemed to move, yet her words rang clear on the cold air. 'I will not submit.'

'Then let there be battle between us.'

'There can be naught else but battle,' the woman agreed.

Meglan lifted his sword.

The kinsmen and mariners were ready, anger high in them.

'VIN-AD-IA,' Meglan shouted. 'VINADIA.'

The Smerteans called out his father's name in unison, as if revenge was still their motive for invasion.

Meglan swung down his sword.

217

The crescent split into two segments, facing both forth and backward, like a blade laid crosswise to the track. When Meglan lifted his sword again, the Smerteans attacked.

Meglan propelled himself straight at the Mother Hag. She swerved the chariot, horses rampant in the shafts, and heaved it round on him. But the young man had covered ground so rapidly that she could muster no distance for a charge. Reins in her mouth, head cocked, she showed him her teeth as if this moment was a zenith of delight. Knees spread against the cage, she harried him with an intricate combination of spear thrusts and sword parries. Her spear narrowly missed his heart. Her sword clanged against his own and, deflected from its arc, severed the neck of a kinsman who trailed on his chieftain's heels. The chariot-wheels were stubbed but unspiked. Meglan stepped close to it as it thundered past, reached for and caught the gate-hasp at the rear and was almost jerked from his feet.

The chariot heeled and flung him like a cockleshell across the snow. His targe buffered the worst effects of the fall. He rose again at once. Two mariners had tackled the chariot now. Fists on the gate, shields drogued on the ground, they groped for the linchpins at the rear of the yoke. They dropped suddenly. Meglan saw that their fists had gone from their wrists, stumps cut clean as winter beef. Blood jetted out. Rounding sharply on one wheel, the woman flew at them and finished them with her blade before they recovered from their amazement.

The kinsmen were undeterred. Another stalwart seized his chance, snatched the hasp and tucked himself below the gate's ledge, riding, prising the hinge with his dagger. The gate swung open. The kinsman prepared to pendulum inward and knife the hag in the liver. She did not appear to have remarked the man's ruse, or to pivot round, yet her weapon somehow speared his mouth. He pitched back and died before he struck the ground.

'The horses,' Meglan yelled. 'Kill the horses.'

Running again, he bisected the circle of the chariot's turn. The rest of the fighting had spread out wide. The sisters were under harassment too, though quantities of dead and wounded attested to their uncanny strength and prowess with weapons.

218

Deducing his intention, the Mother Hag came wide out of her turn and backed the chariot for a straight attack. Five kinsmen and a mariner, straddled and keen, strung out on the sward to intercept. Swaying in the light cage, she lashed the horses with the reins as the first bold kinsman grabbed the bridle-bits. At speed, the heroism was wasted. He pitched under the hoofs and did not rise again. A second buck drove in low with a throw-spear, tearing a wound in the belly of the offside mount. In return he sustained a swift and fatal thrust from the spear. The others let the chariot hurtle past. It was Meglan who found the weakness that brought the cage to earth.

Standing directly in the path of the charge, he judged his distance, swung the targe and cracked the boss against the muzzle of the beast. It sheered away, widening the gap enough for Meglan to leap up and swarm onto its neck. The spear darted out over the prow like a tongue. But he deflected it with the targe, caught the shaft and hung grimly on until the horses shied and bickered and were slain by clustered kinsmen. Slumping dead between the posts, the animals keeled the cage far out of kilter, locking Meglan and the Mother Hag in the midst of a tangle of reins and shattered wicker. On the spear-shaft still, he was just beyond the range of her sword. Her strength was enormous, though, and she lugged him up on the end of the spear like a fish on a fork. He snapped out the strap of the targe and flung the shield full at her. Striking her breasts, the shield knocked all breath from her lungs. The spear-shaft flagged. Meglan drooped to the bloodied crupper of the horse and lunged into the chariot over the prow, smiting wildly with his sword.

But this was not to be the moment of contact, the final fatal mating. Her dirk bared his cheek, cutting through his gum to the bones of his teeth. Fierce pain distracted him. The woman hopped through the chariot-gate and, winded though she was, felled four Smerteans as she hobbled the road to where the remains of the sisters' chariots lay wrecked. She slew with such easy grace that Meglan no longer doubted her choice of odds: yet she would surely tire in time. She could not absorb strength from the earth as goddesses of yore supposedly did. The Mother Hag was mortal. She would bleed and die, give her flesh to the gulls and her soul to the sky just as he would if he was smitten down.

Ripping shreds of leather from his breeks, Meglan stuffed his mouth with them to absorb the blood-flow which threatened to choke him. Champing, he brandished his sword, strapped his targe to his forearm and marched forward to join his comrades.

All things were equal now. The hags were on the ground, standing hip to hip against the broken chariot wheels. It was the hour of trial, when strength would be pitted against experience, discipline against devotion, order against intrigue. Male would oust female, youth overthrow age, of that Meglan was convinced, though even he could not predict the outcome of that last combat in the snow.

They moved away from the sea, crawling at first, then walking and finally running to be clear of the returning sound of Volsas which, Harkfast said, would soon disgorge the debris of the Smertean ships and spread it wantonly along all the mainland coasts. Saddled on the mare, the Druid clung to the saddle-bow as if all life had been drained from his body. Dreams and weather-working had fatigued him beyond measure. It was not until the band had camped and Domgall had built a fire and boiled soup from makings in his pack that Harkfast recovered enough to talk.

The night was bitter with the coming of winter. Only the glow of the fire cheered them. Gadarn felt the cold badly and Ruan had given him his cloak out of sympathy for the Roman's shivering. Though the events of the past days had numbed them, the horror of the unlocking of Volsas was too disturbing to be spoken of. Many months would pass before any of them dared mention it; even then it would be guardedly, a reference to a shared nightmare. Of them all now, only Ruan, Slan and Harkfast seemed to have much stomach to continue the adventure, the quest for power and the revival of the kingship.

As the night deepened and one by one the others slept, Gadarn, Domgall, Bellerus and even Mungan, conversation drew the young man, the smith and the Druid close.

'Is it all over yet with the Mother Hag, Harkfast?' Slan asked, out of a moment's silence.

'It will be by morning, Slan. It was her wish that she should die in battle.'

'Pah! Against a morsel like Meglan.'

'Nay, Slan, do not condemn Vinadia's son,' said Harkfast. 'I think he will learn to be a warrior today. The Mother Hag would not have chosen him if he had not, ultimately, been worthy. He is, poor mariner, a little lost on land, that's all.'

'Would that he might survive,' said Ruan. 'I would despatch him myself, willingly.'

'I have more than fighting to ask of you, Ruan,' Harkfast said. 'Ay, and of you too, Slan.'

'The Hand of the Warrior Huntsman?' Slan said. 'Will we win it, do you think?'

'Ay, we will win it,' said Harkfast. He stirred the fire and thrust a fresh branch into it. 'Those who dare to challenge are those who dare to win.'

'And you, young King, will you have the nerve to go beyond a confrontation with death?' asked Slan.

'Talk is easy,' said Ruan. 'But I have seen death now, and I mark it as having no significance.'

Slan and the Druid glanced at each other.

'Rebellion and power stop at that line,' said Slan.

'Significance,' said Harkfast. 'That is a word of no meaning at all, fosterling. Tomorrow we will leave for an encampment I know of in the mountains of the east. We will lie up for the winter.'

'And then?' asked Ruan.

'We will join with King Cleve and his knights in Fortreen and travel far to the south with them in search of Nudd.'

'He will not be silenced like the voice of Volsas,' Slan said. 'He must be taken as he roars.'

'I will take him,' Ruan said. 'I promise you, Harkfast, that you will be Druid to a king again, a great king, a king of all the Celtic peoples.'

Harkfast nodded. 'But?'

'I require the morning for my own,' said Ruan.

Again Harkfast nodded. 'The Frankish girl?'

'I want her.'

'Of course,' the Druid said. 'It is in how you want her, Ruan, that the "significance" lies.'

'I may make her my queen.'

'If you wish. But be wary of this distant loving, Ruan. It smacks dangerously of an ideal of love that we cannot now afford.'

'I'm in no mood for riddles. I want her,' Ruan said, dogmatically. 'I shall have her.'

'Yes, Ruan. Yes.'

Ruan rode hard on the corn-gold mare and reached Vinadia's Dun shortly before noon. The walls and hedges were deserted. No guardians hailed him from the posts, or skulked under cover to keep him in sight. No spears or arrows whisked past him as he steered the mare through the unprotected gate and stepped her cautiously across the compound. No women, children, dogs or elderly men challenged him or gave him pause. The smoulders under the cooking hooks burned low and the pots themselves were gone. Smoke from the holes in round-house roofs was hardly visible. The settlement had been abandoned, its citizens fled to hills and forest. Though snow-grains no longer filtered down from the pig-iron sky above the province, across Rhea Sketis was screened by lowering cloud. Ruan could not tell what tragedies had occurred on the isle across the water, or why the Smertean guard had abandoned the dun so hurriedly.

The Royal Broch was lagged with powdered snow, fissures laced with it, crannies packed. It stood up pale as glass against the sky and seemed of one substance with the firs and leafless birches, all stripped of dimension on that dim and sunless day. There were no sounds at all, except the loudness of his horse's plodding and the jangle of his armoured bits. When he halted, he could hear nothing but the creak of an alder branch in the copse behind the dun. He stared up at the battlements.

There was no fire-watch and no sign of wardens. He tethered the mare by the door and, unsheathing his sword, entered the dark place. Steps ascended jaggedly, cutting through floors which, like decks in sophisticated ships, layered off the conical interior. Here and there a torch spluttered, close to the butt and acrid. Below him the open door spilled a puddle of clean daylight on the ground—then it was gone, and he was above the level in an empty armoury. He climbed on, came upon a stair built from flint slabs which, curling in upon the timber spiral like a conch-shell, led to a strong door of oak studded with iron rivets. He pushed it cautiously with his foot.

It opened. Ruan entered Vinadia's private place. It reeked of thyme and withered pine and of the fleeces which littered the floor. It smelled too of other things, corruption, decay, a sick fleshiness which the guttering of pitch-brand did not purify. Though there was no one in the room, he could make out sounds now, strange sounds, a scuffling and chirruping like a dormouse in underbrush or a sweetmart imprisoned in a straw cage. Warily he crossed the floor and touched the inner door with the tip of his sword, let it swing on oiled leather hinges. He looked through at scattered sand, an untanned bruin-pelt, broken wine jars and an upturned coal-grate which mixed its cinders with the rest and saw where the sounds originated.

She was crouched in a corner of the wedge. Her head lolled to one side like the seed-pod of a big moonflower, bending her body from the waist. Her legs stuck out across the sand, and her hands cupped her belly. A moment elapsed before Ruan recognized that the broken thing was all that remained of the Frankish princess. No visible marks marred her body, no stain, burn or cut; yet she had been brought so low that her wits were blown like syca-more pods on the wind, and the dignity which had supported her spirit in duress was scattered beyond regathering. Tenderly he stooped and took her face between his fingers. She did not look up. Innocent in madness, her sensuality was transformed into beauty.

Ruan could not imagine what horrors had driven her so far

from reason, so far from fear. She was not afraid of him. She did not flinch from the touch of his hand upon her nakedness. She was beyond apathy, travelling dominions of her own imagining, playing again in childhood groves bathed by a saffron sun, perhaps, or paddling in the turquoise seas of virginal youth, strolling the loamy rows of vineries which, so he had heard, saturated the river-courses south of Gaul. Wherever her mind had found refuge he could not follow nor persuade her to return. Her spirit had already passed from her body. All that he could touch was the shell of a woman already dead. The thin and muted piping in her throat was the equal of the curlew's song as it dies on the wing and plummets down to earth. It was her prayer to gods unknown to leave her soul where now it stood, and let her body rest. And when Ruan took away his fingers, her head fell and black hair, lank with sweat, curtained her eyes. He thumbed her lids, gently closing them before the radiance was lost. He lifted her in his arms, carried her down stone stairs and wooden steps and through the pool of daylight into the winter air.

He buried her in soft soil on the shoulder of the stream under the boughs of leafless birch-trees and close to the roots of a larch, wrapped in his own cloak and facing east, which, Harkfast had once told him, was the way of burial for Franks. He did not pray over her, or weep, and left no posy but the snow. He did not bury her alone, however, but strewed in the grave the last poor trinkets of his own naïveté, forgetting that he did not even know her name.

In the wayward days ahead of him, he would think of her often and regret that rashness had not burned more brightly and sent him back alone and gallant to take her from the broch in blood. Though there would be other maids, he would want none as much as she. His boy's blood had cooled through dreams and nightmares as a sword is annealed in oil. If this was the lore of the hero, he wanted no share of it, or of the lot of kingship: and yet, and yet—he was more royal now than he had been before, for the portion of a king is sorrow and out of that sorrow burgeoned strength.

He walked slowly across the compound to the mare. She

224

watched his coming curiously, silently. He stroked the animal's nose, and found it warm against his palm.

From Pasard, Gadarn, and the Mother Hag, now from this dead princess who had brushed the surface of his destiny as a moth brushes the brow, he had acquired learning which was not written in runic lore or passed down in the murmurings of Druids, anywhere. Could he learn more from Nudd, the Warrior-Huntsman? Was this the kernel of all power, this process of learning, this winnowing of the guiltlessness of youth, a harvesting of knowledge deep and secret within the fibres of one's soul? If ever he found an answer to that question then the search itself would end, for in life—even in death—there are no endings, only innumerable moments of beginning. Which was the greater magic, to learn and to survive in sanity, or to encase the mind in constant icy dreams? The man who could work a magic of the winds, call down an avalanche or stir the sea to rock-hard ice, who could dream of tomorrow and interpret the past, could he for one instant call back the maiden from her sweet-tempered death?

It made no matter now.

Ruan swung on to the mare's back, took the reins in his numb fingers, and plodded down from the abandoned broch. He looked not up nor round him but fixed his gaze on the unfurling crust of snow upon the ground before the hoofs. He would have passed the round-house in a daze, if the girl had not called out to him.

'Warrior,' the shrill voice cried. 'See, warrior, *we* are here.'

He halted.

She stood by the door of the house, her hand upon the hide, holding it coyly apart. Within were the glimpses of a fire, a polished jar of mead mulling by the hearth-stones, drinking horns laid out, smothered fleeces, the younger queens and concubines set out like market goods displayed.

'Who are you?' he asked, dully.

'I am Masena.'

'Masena?'

'You widowed me,' she said, smiling. 'But I do not mind. Vinadia was fat and cared more for his knives and whips than he ever

225

did for me. Come, come within and rest where it is warm.'

'No,' Ruan said.

'You have nothing to fear from us,' the girl told him. She had a sharp, vixenish face, pretty in its way, but hollowed by hidden cruelty. 'Boud has gone—flown like an old goose.'

'Boud, Meglan's mother?'

'When the coracle arrived from Sketis this midmorning, carrying two wounded kinsmen with the ferryman, and she heard the news, she packed her treasures and rode off in a dither of feathers, along with all the others.'

'What news?'

'I thought you were there, on Sketis?'

Ruan shook his head; he could not be bothered to explain.

'Ah!' said the girl. 'Then you will not have heard how our "gallant" countrymen were beaten, routed indeed, by elders and ancient women.'

'I . . . Nay, I have not heard.'

'Burned all our boats, slaughtered our kerns and borrowed spears, and, just this morning, I believe, killed Meglan and the wolf's share of his bawdy mariners.'

'Meglan is dead?'

'Not alone, of course. I mean, he took company with him; all the ancient women, even the queen of warriors herself.'

'Not one left alive?'

'Not one,' said Masena. 'The old women fought like she-cats, so the ferryman said, and burned all our boats to boot. So there are our men, what's left of them, stranded on that accursed, meatless isle, and there they may stay. We do not need them here, to wail upon our laps and console themselves with our favours. Nay, we are more worthy to serve conquerors than conquered.'

'I am no conqueror.'

'But you are fair, and strong-bodied, and have sadness on you. Did you bury the black-haired Frank?'

'Ay.'

'How did she seem? Bloodied, or unmarked?'

'Unmarked.'

'It is the worst way,' said Masena, shrugging. 'But she is dead, young warrior, and we are alive. Step down and rest. Let us salve your sorrows and minister to your wounds. Step down.'

'Nay, I have business,' said Ruan, 'in the south of the land. I have business there with friends.'

'The golden one, he is your friend: *he* would step down,' Masena said. 'See.'

She parted the curtain wider. In spite of himself Ruan stared into the luxurious interior and felt a weak plaint of longing somewhere on the surface of his nerves: women fair, and women sallow, painted and garbed in finery, their eyes hot like the eyes of beasts in caves, and their long pale arms beckoning. Masena slanted her leg across the entrance-way, and let her robe slide down her thigh and part.

'See,' she said again. 'Honey for the eyes.'

Her body was milky and shaven of all hair, so that the slit showed pink on the mound of her belly.

'We are for *you, all* for you, young conqueror, young *King*.'

Her voice was sibilant as grass, and whispered more enticements to him. But Ruan did not hear, for the wind came in a wintry gust from the north and shook the thatch and made the smoke rise in a billow from the dome and that was more to him than pandering, that signal of motion, that call to a journey which would not wait for pleasure, but might lead him on to joy.

Clapping his heels to the mare's flanks, he shook the reins and gave the steed her head. She bore him swiftly through the gate. He took the path which would carry him south to the appointed meeting place.

Behind him the queens screeched and the concubines shouted filth at him. He could not hear them well and paid no heed, riding low and staring straight in front. Nor did he glance at Sketis where the cloud was down and, in the womb of the forge, unknown to Ruan, the seed of the fire-child slept.